I0662323

# I Worshiped My Car

Mark E. Mitchell

*Ark of Ages Publishing*
*harktheark@gmail.com*

...It was dark, about 9:30, when I saw the next hitchhiker. Ordinarily I don't pick people up at night, but it was raining again, a heavier rain than before, and the wind was blowing...

...The long overcoated, thickly spectacled, wild eyed person put his head in the doorway, then looked down at the napkinned seat. "No," he said. "The car's clean..."

"It's okay, I tell you. No one else is going to pick you up in this weather....

...I grasped his arm and yanked. "Just get in."

"...I'm cursed!" he said, once he was facing forward with his feet on the floor. I could smell the odor of wet B.O. (at least two days of ripeness, I would guess) buried under the long blue overcoat. He continued to hold his arm.

"...I'm trapped by an idolater!" he said, his tone loud enough to sound clearly above the pounding of the rain, but otherwise without expression or inflection. "He worships his car, he worships his shower, he worships his own face!"

"Look Bud, I don't know what you're talking about—"

"He doesn't know my name so he calls me Bud. I'm cursed!"

In spite of myself, I smiled. *How'd I ever get this stinky nut in my car?..."*

DEDICATION:
To all my friends and family who provided the life
experiences I have drawn from to know the characters
and situations in this book.

### Author's Note

This book is the first in a series of four. The first three books could easily be labeled a trilogy, even though books of this genre are not usually presented that way. The fourth book is a companion to all four, and could be read concurrently with the first, second and third. However, since it contains much narrative that is unique to itself, it probably ought to be read after the other three, especially since it is set fifteen years later than the third book and thus gives away the ending of the trilogy.

# *Chapter I*

## Covenant

*Richmond, Virginia*

"Hey Dad."

"Hey Mikey." My father's voice sounded a little bit strained.

"I've got good news and–"

"I'll take the good news. Maybe it'll give me strength for the other."

I chuckled. "All right. I got up four hundred today."

Stunned silence. Then, "Free weights?"

"Nothing but."

"I never got higher than three sixty two."

"I know, Dad."

"Had to beat the old man, huh?" Was there a note of bitterness in his tone?

"No! You know it's been my goal since I was seventeen."

"Yeah. Congratulations. What're you gonna shoot for now?"

"Ten reps. I'm going to impress my wife with it."

"What's that supposed to mean?" He didn't sound as hopeful as I thought he would.

"I got engaged today."

"To whom?"

"C'mon Dad. You remember. I brought her home at Thanksgiving."

"Oh, you mean the impossibly built goddess with perfect blond hair?"

"Dad! Yes, that's Tiffany all right, but aren't you happy? You're finally going to have a chance at a grandchild."

"You'll hafta adopt. She's never going to submit to pregnancy."

He was probably right, but I wasn't going to let him know it. "Oh, what're you talking about? You sound like I'm giving you bad news or something."

"Well, what *is* the bad news?"

"There isn't any. You interrupted me before I could say *better* news."

"Oh."

"What's up, Dad." Aren't you overjoyed?"

"Well..."

"What?"

"How do you know she's right for you?"

"I've known her for two years now.  We've been dating steadily for six months."

"And–?"

"And what?"

"What qualities does she have that makes her fit to be the mother of my grandchildren?"

I coughed in amazement.  "What in the world are you talking about?  She's the prettiest woman I've ever seen, she's smart, she has a good sense of humor, she has–"

"You mean she laughs at all your jokes."

"What's going on, Dad?  You're acting like you don't want this!"

Long pause.  "I have some news for you, Mike.  I've been putting off telling you, and now is about the worst time I could pick, but I've gotta do it now."

My heart dropped down into my shoes.  *He's going to tell me he has cancer or something.*

I could hear my father take a deep breath.  Then another.  Then he cleared his throat.  "You've heard me talk about my friend Salvy, haven't you?"

*What does this have to do with anything?*  "I think so.  You knew him in college, didn't you?"

"Yeah."  Another pause.  "He came by the office today."

"Cool."  My dad's office was at headquarters, on the other side of the country.  I'd been working in the Richmond branch for three years.

"Wait'll you hear what he said before you say

anything, Mikey."

I knew from the distressed expression in his voice that he was talking about something serious. *What in the world would Salvy have to do with this?*

"I'm waiting. And it better be pretty good to keep you from congratulating me. You've been on me to get married and settle down for what—six years?"

"More or less. Believe me, Mikey, this isn't easy for me. You'll see as soon as I can force it out."

There was a knot in my stomach now. "Hurry up and force it out then, Dad. You're making me nervous."

"That's two of us." Another pause. "Salvy had an old piece of paper. It uh—had my signature on it."

"What'd you sign, Dad?"

"It was kind of a promissory note."

My throat was suddenly so dry I had to swallow twice to get it to let my voice through. "How much?"

"It wasn't 'how much.' It was more like—'what?'"

"Dad just say it. This is killing me."

"I'll tell you the story. I was three days away from graduating, and I had a job lined up. Fifteen hundred a month, which wasn't bad in those days, but I didn't feel good about it. It was with an engineering firm and everything, but–"

"What does this have to do with–?"

"Just let me tell the story and you'll understand. It was mainly dirt work, and I wanted buildings and bridges. I knew I was lucky to have it, but still I continued  looking through the help wanted ads in the paper. And then I saw it."

"What?"

"My future. Bruce Staley found me with an ad in the classifieds."

"He's the one that sold you the business–"

"Right. I still have the words memorized. 'Bring ten thousand clams and a degree in civil engineering and I'll make you my partner. 555-6787.'"

"It sounds like a scam."

"Today it would, but back then things weren't so bad. Just to see what was going on, I called the number. Bruce answered the phone himself. He'd had to lay off his receptionist that day. From a financial standpoint, his business was dead in the water."

"I still don't see–"

"Hold on a minute more. He was broke, but it wasn't really his fault. He'd loaned some money to a brother in law, and the guy had taken the money and left Bruce's sister."

"Haven't you warned me against–"

"Yes, and that's why I haven't told you the whole story before. But I gotta tell it now. Anyway, he'd just made a bid on a complex of four oil and gas refineries. If he could land the job, he'd be set for a long time, but he had to have some cash to keep afloat until his bid came through. For ten grand, he was willing to make me a full partner."

"Right out of college?"

"Yeah, well, he was desperate. And so was I. He

was doing exactly what I wanted to do, and he was offering me an incredible opportunity. I told him I'd get back with him that evening."

"But you didn't have two nickels–"

"I know, but I wanted it so bad. When I hung up the phone, I put my head in my hands, trying to squeeze out an idea. If I were to borrow from every person I knew, I might be able to–"

"Salvy gave you the money, didn't he?"

Pause. "Yeah."

"Where'd he get it?"

"He was as poor as I was– I thought." Another pause. "But he did have something. It was something I'd only read about before that."

"What was it?"

"His mother's dowry. Salvy was from an old Spanish family, and his mother had married his father the old fashioned way: with her father supplying a dowry for his daughter. The money had just sat there for years, but when Salvy came to UCLA, his parents had put it in a trust to get him started when he graduated."

"And he gave that to *you?*"

It sounded like my dad was crying when he answered. "Yeah. When he asked me why I looked so agitated, and I told him about my conversation with Bruce and how bad I wanted the position he was offering, he didn't even hesitate. 'Call him back and tell him you'll have the money tomorrow afternoon,' he said. 'I can get you the money as soon as my commencement is over.'

"When he told me about the dowry, I told him I couldn't take it. What was he going to do?"

My dad paused for a long time. I could hear him breathing, heavy and deep. "Salvy just shook his head. 'When someone wants something as much as you want this job, you deserve it,' he said. And no matter what protests I made, he stood firm."

My father cleared his throat. "If I had been serious in insisting he not give me that money his dead grandfather had given his now dead father (it was almost like it was sacred money, for his family alone) to help *him* when he finished college, I would have talked him out of it. But I wasn't thinking of him. I was only thinking of how much I wanted to be Bruce Staley's partner."

"What were the terms of the loan, Dad?" I could feel a cold chill gripping my spine.

"He didn't make any terms. I did."

"What were they?" I could barely speak.

"Let me read it to you. 'On this eighteenth day of May, 1980, I, Jacob Frank Marson, being of sound and grateful mind, do hereby swear to my eternal friend, Iago de Maria Salvadore, that I will grant to him any request in my power to fulfill. This oath extends throughout my life, into the lives of the heirs of my body, until it is fulfilled. This I deliver with a most solemn oath and in the fear of God, upon my word of honor.' Then I signed it. I even went to the bank and had it notarized."

"Dad!"

"I know.  And you know what happened to the money.  I bailed Bruce out with it, and we got the refinery bid, and ten years later he sold out to me for a million dollars.  For twenty nine years, it's seemed like the most wonderful thing that could ever happen to someone."

"So Salvadore needs money now?"

"I wish.  If you could have seen the anguish on his face when he came in today, this wouldn't be as hard on you as it's gonna be."

"For heaven's sake Dad, just tell me!"

"Salvy's done very well for himself.  He owns a chain of  gourmet restaurants now, down in the San Diego and LA areas.  I'd say he's worth ten million."

"Then what in the world does he want?"

"All he said was, 'Hi, Jacob.'  Then, really slowly, he handed me an envelope.  All it had in it was a piece of paper, and I knew it as soon as I saw it."

I could hear my father breathing heavily.  "Underneath my signature there was more writing.  Let me read it to you."

Finally!  This had taken so long, I was ready for anything.  Or so I thought.

"'I, Iago de Maria Salvadore, being of a sound mind on this 26th day of July, 2009, do hereby request the promised boon of my lifelong friend.  I would have Jacob's son Michael marry my daughter Olivia."

\*_____\*

*Los Angeles, California*

"What do you mean you've found me a husband?" I knew by the helpless expression on my father's face that I already had him on the ropes.

"You haven't made too much progress by yourse–"

"What business is it of yours?" I put as much vituperation into my voice as I could.

"You're my daughter–"

"This is modern days, Daddy." I laced my tone with sarcasm. "Women make their own futures."

He didn't back down. "Everything you do makes you unhappier. I chose to intervene a little."

"A *little*?"

"I know what's good for you–"

"So you're an expert in making women happy. How happy was my mother's life?" She had committed suicide twelve years earlier.

"A lot happier than yours."

"Oh, right. That's why you lock yourself in your room every day."

Arguments with me didn't work, and he knew it, but he wouldn't let this one alone.

"It so happens that I like my time alone more than–"

"Well, it so happens I like being alone too."

"That's not true Olivia."

"So are you suddenly my psychiatrist?"

"I'm your father and I care about you."

"You care about me so much that you are willing to

sell me off in marriage to a man I haven't even laid eyes on?" The tears rose unbidden to my eyes for just a moment.

I steeled my jaw and continued, "Arranged marriages fell out of vogue a long time ago. They're probably illegal by now, and if they're not, they ought to be."

He sighed and his shoulders fell ever so slightly. I had beaten him once again, but there was almost no satisfaction in it anymore. "You can't make me do it."

"No Olivia, I can't make you," he said, his voice filled with resignation. "But it's what you *should* do. How many men have you been with? Have they made you happy? You don't know how to find happiness, but I do, so I'm helping you because I love you."

*I hate you. You have no idea what life is really like – especially for me.* "Stop trying to love me then. If this is love, I think I'll do without."

"His name's Michael Marson," he said, his voice very soft. "He's the son of my best friend."

I opened my mouth to answer, certain something nasty would come out, but he had already turned around and left my room.

# *Chapter II*

## Stink Bomb

*Richmond, Virginia*

I felt like I'd been punched in the gut. With a battering ram. "What?" I finally managed to gasp, like a drowning man taking an uncertain breath.

"You heard right," he said.

It took me a few breaths to be able to spill out my outrage. "That's the craziest thing I've ever heard!"

My father didn't say anything. And his silence said more than anything he could have said. The few phrases from the document he had just read lingered in my head, tormenting me with their gravity, seeming like bars of a cage that was being lowered over the top of me.

*How much am I obliged to honor my father's oath?*

As much as I wanted to deny any responsibility for my father's foolish promises, phrases like w*ord of honor, in the fear of God, my eternal friend,* bounced around in my mind, refusing to leave.

But how could a man I had never met before be allowed to control my life? I had a new fiancee, I had my own life. I was a civil engineer prodigy, managing the Richmond office at age twenty-seven, and doing a great job of it too. My life was before me, each day was loaded with incredible things, and tomorrow was– what was tomorrow? If I ignored my father's promise, I'd feel guilty every day of my life, but if I honored it, I would cut myself off from everything I treasured.

For a long moment, I said nothing. One side of my mind was saying *what right does Salvy have...?* but the other side was simply staring ahead. *What would happen if...*

No! I was not going to allow some– *why am I angry?*

I took a deep breath and spoke into my phone again. A part of me wanted to scream into his ear, but the other part wanted to keep quiet. As a result, the average of the two parts came out: "This is hitting me pretty hard, Dad."

"I'm sure it is." Those were his words, but the expression in his voice said *this is not the reaction I was expecting.* And somehow, there was comfort in that. He was expecting me to rave on in my anger, and my quietness had surprised him.

"I'm pretty caught up, Dad. I'm going to take the rest of the day off and think about this."

"Hold on a sec, son. Salvy told me why he's making this req–"

"At this point, I don't care. Just let me ask one thing that I've only assumed. You trust Iago, de Maria Salvadore, don't you?"

"As much as I trust anyone, including myself."

"Good enough. I'll call you back."

"Mikey, I'm really amazed at the way you're responding to this–"

"Me too, Dad. I'm not making any promises or anything, but my feelings are deeper than you might have thought. Maybe I'll tell you about it later. Maybe not too."

A call was coming in. Tiffany. Great.

"Talk to you later," I said, and punched the green button. I took a deep breath. Then another.

"Hello, Mr. Magnificent."

Up until a few minutes earlier, that had sounded really good coming from her. (I sometimes called her Ms. Fantastic) But I cringed this time. "Um, Tiffany, I just got a call that threw me for a loop."

"What–?"

"I don't want to talk about it yet, until I have time to sort things out. I'll call you later."

"All right." She sounded petulant. "I just wondered if you wanted to go hot tubbing after your workout."

"I don't know. Probably, but I can't say for sure yet.

I'll let you know in an hour or so."

"All right. I'll call back."

"Okay. Talk to you later, Astoundingly Beautiful.."

She giggled. "You do have a way of putting things."
Click.

I breathed deeply. Her voice was melodious and low,
utterly sexy, matching her appearance. She turned
everyone's head that saw her. When we walked down
the street together, it was like a shot of pure adrenaline.
Just from talking to her, the importance of my
conversation with Dad faded...

*Word of honor, fear of God, as much as I trust
anyone, including myself.* The words intruded
themselves into my mind again.

And I realized something. I had read those words
before, several times, but they had never applied to
anything about me. As I heard them the way my father
had used them, when he was younger than I, it felt
strangely like my longing to equal or better him with my
bench press. I wanted to have words like that apply to
my life.

Why? What more could a man like me want? I had
the perfect job, the perfect body, the perfect car, the
perfect house, the perfect girlfr– fiancée...

When I had called my father it seemed like
everything. Now, I felt a little bit difference...

Impulsively, I picked up my phone and dialed a
number. "Hello."

"Nick? Mike here. How's it going?"

"You got news for me, man?"

"Well, yes."

"Whaddya mean, *well* yes?  Did you arrange a knot tying or didn't you?"

"Well, yeah."

"There you go with that 'well' again.  What's it mean?"

"That's why I called you.  Yeah, I got engaged, but–"

"But what?  You've got good times ahead of you."

"Calm down a bit.  I called my dad to tell him, and he laid something heavy on me."

"Does he have cancer or something?"

"That's exactly what I thought, but no.  Believe it or not, it's worse that that."

"Like what?"

"Like some dude he knew from college wants me to marry his daughter."

"Sure he does.  Successful, good loo–"

"Not at all.  This guy's only seen me once or twice, when I was a kid, and as far as I know, doesn't know anything about me."

"Then why–?"

"Thirty years ago, my dad promised this guy he'd do any favor he asked of him.  He gave his word of honor."

"What?"

"Does that term hit you strange too?"

"Well, the way you said it–"

"Why am I even thinking about this, Nick?  I've got everything."

"You want a word of honor, don't you?"

Nick was like that. Seeing right to the heart of the matter.

I paused. "Yeah, I do."

"So you think your life's a bit shallow, huh?"

Ouch. "Do I?"

"What're you doing right now?"

"Nothing. I've decided to take the rest of the day off."

"Meet me at the Plug n' Chug in twenty minutes. I'm buyin.'"

"You don't need to–"

"I'm buyin!'"

"All right. Make it thirty minutes, though. I've got to give Casey a little bit of instruction.

"Fine. See you there. And don't eat anything before you come."

"Why would I do that?"

"So you can honestly tell me you're not hungry when you don't like the sandwich I'm ordering for you."

"Nick!"

"You've done it to me before."

"Oh. I didn't think you'd noticed."

"You know me. I don't miss nothin.'" I recited the last phrase with him. He hung up.

Nick was an unlikely friend I'd met the first day I came to Richmond. After traveling for most of the day, I'd arrived at my new office midway through the afternoon, and finished unpacking my van by five or so.

As I was stuffing some of the files into the cabinet, I suddenly realized I hadn't eaten anything since breakfast at six o' clock that morning, and I was famished. I'd asked Casey, my new secretary, for directions to a place where I could grab a quick bite, but as I drove around the unfamiliar streets, what had seemed initially like easy to follow directions became a mire of contradictions. A few minutes wandering had taken me to a side street with a greasy spoon hole in the wall dive that had cars parked all around it. At that point, my appetite was desperate enough to not care about appearances, so I'd gone inside.

The place was packed, except for one table where the skinniest guy I'd ever seen was sitting. He had a bald head, with a scraggly beard that had wisps reaching to the bottom of his chest. His clothes were out of style by so many years they were almost back in style, with bell bottomed pants, and a shirt unbuttoned down to his navel, showing off chest hair that had to protrude out as far as his chest was deep. When I first saw him, he was eating a sandwich that was piled so high with meat, cheese, lettuce, tomatoes, it looked like he had to unhook his jaw to bite down squarely on it. It was slathered with some kind of topping, probably mayo and mustard, that oozed off the bread in a yellow white river and mixed with the hairs of his beard.

In spite of my hunger, I watched in fascination as he ate the whole thing, which had to weigh a significant percentage of what he did. I continued to watch as he pulled out a moist towelette from his pocket and meticulously cleaned his beard. He noticed me as he was finishing.

"Hey, newcomer," he said, in a voice loud enough for the people in the cars going by to hear. "I'm the only one that's got room at my table."

"That's because nobody wants to get sick from watching you eat, Nick!" an anonymous voice from the crowd had shouted. It was good natured enough in its tone, but it was absolutely true, of course. Still, I didn't have much choice if I wanted to eat. And it looked like Nick was finished anyway.

So I sat down. Before I could get myself situated, Nick called out, "Hey Bev! Get my friend and me another one of what I just had! I guarantee you'll like it," he said as he slapped a ten dollar bill down on the table.

They must have had the sandwiches ready made, because less than thirty seconds later, to my delight, a sixtyish appearing woman appeared, placed a tray on the table, took the money and left without acknowledging either of us. "She doesn't want to encourage me," Nick said, smiling, and showing a mouth full of perfect teeth. He was no more than ten years older than I.

"Is that a possibility?" I asked.

He grinned again. "Well, no, but she doesn't need to know it," he said. "If you got time, wait till the dinner crowd leaves." I could barely understand the end of his sentence, because he'd bit into the dagwood in front of him as he finished speaking.

In spite of his awful manners, the sandwich did put out an enticing aroma. Tucking a napkin from the table under my shirt collar, I took the behemoth of food into my hands, opened my mouth as wide as I could, and took a bite. It was delicious. For a few minutes, I tried to match Nick bite for bite, and I might have been able to do it, except I was unable to ignore the sauce that built up on my face with each chomp. As a result, Nick finished well ahead of me.

"Do you think you'll want another one?" he asked, watching the food go from my hand into my mouth like a hungry dog. He was cleaning his beard again.

I shrugged and finished chewing and swallowing the current bite before I answered. "I don't know. I'm not done yet."

"Two more, Bev!" Nick called out.

"I don't think I can eat another one," I said, dismayed.

"Don't sweat it," Nick said. "If you can't finish it, I will."

And he did, along with his, at least his third. Each time when he finished, he cleaned his beard.

"How in the world do you eat all that?" I said.

"Don't you mean, where does it all go?" Nick said, flashing his brilliant smile again.

"I suppose so, yeah," I said.

"My stomach has learned the art of interdimensional

transfer," he said, without a trace of his smile.

"Hmm," I answered. *Where are those three and a half monsterwiches I just saw him consume?* My belief in the conservation of matter was being seriously challenged.

That was on a Friday night, thirty months earlier. Since then, I hadn't missed one Friday at the *Plug and Chug.* Each time I went, he was there, and every time, in spite of the fact that I was making plenty of money, he insisted on buying. My protest and his vehement reply were part of our ritual.

Twenty-eight minutes later, I was there at the same table as the first time, the only one I used. The crowd was heavy as usual, with some of the faces quite familiar and some not quite so familiar. I loved the place.

Tiffany didn't though. I'd only brought her once, and she had sat next to me at Nick's table. She had only managed one bite of her sandwich before she stood up and walked out, claiming she needed fresh air. I had eaten my sandwiches (I was handling two at that point) more quickly than I liked, and went to find her. Since then, she had tried to get me to do other things on Friday nights, but every time, I told her I would love to have her with me at the Plug and Chug. I wasn't going to give it up.

*Why? The food's usually good, but lots of places have good food. It can't be the atmosphere, could it? Could Tiff's dislike of this place make it more desirable than it would have been?*

Maybe. But mainly I like Nick. Like the restaurant, he's different from anyone else.

A moment later, I felt his hand on my shoulder. "Two minutes early, eh?  Couldn't wait for the lunch I'm buying?"

He sat down in his accustomed seat, across from me. "Bev, these two young men at my table want the Stink Bomb."

"No one *wants* the Stink Bomb."

Nick held out his hand. "Don't listen to her. She doesn't know jack."

Unlike my usual experience at the Plug and Chug, the Stink Bomb took a long time to prepare. When Bev finally brought it out, she had a large, florescent orange clothespin squeezing her nostrils together. After she set the tray down, she cleared her throat. "Ladies and gentlemen," she said in a surprisingly loud voice. Her face had no more expression than ever. "We need  to applaud these two men.  They  are about to attempt the Stink Bomb, (tendrils of unpleasantness *were* wafting up from the plate into my nostrils) willing to brave the Limburger Cheese in order to experience the most magnificent sandwich in the world."

There was enthusiastic applause from the crowd, about three fourths capacity.  A few mean spirited calls also, something like *you can't stink any worse, Nick.* Which was unfair. He didn't stink.

Somewhat reluctantly, I took the sandwich in my

hand and held it up. The odor from the Limburger, originating from the sandwich in my hand, seemed to linger over it like the green cloud from legend.

Nick was watching me expectantly, but I noticed he hadn't even taken his sandwich in his hand.

*I'm not going to eat something Nick won't*—but why not? It wasn't going to poison me. If it tasted bad, it was supposed to teach me something. Besides, the whole restaurant crowd was watching me, and had already applauded my courage. I couldn't let them down.

I bit into the sandwich. I admit, though I was trying to keep a straight face, inwardly I was wincing like I had my hand over a flame. This was not much different from the bitter drink the warriors of ancient time had to quaff to prove their bravery...

My anticipation and jaw tightening kept me from tasting the first bite until it was going down. Only at that point did I realize the sandwich wasn't awful. In fact, I found when I tasted it again, it was not bad. No. The third bite confirmed it. It was tasty. Not just tasty. Delicious, I found with the fourth and fifth bites. The most delicious sandwich I had ever eaten. By the time I reluctantly put the last bite in my mouth, sorry it had to be over so quickly, I realized it was the most delicious *food* I had ever eaten. Intense. Astounding. Unbelievable, almost surreal.

In one neutral corner of my brain, I noticed that the people were applauding enthusiastically, including Nick and Bev.   And it's a little difficult to describe my feelings.  I felt a strange sort of guilt, having people cheer for something that had ended up being delightful rather than what we had expected.  At the same time, I resisted that thought, not wanting to waste any portion of my consciousness on anything except savoring, relishing, *basking* in my gustatory experience.

Slowly, I became aware of  a hand on my arm.  It was Nick's, and he was pulling on me.  Somehow, I had ended up standing.

Shaking my head to orient myself back to life, I sat heavily.  "What in the world was in that thing?" I asked.

Nick smiled.   "Have you noticed I haven't eaten my sandwich?" he said.

I nodded.

"Well, you gotta admit, that's unusual.".

I nodded again, with probably more vigor than was polite.

"It's not that I didn't want it, you know."  He said it almost defensively.

I held out my hands, conceding, but also placating.

"What did you learn from that experience?"

It took me about ten seconds to think up an answer. "I've learned that our first opinions about things aren't always right."

"Good," Nick said.  "What else?"

"Goodness can sometimes be disguised."

"Excellent.  Anything else?"

I thought some more.  The principle he was trying to

teach me seemed to be deeper than what I had expressed.

This time I spoke slowly. "You can't truly know a sandwich until you eat it."

It was like I had turned on a light in his eyes. "Yes!" he said, so loud, many eating heads turned to look. He leaped to his feet. "You did it! Mom!"

*Mom?*

A moment later, Bev appeared at our table. For the first time in my memory of her, she was smiling. She had a lovely smile.

"He got it, huh?" she said, leaning down and kissing my cheek.

*What in the world...?*

Nick nodded enthusiastically. "Looks like it."

"Does he graduate?"

"Yeah."

"What is going on?" I felt frustrated and delighted simultaneously.

Nick stood up and took my arm, pulling me to my feet with one hand while he held his still untouched sandwich with the other. "Where're we going?"

"Graduate    School," Nick    and    Bev    said simultaneously.

They led me into an office behind the kitchen. Nick pushed me into a chair on one side of the large desk on one end, and then went around and sat in the chair on the other side. He moved a couple of papers from the middle, a little closer to my side, revealing a metal tray set into the wood of the desk. This he wiped down with a moist towelette, which he took from a huge supply in the top desk drawer. With a little bit of a flourish, he placed his sandwich on the tray.

"What is the physical appearance of this sandwich?" he said.

"Nick, what's going on here? Is it all right with management that you're using this office, or–" the truth hit me like a face slap– "you own this place?" *How could I not have seen?*

Nick nodded, but he did not look up. "What is the appearance of this sandwich?" he said again.

All right. I'd play along. "It's got darkish appearing bread–" I began.

"Pumpernickel," Nick said. He took off the top bread covering and placed it on the tray beside the larger bulk. "It doesn't have an odor like Limburger, but it has a stronger taste."

The next layer was a red colored sauce, with some exotic name I don't remember. The next was the cheese. Each time we identified a layer, Nick would slice it off the body of the sandwich, and place it on the pile that had started with the top slice of pumpernickel.

By the time he was finished, he had identified ten different layers, and had remade the sandwich upside down. Then he took it in his hand, smushed it a little flatter, put it to his mouth and took an enormous bite. While he was chewing, he waved it at me.

"I worked on this for six months before I felt

confident enough to put it on the menu," he said, barely understandable. He sprayed crumbs as he spoke. "I researched all the complementary tastes, all the textures, all the smells before I started. I wanted it to stink just like it does, but I needed to weigh the value of ideal texture with the power of the taste. The weight, the feel, the balance also needed consideration."

I raised my hand. "Why did you have it stink?" I said. "How many people are going to buy a sandwich that smells like that?"

"I didn't design it to sell a lot," Nick said. "I designed it to teach."

"Teach?"

"What you just learned."

I looked down at the desk for a moment, while Nick happily devoured his magnum opus.

"So I get to know a sandwich for what it is by knowing the ingredients and eating it. Now I know how to deepen my relationships with food. How–?"

"Think a little bit before you say any more, or I'll flunk you."

"Give me a hint."

"What happens when you really savor something, all the way down?"

Okay. This pulled me in a more productive direction. "I eat it slowly, identifying each component, both individually and together, becoming acquainted, then intimate with the interactions of each part with the other parts, appreciating the food with its appearance, its texture, its aroma, its taste."

"Good. You're getting there. How will you think about it subsequently?"

I thought a moment more. "With great reverence. Each time I think of it afterward, I will want to savor it again, to become even more familiar with it, more attached to it, more *committed* to it."

I could tell by Nick's expression that he was pleased with what I was saying. "And what would your commitment to this sandwich be?"

"That I was allowing it to become part of me, something I carried with me at all times, something that became part of my personal definition."

"All that for a *sandwich*?" It was a question *I* wanted to ask *him*.

But, since he was asking me, I would answer. "It honors the sandwich and me to have such a bond. Hereafter it will be part of my personal definition that my favorite, most cherished, most revered food is the (I cringed just the slightest amount) Stink Bomb." I hesitated a moment. "It seems a little premature for me to say this about my relationship with a sandwich I've encountered only once."

Nick nodded. "Fair enough. But you've learned what I wanted you to learn. Why did I want you to learn it?"

The question seemed casual enough. Sure. "Because you care about me. More than that. Because you care about—everyone."

I suddenly found my face hot. "I've known you two and a half years, Nick. Today I find out you own my favorite restaurant of all time, and only now I realize you're a teacher. Where'd you go to college?"

He flashed me his smile. "Dartmouth, '95." he said. "Philosophy., M.A."

"Nick, I'm ashamed," I said.    "I haven't cared enough to think beyond myself."

He held up his hand. "Don't sweat it. Every time we got close, I steered it away."

"But if I'd really cared–"

"'Sall right, bro. You're caring today. Why would I want you to learn about the sandwich?"

"Because it's an analogy about my relationship with people."

"All right. Let's start with Tiffany."

Something about his tone tipped me off. "You don't like her, do you, Nick?"

He shook his head. "I have no personal opinion of her."

At that moment, my phone rang. Tiffany again.

"Hello, Miss Lovely." It was my second string pet name for her.

"How about hot tubbing?"

"Um, what time?"

"After your workout!"

"Oh, yeah. Sure."

"Don't sound so enthusiastic!"

"Well, I still kind of got stuff on my mind."

"Let me come over and cheer you up."

"Well, I'm talking to Nick right now.  If you wanna come–"

"Why're you always talking to him?  What's the matter with me?"

"Nothin.'  But I like to talk to him sometimes."

"All right."  She sounded petulant again.  "I'll see you at five then."

"Cool.  See ya."  I hoped I didn't sound as uneager as I felt.

Nick was watching me closely.  "Do *you* like her, Mike?"

"Of course I do.  I love her.  It's just that sometimes I like–"

"To consider deeper stuff.  Like sandwichology."

"Right.  She's really smart, but–"

"It hasn't sunk in very deep."

Ouch.  "Right, I guess."

"Why do you love her then?"

"Because–"  I started speaking immediately, hoping words would come out, but I was left with just a 'because,' hanging out over nowhere.  "Um, because she's pretty, smart, has a good sense of humor–"

"She laughs at your jokes," Nick said.

"Have you been talking to my dad?"

"We both know you.  What else?"

"Well, she's really knowledgeable about– lots of stuff."

"Like what?"

"Well, she knows everything about fashion and current trends and—everything."

"Are you hearing yourself, Mike?"

"Yeah."

"You want to spend the rest of your life with this woman?"

"Nick, she's got the best body you could imagine!"

"Let's go back to the sandwich. Use the same words, but apply them to her."

"All right. I guess I'll use all her caring about makeup and hairstyles as the Limburger."

"What about the fashion?"

"I know it kind of all fits in the same place, but I care a little more about that part of appearance. I mean, when your attire is right on, people respect you more. It sounds superficial, but it's just a fact that as I move up in my career, having her at my side's gonna be an asset."

He just stared at me. "Nick, this is the first time I've ever thought about it."

"All right. What will you use to counteract the Limburger? In order to work, it has to be something as intense."

"Can I use her looks for that?"

"No, because sandwiches have appearances too. It's the appearance of the sandwich that entices us to try it in the first place."

"Oh. Well, I'm not sure I can find something as intense as the pumpernickel. I don't think–"

Nick held up his hand again. "Look man, I just

lowered this whole thing on you. But you need to think about it."

"I will." I stared at Nick a little. "How'd you end up in this business?"

He pushed back in his chair, put his feet up on the desk, and ate a crumb from off his shirt.

"I wanted to teach the masses, and maybe find some people who thirsted for greater understanding. They have to be people who are willing to overlook appearances and learn from unlikely sources. Today you proved you're that kind of man."

I waved dismissively. "Nothing but a confused young man looking for answers."

"Good enough. If confusion leads to humility, it's doing a good job.."

"Mmhf."

"Look Mike, you've got a chance today to really see how Tiffany measures up."

"To what?" It wasn't like I didn't know, but–

"To what you said about getting to know your best sandwich."

"Oh. Yeah."

\*_____\*

*Los Angeles, California*

"Here's his picture. My father placed a full length photograph of a incredibly handsome, light haired man, with piercing blue eyes, on the kitchen table next to my bowl of cereal. His shoulders were broad enough to notice even though he was dressed in a dark suit, tailor made to fit over his six foot frame.

"What'd you say his name was: *Ken*?"

"Michael Marson."  My father never did appreciate my humor.

"How old is he?"

"Twenty-seven."

"*Twenty-seven?*  What's the matter with him?"

"What are you talking ab–"

"I mean, what's a guy looking like that doing unattached?  Is he–?"

"He's *engaged*, Olivia."

I had him.  It had been too easy.  "*Engaged?*  You're trying to set me up with someone–"

"His father tells me he doesn't think he's in love with–"

"So Michael's father's as much an expert on the feelings of his child as you are.  He's another control freak."

"Olivia, why do you have to say things like that?"

"Why do you have to control my life.?  That guy doesn't want to marry me, any more than I want to marry him."

"He's a good kid.  And how much have I tried to control your life?  You won't let me—"

"And I'm not?"

"Not what?"

"A good kid."

"I didn't say that.  If his dad asks him, I think he will."

"Do you think I'd take someone that does everything his daddy tells him to do?  And someone that was always resenting me for taking away his own choice?"

"How do you know he'd do that?"

"Of course he would!"

# *Chapter III*

## Evaluation

*Richmond, Virginia*

She was wearing a swim suit that would have been modest on most women, but on her it looked designed to showcase her body. As we sat in the tub, a few young men, perhaps deciding they wanted a continuous view of the awesome spectacle sitting next to me, climbed in on the other side of the tub, even though I was fairly certain they had been leaving before they saw her. Tiffany gave no sign she noticed their attention, but kept her eyes fixed on me, like I was Adonis or something. For their part, our enthusiastic tubmates kept their muscles flexed, their necks bulled, their chests outthrust, in the vain hopes a spare glance would chance their way. I kind of felt sorry for them.    They couldn't have gotten any relaxation out of the steaming water.

Unfortunately, neither did I.  The foreignness of the day's events had pressed into my heart, becoming a part of me.   In a sense, I found myself engaged to two women: one my choice and the other, a stranger.  And in a certain part of my mind, I found myself wondering if perhaps my father's choice, (or was it *her* father's choice) might not be the right one.

Tiffany grasped my arm and pulled herself closer to me.   "What's all the disturbance?" she said in her soft, melodious voice.

"Don't want to talk about it now," I grunted, glancing at the oglers.

She looked up, like she hadn't seen them.  "Oh," she said.  Then, one at a time, she gifted each of the young men with one of her brilliant smiles.

Then it was like magic.  As if she had explained our situation to them, the four got up, drunk up one more intoxicating gaze of my fiancée, and left.

Now, in spite of my readiness, I had to talk about it. I realized, somewhat to my surprise, that I had been grateful to the adolescent sightseers.  Now that they were gone...

"This is really bugging you, isn't it?"

I nodded, but now I gritted my teeth too.  "Yes, but there's no reason not to tell you.  It's just kind of embarrassing."

"Talk about embarrassing.   Do you know what

happened to me today?"

*Why's she providing me with an easy out? Is she afraid of something this serious in me?*

"Um, I better tell you about my thing first." Her "embarrassing" stories were almost intolerably dull.

"Okay." Petulance again.

"Um, my dad owed his college roommate a huge favor..." I began.

It took me at least fifteen minutes to tell the whole story, because Tiffany had all kinds of questions, none to which I had the answer. *What's the matter with his daughter?, Is she some huge cow?, What's happened to her other relationships?, Don't you see this is nothing but a set up?, How much money does she have?,* but the question that she asked the most often, and the one I dreaded the most: *Why didn't you just tell him **no**?*

I think she must have asked it seven or eight times, and each time, I stammered out something utterly without conviction, that she did not hear anyway. "Well, uh, he brought it up so suddenly, I was totally taken off my guard."

The plain truth suddenly occurred to me. *She keeps on asking the question whose answer she fears more than anything. She trusts me enough to believe I won't dare say it, even if it is true: Because you're inadequate to me. You're only the bread and Limburger cheese of my sandwich. Very expensive, beautiful bread. Tasty? I don't know.*

"Will you come with me to the Plug and Chug?" I had to interrupt her, because she was asking the question again.

I had offered her an escape route for her anxiety. "No, I don't want to go to that *hole*! Why do you always go there anyway? You were just there."

"Nick's my friend."

"Why do you have to meet him there, of all places?"

"It's his restaurant."

"It is?" She was surprised too.

"Yep. And I like it there." I knew this argument was an easier way to deal with the far deeper question we were avoiding, but it was preferable to both of us.

"You go there just to annoy me."

Now was a perfect opportunity to deny something that was somewhat true, But denial would have been a way of placating, which was a way of postponing unpleasantness until we were madder.

"Well, I admit, it makes going there a little more desirable."

"I can't believe you just said that!"

This was an opportunity to get angry in turn, which would have also been an easy way of finishing our discussion. A few rash words, an abrupt parting, discomfort over.

But not for good, and it was too easy. "I'm sorry, Tiffany. But don't all men have something like that?"

She looked at me for a long moment, and the anger faded from her face. "Well, probably, but it isn't polite to bring it up." Then she smiled.

Uh oh. We were back to rational discussion again. I kept wasting all my opportunities for dodging.

I took a deep breath. "All right. Let me be honest then."

As I spoke the words, I looked into her face and saw a wave of anxiety pass over her lovely features. *How can I go on with this?* I closed my eyes. *If I don't now, I might never.*

"Tiffany, my dad gave his *word of honor* to do what this Salvadore asked."

"Isn't that your dad's problem, not yours?" I could hear a note of hysteria in her tone.

I softened my voice. "It feels like it belongs to me." Then, very quietly. "I *want* it to belong to me."

"What do you mean by that?" Her voice was full of hurt.

"I've never given my word of honor in my life, and here my dad, at age twenty-two, gave his."

"He was just a dumb kid saying words."

"No he wasn't!" Vehemence in my reply. "When he read it to me, it felt *real*." Softer this time.

"It was real to him, not you. He can't go around dictating your life like that."

"I guess the question is, do I have any responsibility to uphold my father's honor?"

She was quiet for a moment. "It's not fair."

I didn't say anything. I didn't exactly know what she meant.

"What's the matter with me?" Tiffany said in a small voice that tore at my heart like claws.

And that question, more than anything else, weakened my resolve to protect my father's honor. Tiffany had asked the question that both of us had been trying so hard to avoid. *If she can face her own inadequacy so well, then Tiffany's pumpernickel is courage.*

"Nothing," I said. "There's something the matter with me."

But that wasn't true. There was the potential of a problem in her. *Is there the remotest possibility that telling her the absolute truth will do her, or my current situation any good?*

I bit my lip—hard. Certainly, saying nothing now had the potential of causing problems in the days to come. But how could I do it?

"There is something the matter with me," I repeated. "But I don't know how I'm going to tell you without making it sound like there's something the matter with you."

Tiffany shook her head. "Don't say anything more, Michael," she said. "I'm not ready to hear it."

"The last thing in the world I want to do–" I began, but she covered my mouth with her hand. "I know."

I took her by the shoulders. "At least let me say this much. I have to do this."

"Do what?"

"I have to find out the answer to my question. Is it

my obligation to fulfill my father's word of honor?"

"How are you going to find it out?"

"I don't know." I hesitated a moment. "But I will."

"What do I do in the meantime?"

"What do you want to do?"

"I want this to be over with as quickly as possible."

"I don't even know where to begin. But I wouldn't be able to take this for very long. No more than a week."

"Does that mean we're not going to see each other for that long?"

I shrugged. "I don't know. Probably not."

Tiffany sighed. "This all seems so crazy. A nut from your father's past–"

"No, Tiffany. I wouldn't consider this if he were a nut. In a way, he's responsible for my dad's career, for all the people who've been successful because of it, for my job as well."

"How much am I worth?"

"Aw, c'mon Tiffany. You're worth everything. It's just that, it's like my father swore an oath, and maybe I'll be cursed if I don't honor it."

In spite of the hot water, Tiffany shivered. "You don't really believe that, do you?" she asked.

"Kind of."

"Why?"

I thought for a moment. "Because my dad taught me my word is the most precious thing I have. By it my worth is gauged."

"What does that have to do with–?"

I shook my head vigorously.    "Tiffany, my dad taught me that.  If I believe it, aren't I obliged to honor *his* word?"

"But Michael, he gave his word without knowing what Salvadore would ask him to do!  What right does anyone have to–?"

"No Tiffany.  I still have to honor it.  It does seem kind of crazy, but I get the feeling I'll hate myself for the rest of my life if I just ignore it."

"No matter what the request does to us?"

Ouch.  Direct hit.

"Um, of course it matters, but I still have to look into it."

"Whatever."    Tiffany turned her head and looked straight ahead.

There really wasn't anything more to say, even though I think she was expecting me to try to reconcile.  It was too good of an opportunity to let me finish up this interruption and get back to my life.

So I stood up.  "I'll stay in touch," I said.  I climbed out of the tub and went to the locker room.  The last I saw Tiffany, she was staring straight ahead, her face expressionless.  It could have been sweat or tears I saw on her face.  I still wish I could have been more graceful.

\*_____\*

*Los Angeles, California*

It really bothered me.  I had not burned his picture.

In front of my father, I had wadded it up and thrown it away, but I had retrieved it and even ironed it when he had left. This guy this Michael Marson, looked to be the most everything man I had ever seen. It wasn't exactly his handsome face or Apollo-like figure either, although they were hard to ignore. There was a look of confidence in his mien, a look of genuine friendliness, a look of interest, a look of *awareness,* but there was also a look of innocence.

This must sound quite foolish, me extrapolating all this from a mere photograph, but that's what I did, and I spent about two hours doing it, before I got up the next morning. My father never bothered trying to rouse me before 10:00, so I didn't have to worry about him coming in and surprising me in the middle of actually caring.

This is embarrassing too, or would be if anyone but me were ever going to read this. I was actually out of bed and dressed in my exercise outfit before 9:00 that day, which means I was awake before 7:00. Michael the archangel looked like the type of fellow that would get up early.

I knew he was out of my reach. Not because he was engaged. It was because what my father had said about me was exactly right. I couldn't hold on to a relationship. Even if this guy were to give up his lush babe of a fiancee, (I didn't know what she looked like, but it was a safe bet) and bow at my feet, I'd kick him in the head. The more I liked him, the harder I'd kick.

# *Chapter IV*

## Departure

*Richmond, Virginia*

Feeling somewhat like a coward, I showered and dressed and made no further effort to see Tiffany. I was going to give this matter my attention. Tiffany was complicating it by suddenly showing depth I hadn't suspected in her. And it was complicated enough.

But I stopped as I gripped the door handle of my scratchless Corvette. What was I doing this for? Why was it seeming so much like me punishing Tiffany?

*Because I'm not sure I love her. I suspect I don't.*

There it was. I'd put the thought out of the discomfort of whispers from my unconscious into broad daylight.

*Why would I not love Tiffany?*

I don't know how long I stood there, with my hand on the door of my car, considering my question. The only thing that goaded me back into action was the thought that she might come out of the recreation center, and I'd have to say something to her.

So I got into my car. I remember starting the engine, and I remember going to a gas station and filling up. But my mind was considering my question, and I felt a pure beam of concentration upon me. I wasn't going to interrupt it, because I knew, if I followed it, enlightenment was on the other end. If interrupted, it might not come again.

From the gas station, I started driving. I didn't have a destination in mind, but I know I didn't want traffic to distract me, so I got on 64 and headed west. A little ways north of Charlottesville, I had bought a cabin a year earlier, and I think I decided, somewhere in my secondary thoughts, that I would head there and hole up for a day or two.

But I kept the concentration beam with me. *Why would I not love Tiffany?*

She was beautiful—exactly. Her physical appearance was almost overwhelming. If she had been in the beauty contest between Athena, Aphrodite and Hera that Paris decided to the great detriment of his people and his city, he would have been hard pressed to pronounce Aphrodite the winner, despite her bribes. Tiffany's features were perfectly symmetrical, her eyes large, luminous, the color of the sky on a perfectly clear day, a startling blue. Her nose could have enhanced the face of Helen herself, her cheekbones—well, everything was perfect. And she was a true blond.

We had met on a blind date, that Randy Mart, my accountant had arranged. She was the sister-in-law of his wife's sister, and had just finished up her MBA, with her undergraduate in Fashion Design. Three months after graduation, she had a successful Internet business going. Our first date had been at an Art Show, and I had been instantly impressed with Tiffany's knowledge and insight into the various forms of art expressions. In fact, I had been a little intimidated.

But it had been great fun. Here I was, walking through an art gallery side by side with a goddess of beauty who also appeared to be the goddess of wisdom. I could actually feel the stares of the others in the gallery, men and women, as Venus and her not too hard to look at escort strolled in front of them all. We served as better replicas of Adam and Eve than the First Parents statues featured in the front of the display.

So there we were, appearing like the perfect couple, (everybody said so) both of us unattached, and– things just happened from there. Four months after we started dating, we began talking about marriage, and eighteen months after that, (looking back, it seems remarkable we dated without commitment for so long) we were engaged.

I was cruising along the highway, going about seventy, with plenty of accelerator left. The car was running perfectly, a true joy to drive, allowing me to think, to remember, to relive the experiences I needed to scrutinize my heart.

Everybody thought we were the perfect couple. Who was everybody? Tiffany's brother, Alex, Cynthia Mart, Randy's wife, Randy, all of our friends. They said it nearly every time we were together.

And it kind of bothered me. What made us the perfect couple? Our looks? And whose fault was that? It's true, we both worked hard at it, but we were both physically well favored. It was, more or less an accident that had nothing to do with intelligence, character, disposition, creativity, compassion, humility, or any other quality that determined the suitability of a person to be part of a good relationship.

More times than I could count, virtually every person I knew, except my father, had told me "you ought to marry that woman."

Why? Of course I was attracted to her, and of course I liked the attention her looks, and perhaps our combined looks brought us. But it kind of bugged me that everyone around us assumed it was a foregone conclusion we would be together. It was pressure I didn't like...

Why not?

Was I afraid of commitment? Here I was, twenty-seven years old, having put off marriage and family until I was able to support them well, and along comes a lovely woman willing to marry me and be the mother of my (probably adopted, and that didn't sit quite right with me) children, and I was throwing down roadblocks.

Had I had other girlfriends that would have been good marriage candidates? Using my knee to steer, I counted off on my hands. Leila, six months. Cynthia, three months. Desdemona, eleven months. Kylee, fourteen months. Megan, two months. Every one of them talked about marriage. Were any of them good candidates?

Without question, each of the five were more qualified in the traditional way, and each had more mothering skills than Tiffany. Why did I choose to advance my relationship with Tiffany when I'd been with five more prepared to be a mother? It hadn't occurred to me before.

The implications of the thought were quite uncomfortable. *Why am I setting myself up to fail? Because unconsciously, I didn't want to marry her. The mismatches were enough to sabotage the relationship before I made it permanent.*

That means I was looking for the announcement from my father. Why?

I didn't have an immediate answer, so I settled myself into my seat, put both hands on the wheel, and drove for a little while. It felt good to drive this machine, so perfectly tuned, so smooth, so *head turning.* I liked that as much as anything.

*I like people to notice my car. I like people to notice me.*

*Yes!*    This was coming close to uncomfortable territory, but I pressed on.  *When people notice me, I want to notice them noticing.  I want them to see my appreciation of their attention.*

Aha!  *When I have a girlfriend, especially a fiancée, I'm not free to respond to someone else's attention.  I'm bound by my loyalty to–*

Why should I care so much for the attention of someone I don't know, when I have the full attention of someone I do?

Because the superficial relationship is safe.  The further I go into commitment, the tighter the bands that bind me.

Bind me?  To what?

*To the risk that someone might discover the me I fear to show to the world.*    I had to wrench the realization out of myself.  *What do I fear to show the world?*

Nope.  I wasn't ready to go there yet.

Tiffany and I had done all kinds of things together.  I attended her first fashion show, well, mainly I sat at her first fashion show eating sunflower seeds.   Tiffany wouldn't have let me get away with it if she'd been sitting by me.  She'd gone with me to a car show, which had been great, except maybe for her.  We'd eaten at every possible nationality of restaurants, and in every case, except for the Plug and Chug, we had mutually enjoyed it.

But I realized our activities had mainly been parallel, not mingled.  We shared very little common interests, and—suddenly it came to me clearly. Other than my enjoyment of her physical nearness, which was inevitable, I didn't enjoy our times together. *If it weren't for her intense femaleness, her sheer womanhood, I wouldn't especially like being with her.*

There. I had admitted it. *I don't like Tiffany.*

No. Wait a minute. I like her as much as I like anyone. It's just that–

*But is that necessary in a marriage?* I looked down and saw I had crept up to 80. I eased my foot off the accelerator, then slipped back into my concentration.

Not strictly necessary, but obviously helpful. Still, two people committed to each other can find things in common. Or create them.

Ouch. I had been almost succeeded in justifying myself. But I wasn't going to do it. A lot was right about Tiffany.

My phone buzzed. "Hello."

"Isn't our engagement *your* word of honor?" Click.

*Really* good point. I thought about it for a few moments. Would calling off our engagement be tantamount to placing my father's word of honor over my own?

No, I didn't think so. *Marriage* would be my word of honor. Engagements, I decided, was a very ingenious way of postponing two words of honor until both were ready to give them.

Still, it was a good point, and showed Tiffany was thinking. More than I thought of her doing.

Hmm.   Had I answered my question yet?   Why would I not love Tiffany?  I bit my lip, trying to force more thought, more clarity into my brain.

It was kind of strange that every time I thought about her qualities, her physical beauty was the first thing that came into my mind.  It wasn't all she had, but it was the most obvious.

*When have I ever seen a strikingly beautiful woman that focused her life ultimately on anyone but herself?* It was not a completely fair question, because I hadn't really known anyone as incredibly lovely as Tiffany until I met her, so I had formed most of my impression from Hollywood.  But it was sitting there in the back of my mind, all the time.  It was stereotyping on my part, I know, and I felt somewhat bad, but nonetheless.  Since I had met her, I don't know how many times I wondered how I'd feel for her if she were just pretty, or maybe even plain.

So I drove, thinking of Tiffany.  Her face and body were so incredible, how could I think–?

But being away from her cleared my head.  As the distance between us increased, it seemed I became more and more able to separate my true feelings from my feelings of—it is very hard to describe what my emotions, my impulses, my *passions* were.  They make my relationship with her sound so cheap.

My phone buzzed again.  At that moment, I would have rather thrown it overboard then to endure another of Tiffany's barbs, but I don't do things like that.

"Hello."

"It's Dad, Mikey."

My relief brought more enthusiasm than I was feeling into my voice. "Oh, hi!"

"How are you doing?" I could tell he was speaking carefully, trying to determine my mood.

"Okay," I said noncommittally.

"Have you thought about–?"

"Are you kidding? Dad, I haven't thought about anything else!"

"Does that mean you're actually considering it?"

I drew a deep breath. "I'm not ready to answer that yet."

"I know a little bit more," my father said.

"Will it make my decision any clearer?"

Now I heard his great intake of breath. "I don't know, son. I can send you a picture of her, if you want."

I hesitated only a moment. "Yeah, that'd help a lot. But how could she be anything but a dog?"

"I'll send it to you."

"She'd have to be unbelievable to have her picture make a difference."

"So you don't want to see it?"

"No, send it along. I wouldn't dare even think about this without it. But how can anyone compare to Tiffany?"

"Different kinds of beauty, son."

"So she's one of *those,* huh?"

"Don't judge until you see."

"All right.  Look Dad, don't expect anything out of this.  I'm almost sure I'm going to make my decision this evening.  And it won't be in favor of this harebrained scheme."  I was being a little more harsh than I liked.

As I ended the connection, I saw the Highway 250 exit was only ten miles ahead.  I'd take it north and west to Hwy 29, the Seminole Trail.  My cabin was northeast of there, just past Westmoreland, on the river.

Storm clouds were darkening the western sky.  In a half hour or so, it would be pouring rain.  It was going to feel really good to lounge on the veranda listening to the rain pound the roof, watching the lightening and hearing the thunder.  Nothing felt more secure than watching the elements battle from a safe location...

*_____*

*Los Angeles, California*

I was standing in front of a mirror, dressed only in my swimsuit.  I didn't really want to look, because I was only gauging how *he* would judge me, and I doubted I would ever see him.  Separating myself out from my body (I had begun doing it at age five and had become adept at age eight) I looked objectively at the woman in the glass.  Although I called myself fat, she was a little on the too slender side, even though she managed to hide it effectively with her wardrobe.  Her hair, reaching down past her waist was deep brown, almost black, and her eyes were also dark, large like a deer's.  Her high cheekbones and arched eyebrows focused attention  on her eyes.  For a woman, she was on the tall side, five foot eight and a half, weighing a scant one hundred twenty-two pounds. Her lips were surprisingly full for a woman so skinny, and her smile revealed perfect teeth and a sudden radiance. (The radiance troubled her, because it was so opposite to her true character) Her nose was the spoiler. It was too narrow, and it hooked unforgivably. She had been planning to have plastic surgery on it for years, but it always seemed too painful and inconvenient. Now here she was, needing it perfect, and here it was, hooking right in front of her, utterly without permission.

Slowly, I let myself back in. *He's never going to love me with my nose like this. And why should I care anyway?*

# *Chapter V*

## Car Lovers

*East of Charlottesville, Virginia*

Someone was standing at the side of the road. As I came closer, I saw it was a man, dressed in work clothes with holes in the knees of his jeans. He had a backpack over one shoulder, and his thumb was out.

I picked up hitchhikers occasionally, according to how they looked and felt as I approached them– but so close to my turn off—it looked too much like this rain was going to hit sooner than I wanted it to. I would feel bad if this fellow was drenched because I didn't stop. So I pulled over, just a little bit beyond him.

He came up with a huge smile on his face. " Powder blue Corvette!" he said as he gingerly sat down on the seat, holding his backpack on his lap. "This is a

'63, isn't it?"

"Yep," I said, unable to keep the pride out of my voice. A little excessively, I pushed down the accelerator, pinning our backs to the seats.

He cleared his throat. At that moment, the first raindrops hit the windshield. I turned on the wipers, with their one week old blades, and turned to look at him. His face, full of animation, reflected my own enthusiasm.

"I'm actually riding in Corvette's masterpiece," he said in slow, reverential tones. "In my opinion, GM's masterpiece." He was thin, with an Adam's apple that bobbed up and down while he talked.

I found myself immediately warming to one of my pet subjects. "Not many know that. Most people look at some of the showier years and think that's what Corvette's all about." I stuck out my hand. "Mike."

"Cliff," he said, shaking my hand heartily. "And thanks for the ride. My brother's going to be jealous."

"You guys know a lot about cars?" I said. The rain was coming down hard now. I turned the wipers up one speed.

"Everything before 1980," he said, laughing. "After that, it seemed like they all looked either the same or like rehashes."

"Isn't that the truth?" I said. "And fuel injection's a great thing, which Corvette did first. Everything after that was just plain old copying."

"Right!" Cliff said passionately. "I can tell you're a

man who knows his machines."

We were instantly friends. As the rain flooded the windshield faster than the wipers could clear them, we drove, starting sometime around Henry Ford and working our way forward to present times. Cliff knew more about engine design than I did, but I've never met anyone who could best me in knowledge of body styles.

After a half hour, we drove out of the rain, and I realized I'd long since passed up the 250 exit to Charlottesville. Oh, well. I wasn't in any hurry. I'd catch the second one and backtrack a little.

Unfortunately, we started sharing our views on foreign cars, arguing about the merits of Farrari, Mazeradi, Lexus, Bentley, Mercedes and Rolls Royce, Honda and Toyota, and our conversation got so animated, I drove right by the other 250 loop exit. At that point, we were only an hour away from Cliff's destination, so I decided to come back after I let him off.

The hour passed incredibly quickly. In fact, when he had me stop at a farm exit in the middle of nowhere, I couldn't believe we'd been driving more than two hours. I sat there with the motor running an extra fifteen minutes while he finished telling me about an old Dodge he had that went everywhere and forever. I actually shed a tear or two when he told me how a tree had fallen on it in a tornado.

"Do you want me to drive you to your home?" I said, noticing there were no houses in sight.

For just an instant, he looked uneasy. "Naw. It's uh —kind of a wreck."

"Look man, I don't care–" I started to say, but he had already disappeared over the embankment.

So I pressed down the accelerator and my car flowed back into the freeway traffic.

For several minutes, I just grinned while my Vette rolled down the road, smoothly as glass. Eddie, my mechanic, knew 60's vintage GM's so well he advertised himself as an expert, and had been able to limit his business to nothing but. He knew my car's problem by its sound as it rolled into his yard, and more often than not, he had the parts it needed. He chastised me for not reporting every change and every noise, and he charged me double for problems he found that I knew about and did not report. If he found anything wrong, he always fixed it, without my approval. I loved him.

Eddie didn't do body work, but he did not tolerate dings and dents. When I took my car in, he would mark the most obscure ones, with chalk and charge me five dollars per mark. I learned his lessons quickly, and kept the body nick and ding free, bright blue and shining.

Now it was gunning forward, cruising effortlessly at 75 miles per hour, getting 25 miles per gallon, more than 7 miles per gallon better than most others. Adjusting myself a little in my seat, I pushed down on the gas just a little, working up to 85.

"What a great guy!" I said to myself, remembering

the animation on Cliff's face when he sat in my car. Moment by moment, I reviewed our time together, relishing all his observations, all his compliments. It had been a really great time. He had validated all the work I had done, all the hours I had spent making my ride perfect.

"What a great guy!" I said again. "He–"

Wait a moment. *What evidence do I have that he's a great guy?*

*He likes cars. He knows a lot about cars. He cares a lot about cars. Is that the requirement for being great?* It was a ridiculous question.

*I don't know his occupation, I don't know his convictions, I don't know his work ethic, I don't even know his last name. Do I really think he's a great guy?*

So why'd I say it twice?

Because he was interested in what I like. He might be an axe murderer, his name and mug shot might be in every police station across the country, but he's a great guy because he shares my interests. How much does interest in cars have to do with someone's level of goodness, nobility, loyalty, productivity or value? Is it possible that Hitler or Stalin was equally interested in them?

It was an uncomfortable thought, but it was something I needed to consider. *Can I feel the value of people even when they did not share my passions? Can I objectively evaluate for qualities of worth, someone who believes differently than I do?*

With these thoughts burdening me, I drove on, so absorbed in my conundrum that I did not notice I was speeding every further away from the turnoff to my cabin. Only when I came to the junction between Highway 64 and 81 did I notice what I was doing.

*I'm trying to leave! Get myself lost so far Tiffany won't be able to find me.* As if in answer to my insight, my phone buzzed again. But I was passing a parked patrolman at the moment, and knew my car was conspicuous enough that his attention would likely be on me. (He had the decency to be parked at the top of a long rise, so I was only going 68)

Once I was safely by, I picked up. It was Tiffany. "Where are you?" she said.

"On the Highway," I said. "Taking a drive."

"In your powder blue *Corvette?*"

"It's the only car I have," I said, taken aback by the bitterness in her voice.

"When are you coming back?"

"I don't know yet, Tiffany. Pretty soon, I think."

"Well hurry up and make up your mind so I can get on with my life." Click.

Her sudden endings to our conversations were making it easy on me, even though I know she was trying to shock me with her abruptness. "I love you too," I said to nobody.

I'd been on the road somewhere between two and three hours by the time I pulled into Lexington. Hungry, I pulled over at a Taco joint, bought enough to get me by (everything was a disappointment after the *Stink Bomb*) then did a little stretching after I had eaten. It was twilight, and I was a long way from home, and now a long way from my cabin.

*I'm heading west,* I thought as I ate my burritos. *For what? I'm leaving behind an incredible, sweet, bright girl, for what? A twenty-nine year old promise, my father's word of honor, an old friend's moral debt—and his daughter.*

"What's the matter with her? Is she tough to look at–?

All I needed to find out was to park somewhere with good reception and download her picture on to my phone. Then I'll be able to tell—

No. I wasn't going to do it. I suspected that my relationship with Tiffany was based on that, and even now, though there might be more to it than that, I could not tell because of the physical part that blinded me to all the other qualities she might have. With someone like Tiffany, it was hard to avoid, but since I was starting out here, and I had the luxury of having never seen the girl some people wanted to be my wife, I wasn't going to let my feeling for her be colored by her looks.

I was certainly far enough away from home that I couldn't be tracked. All I needed to do was to check into a motel, turn off my phone, and continue my thinking until I had discovered–

What was I trying to discover? Whether I should

marry Olivia Salvadore or Tiffany Bailey?

No. It was more of a quest than that. I was going to discover, before my journey was through, the meaning of my life. My father had given me insight, Nick had given me (much) more, and now this Cliff, (albeit unwittingly) had added to my self understanding. His teaching was painful: *Commonality with another has nothing to do with goodness.*

*Now wait a minute.* A discordant voice inside me tried to argue. *That might be true some of the time, but it was like our minds melded or something. Isn't that kind of camaraderie something really good?*

*What import does the commonality have? What good will it do the world?* I can't say whose voice was arguing back. It was one of the angels on my shoulder, but which one?

*Well,* the car side of me said, sniffing, *if two people like that got together with their ideas, they could make a lot of people happy.*

*Happy over what? A shiny, souped up car?*

*Well, yes.*

*I rest my case. Find something better to do with our money.*

I rubbed our chin. I could easily sympathize with everything the car defending voice had said, but whose was the other one? *Is it the dominant part of me? Is it right?*

*\*_____\**

*Los Angeles, California*

I was making a list of the qualities I needed to develop when my father came into my room again. He was carrying something in his hand. I would have thought it was some kind of gift to placate me, but it was only an old piece of paper.

"Here," he said, handing it to me without a greeting.

I scanned it. "What?"

"It's the agreement Jacob signed when I helped him."

"Why would I care about–?"

"Read it." His tone was impervious, but gentle at the same time. "Please."

So I read it, aloud. "'On this eighteenth day of May, 1980, I, Jacob Frank Marson, being of sound and grateful mind, do hereby swear to my eternal friend, Iago de Maria Salvadore, that I will grant to him any request in my power to fulfill. This oath extends throughout my life, into the lives of the heirs of my body, until it is fulfilled. This I deliver with a most solemn oath and in the fear of God, upon my word of honor.'"

I looked up. "Why'd he–?"

"Doesn't matter. I have faith in him."

"That he's going to get his obedient little boy to drop his babe and come after fat, hook-nosed me?"

My father looked me in the eye without flinching. He didn't do that very often. "I'm given Michael Marson the opportunity to marry my lovely daughter."

His tone was neither patronizing nor flippant. To my complete dismay, I found my eyes filling with tears again. I couldn't let him see it. "Get out of here," I said. I tried to put anger in my voice, but it cracked, betraying my emotion. I saw a slight smile on his face as he turned and left.

And I knew why. For the first time in my memory, he had won. *Never again, Daddy,* I breathed. *Never again.*

# *Chapter VI*

## Idolater

*Between Lexington, Virginia and Charleston, West Virginia*

It was dark, about 9:30, when I saw the next hitchhiker. Ordinarily I don't pick people up at night, but it was raining again, a heavier rain than before, and the wind was blowing. It didn't seem fair that I would be cruising in my warm car while someone I could help was freezing outside.

I'd taken a pile of napkins from the Mexican place where I ate and now I put them on the passenger seat to protect it from the rain.

The long overcoated, thickly spectacled, wild eyed person put his head in the doorway, then looked down at the napkinned seat. "No," he said. "The car's clean."

He was dirty and bedraggled, and for an instant, I was willing to let him go. But wait. "Get in," I said. "Don't worry about the seat." (I must admit, the words sounded strange coming out of my mouth)

The man looked me in the face. "No," he said, backing up, a determined look on his face.

"It's okay, I tell you. No one else is going to pick you up in this weather."

He hesitated, a slight look of confusion apparent even in the faint light of my overhead. "I don't–" he began, but I grasped his arm and yanked. "Just get in."

I was strong, but I hadn't pulled hard enough to make a difference. The man tumbled into my passenger seat, then instantly took his arm and grasped it tightly while situating himself. In the process, he scattered the napkins, shredding the ones underneath him, grinding them into the seat.

"I'm cursed!" he said, once he was facing forward with his feet on the floor. I could smell the odor of wet B.O. (at least two days of ripeness, I would guess) buried under the long blue overcoat. He continued to hold his arm.

"What're you talking about?" I couldn't see his dark, shadowed face clearly, but I could tell he was staring straight ahead without even acknowledging me.

"I'm trapped by an idolater!" he said, his tone of voice loud enough to sound clearly above the pounding of the rain, but otherwise without expression or inflection. "He worships his car, he worships his shower, he worships his own face!"

"Look Bud, I don't know what you're talking about–"

"He doesn't know my name so he calls me Bud. I'm cursed!"

In spite of myself, I smiled. *How'd I ever get this stinky nut in my car?"* Where're you headed, Bud?"

"I'm all that redeems him from his worship of false gods. He wants to be rid of me, but he'll take me to Charleston."

*Charleston? That's over a hundred fifty miles away!*

"He seeks to waffle on his kindness."

"What?"

"The idolater would rid himself of his redemption."

I would have stopped the car and ordered him out, but I couldn't do it when the rain was pounding on the windshield so hard I could barely see. Besides, other than his odor, he wasn't really hurting anything. Charleston was a little over two hours away. Could I stand him that long?

"The idolater will be my brother, stripped of his trappings of wealth. As I, he will be forced to beg for his conveyance. Then will my stink be not so rancid to him."

"What's that supposed to mean?"

"He doesn't believe his passenger. How can a crazy homeless man have aught of importance to say?"

My phone buzzed. It was probably Tiffany, but I wasn't going to acknowledge the call. What would he have to say about her?

"He fears the homeless man's rebuke so he answers not his message."

I still didn't answer the phone. The rain let up a little, and I pressed the accelerator down...

*_____*

*Los Angeles, California*

I always let spiders live. They eat bad bugs, and everybody hates them, a lot more than they hate the bad bugs. It's probably because the Black Widow is their poster child. Black Widows eat their husbands. I can't ever have a husband, because I'd do the same thing...

I reached out and stroked Michael's cheek. It was a little wrinkly, because I'd crumpled it, but it was still beautiful. *If he were to love me, he would be the most desirable of all men I have–*

My father's footstep sounded in the hallway. Quickly (I had planned in advance) I placed the picture flat on the bathroom counter and covered it with my hand mirror. A corner of it showed, but it wasn't too noticeable.

His quiet knock, an apology for disturbing me while taking care of delicate matters, sounded. I laced my voice with irritation.

"What?"

"I just got the rest of the data on Michael."

"So?" How could I say the first thought that came to my mind: *Let me have it. Quick!*

"Thought you might like to look at it."

"Why should I ca– oh, all right." I opened the

bathroom door.     He stepped inside and handed me an
unsealed envelope.     Like a homing beacon, his eyes
found the corner of photo paper protruding from under
the mirror.     His gaze lingered there just a moment
before coming to my face. "Hope it's helpful," he said,
then turned and left.

*Did he know what it was?   It was like he expected it
to be there.* I slammed the door behind him.   Then,
quickly, I opened the envelope and drew out the paper.

Michael Harrison Marson.
Born: August 31, 1982, Long Beach, California
B.S., Civil Engineering: Long Beach State, 2003.
M.S. Civil Engineering: UCLA, 2004.
Junior Staff Engineer, Marson Engineering Solutions
LTD, July 2004-January 2005.
Staff Engineer, Marson Engineering Solutions LTD,
January-April 2005
Chief Engineer, Marson Engineering Solutions LTD,
Richmond, Virginia Branch, April 2005-present.
Height: 6 foot 2
Weight: 202 pounds
Hobbies: Power lifting, fitness, vintage cars, Boggle.
Honors: American Legion Award, Junior High and
High School
Most Outstanding Senior Athlete.
Captain, Long Beach State Football team, 2001-
2002.
Most   Innovative   Masters   Engineering   Project,

Greater Los Angeles area Committee, 2004

"As if someone like that would ever care about me,"
I muttered.

*_____*

*Between Lexington, Virginia and Charleston, West
Virginia*

I had not been able to drive as fast as I wanted
because of the rain. The homeless passenger had kept
up a harangue nonstop, but had never given me his
name. After the initial interchange, he had referred to
me only in the third person as the idolater.

At first, even as he censured me for it, I cursed the
rain and my insistence he ride with me. As far as he
was concerned, I had nothing good in me, except the
little bit of kindness that had incited my picking him up.
Even then, I didn't give him his choice, but had forced
him.

He was truly crazy, and he said it of himself several
times: "Are the words of the crazy man opening the
heart of the idolater?" Fortunately, I never had to
answer him.

As nearly as I can remember, and like I said, he was
redundant, the following is a list of what he said to me
during our car ride in the summer rainstorm:

The crazy man was cursed.

The crazy man was trapped by an idolater who
worshiped his car, his shower and his face.

The crazy man was all that redeemed the idolater.

The idolater was tempted to waffle on his agreement to take the crazy man somewhere.

The idolater and the passenger would have much in common. (Sure)

The idolater and the crazy man would both stink someday.

The idolater thought money answered all of life's problems.

The idolater thought appearance was important.

The idolater's doom was ahead of him.

The idolater loved his father, not his lover.

The idolater thought the unseen was unreal.

The idolater would not always be an idolater.

The crazy man was happier than the idolater.

The crazy man was more successful than the idolater.

The crazy man was richer than the idolater.

The crazy man was stronger than the idolater.

The crazy man communicated better than the idolater.

The crazy man was once an idolater.

The crazy man loved the idolater.

The crazy man was more beautiful than the idolater.

The idolater would someday think the crazy man his good friend. (Sure)

The idolater was being guided by something other than the object of his idolatry.

Each statement seemed to be more outrageous than the one before. Some of the time, I wanted to laugh, some of the time I was so angry I wanted to finish the job I'd started when I pulled on his arm. Underlying all my feelings was the almost irresistible desire to stop the car, reach over him, open his door and push him out into a puddle.

It was the longest car ride of my life. Toward the end of it, the rain let up, and twenty miles from Charleston, it stopped completely. But we were close, and though I had never agreed to take him there, I felt obliged.

His directions, once we got to town, were terse, to put it mildly. He never reproached me as I tried street after street leading to some sort of place. As it turned out, he had me stop in a transition place, where to our left were quite run down homes, and to our right was a modern subdivision. Which one was he going to choose?

I didn't find out. At the corner, the man raised his hand. "The idolater will let the prophet out here," he said imperviously.

I let him out. It was exactly midnight. I sat in my car, facing him, while he stared back. Neither of us moved. *He's not going to do anything until I leave.*

So I left. The last I saw of him, by the light of the street lamp, was my passenger/crazy man/prophet staring at me as I drove out of sight.

I was exhausted. The last 150 miles had been arduous, but I had been driving all day, and I never stayed up this late. Somehow, I managed to find a hotel with a 'vacant' light, checked in, and fell into bed without pulling down the spread, without even taking off my shoes.

Around 3:00, (I knew because there was a bedside digital clock) I woke up enough to take off my shoes, undress and get under the covers. (The air conditioning was on full blast and I had been freezing to death)

Ordinarily, I like seven good hours, but on this occasion, I awoke at 6:30. The words of my second passenger had integrated themselves into my dreams.

"I don't want any more to do with you!" I said as I got up and turned down the air conditioner. Then I was back under the covers, eyes tightly closed, determined to get at least another half hour. But like a song stuck in my head, the words of the madman repeated themselves again and again.

"What'd I do to deserve this?" I cried out, loud enough for people in the adjoining rooms to hear me. "I was giving a needy man a ride!"

But my reluctance to escape the memories seemed to draw them to me. Sentence by crazy sentence, I heard them again.

***[1]

(At this point, I am going to place my reflections and the more in depth conversations in the fourth book of this series, which is more of a handbook to go along with this work as much as anything else. Every time you, as the reader, see the three asterisks, you may go to the fourth book if you are interested. For the type of reader that only wants the action without the insight, here it is)

Somehow, in all my fatigue, I had managed to bring in my phone and cord and plug it in. Now I picked it up and speed dialed.

"Yeah, Mike."

"Hey. I need a couple of your minutes."

"Done, and no charge. What's up?"

"It's scarin' me, man."

"What?" I could hear more concern in his tone than he usually let show.

"How long ago did I eat that sandwich in the– in your shop?"

Nick hesitated a moment. "I dunno. About 20 hours ago, I guess. Do you always get up this early?"

"Did I wake you up? Sorry, man. I thought you'd be up alrea–"

"I'm finally getting a social life." He paused a moment." We were out till one."

"Hey, that's great. I'll call you back–"

"Naw, I was awake, just not likin' the idea. Talk to me."

"After I saw you, I went over and talked with Tiffany. We, or at least I, kind of agreed to not see each other until I got this thing settled."

"Got *what* thing settled?"

"You know, my dad's agreement with Iago

Salvadore. About me marr–"

"Yeah, I know about that. But why would something like that necessitate not seeing your fiancée?"

"I don''t get your question. Because I can't be married to two–"

"What I'm askin' is, why are you even considering this thing?"

"Because I–" I paused. "Because I might want out of the engagement."

"So your dad and this Salvadore and his daughter might not even have anything to do with this?"

"Well, maybe. I'm trying to use this as an opportunity to understand myself, I guess."

"Nothing wrong with that. It's what I was trying to help you with."

"Right. Well, I'm not sure I like how my education's proceeding."

"Tell me about it."

"Well, for one thing, I'm in Charleston."

*"South Carolina?"*

"No, West Virginia."

"What're you doing there?"

"That's kinda my story. Or part of it."

"Tell me."

So I told him about getting in my car and starting for my cabin, then picking up Cliff, my instant liking of him, then–

"You liked him because he admired your car. You didn't know anything about him."

"I know. I've already figured that out. I liked him so well, I drove way past the exit to my cabin, just so we could finish our conversation."

"All the way to *Charleston?*"

"No. I did that with the second hitchhiker."

"Why didn't you just turn around after you dropped Cliff off?"

I don't know. It's kind of like *west* is attracting me."

There was a long pause. "You've got some serious commitment issues, man."

"How do you come up with that?"

"You want to meet this new babe, a woman you know *nothing* about, and that's pulling you across the country."

I gulped. "Umm–"

"And you're willing to give up the perfectly good one you already have."

"I thought you didn't like Tiffany."

"But she's not my fiancée. If you're willing to get engaged to someone, you've gotta like her a little."

"I do like her. I think—I thought—I love her."

"Right.    So you run away to meet someone unknown."

A great indignation rose up in me. I would have screamed it out at Nick, but three things kept me from it.    First of all, I don't usually scream at anyone. Second, even in my anger, I remembered that Nick usually gauged things exactly right.    Also, my innate sense of fairness recognized that he spoke at least some truth.  I swallowed hard.

"Keep talking."

"First of all, I gotta say this.  Why do you think I'm seeing this so easily?  What's a thirty-three year old successful businessman doing with his mother as his only employee?  I could hire three more people and they'd still be overworked."

"Is that your method of meeting girls?"

"Look man, this is about you, not about me."  But there was a chuckle in his voice.

"All right, but when I get through this, I'm going to be the wise one, and I get to take you apart."  I needed to say it, and I meant it.

"Fair enough.  I could use it."  Pause.  "In fact, do you have room at your hotel for a bald man with a long beard?"

We both laughed.  "Let's get back to the rat killing," I said.

"All right.  Do you acknowledge what I just said?"

I'd already forgotten how painful it was.  "Um, I guess so."

"Good.  Finish your story."

So I told him about the mad prophet.  As clearly as before, I recalled everything he said, even reproducing his monotone, high pitched pronouncements fairly accurately.

While I was talking, I could hear Nick's breathing, harder than usual.  "What's up?" I finally asked, interrupting my story.

Another slight pause. When Nick spoke, his voice sounded strange, as if he were suppressing emotion. "You're on a vision quest, man."

"I think so." The truth of his words felt like a jolt through my phone.

"That doesn't give you any excuse for running, but it does mean something's guiding you."

"Wait a minute here. Couldn't I have been guided to run?"

Nick snorted. "That crazy man had you pegged. Now you gotta worry about his prophecies."

"No kidding. This might end up being quite an adventure."

"That's it!" Nick said abruptly.

"What?"

"You're an adventuroholic. That's why you're not really interested in Tiffany!"

"Just looking at her is an adventure!"

"Right. But how long can you look at eye candy before you get tired of it? Your unconscious mind knows that. And your unconscious mind also knows that this daughter of Iago Salvadore has got to be a real handful or her dad wouldn't have had to call in a twenty nine year old promise to get her hitched. Life with her is going to be an adventure from beginning to end."

Just for form's sake, I wanted to protest, but he was usually right, and again, I felt the truth in his words as he spoke them. "Why do you think I crave adventure?"

"Well, good question. Sounds like you have some

more thinking to do."

*A vision quest. This isn't just about checking out my father's choice of my wife,* I thought as I walked to a local variety store, planning on getting a few toiletries and spare clothes. *This journey's going to teach me about me, who I really am. I'm going to learn from every person I meet, and I'm going to learn from myself. When I'm done, I'll have self-intimacy.*

*_____*

*Los Angeles, California*

"I'd like you to take a drive with me, Sweetheart," he said as he was walking by my open door. "You'll be glad you did."

To my annoyance, he didn't stop and wait for an answer. My 'no' was part of my custom and he knew it, of course. Oh, well. I could say it later just as easily.

But that didn't fit right with me. Letting him go felt too much like another victory for my father. I had sworn...

But he had me either way. If I jumped up and ran after him to castigate his socks off, I'd be showing excessive concern, something it was my decided policy to avoid.

A silent growl formed in my chest. This battle was ridiculous, most likely a battle my father did not even know about.

*How can he win these skirmishes if he doesn't even know they exist? He must know, and he's taking great pleasure in his kills. I won't forget...*

As it turned out, he was even more devious than I had suspected. Saturday was my shopping day, and it was my custom to spend several hours wandering through all the local malls, buying rarely and very carefully, but daydreaming extravagantly. Away from home, away from the ghosts of lust and evil that my mother's father had forced upon me, I could, even if it were fleeingly and fragilely, become somebody else, somebody important, somebody talented, somebody *happy*. I knew within the nearest minute how long I could make my fantasy last. As soon as the anonymity and pleasant safety began to fade, as reality and memory forced their way to the front of my consciousness, I would leave.

My father had permanently engaged a taxi for me every Saturday at 10:00 A.M. The driver's name was a cliché: *Mac*. But he didn't live up to the name. Every week, he was smartly dressed in a red uniform, with what looked like a pressed coat, starched hat, white shirt and tie, creased trousers and shiny shoes. He wore dark glasses in all kinds of weather, and he kept the collar of his coat turned up. The epitome of genteel service, he was a throwback to the olden days of chivalry. I think I had a little bit of a crush on him.

On this particular day, he waited in the front seat of Taxi 86, the same one he had driven all those years, no differently than ever, his face expressionless as usual. I had been determined to give my father a stinging barb as I passed him, but wisely for him, he had chosen to stay out of my way. *Smart tactic Daddy. But it means a victory for me.*

Already the feeling of exhilaration was upon me, more than usual, for I had, by ignoring my father, thwarted his plans while I fulfilled my desires.

As usual, Mac said nothing as I situated myself in my accustomed seat, next to the right side back door, buckled my seat belt with a flourish, then bounced a couple of times in pure delight. "Southwest," I said, unable to keep a girlish giggle from my voice. "I want to browse through the doll store."

Mac nodded his head in understanding and respect, then backed out of the driveway, and turned the car around. I slumped down in my seat, breathed deeply, and for several minutes basked in the artificial freedom I was enjoying.

My Saturday ritual had been going on for at least ten years, so I had visited every possible destination many times, and was surprised when I finally looked out the window and saw unfamiliar surroundings.

"What's up, Mac? Why are we–?"

At that moment, I recognized something I had never noticed before. In all the years I had had Mac as my cab driver, I had never asked him a question, and I realized with a greater shock, he had never spoken to me. *Can he even speak?*

My question remained unanswered, because Mac kept both gloved hands on the wheel, both eyes on the road as he always did. He acted like I hadn't spoken,

"Mac," I said again.   I unbuckled my belt, leaned forward and snapped my fingers next to his ear.  It was like I wasn't there.

"Mac!"  This time I screamed it out.  No response.

"Stop the cab!"  Nothing.  "Stop, do you hear me? Let me out of here!"

At this point, I was so puzzled and furious that I lost all thoughts of safety.  I jerked on my door handle, willing to take the road rash to show Mac my frustration.  It didn't respond.

I was weeping in rage.  "When you let me out of this, you're *fired*!" I screamed.

We had turned onto a tree lined side road, with spacious, lovely homes.  It could have been our own street, except we were on the other side of town.  After a few moments, we turned again, this time into a gated drive.  To my complete astonishment, the gate opened, as though it had a sensor that recognized the cab.  We drove for a few minutes, then came to a tree lined driveway, with lovely green lawns on either side, playing fountains of all sorts between the trees.

In spite of my anger, I was fascinated.  *Under any circumstances, this place is worth seeing.*

And a horrible suspicion came into my mind.  "Mac, my father didn't put you up to this, did he?" I said, the accusation as harsh as I could make it.

At least this time he responded to my words, but with nothing more than a shrug.  I would have given him a little more of my wrath, but the scene outside was too remarkable to miss. We had come to the end of the driveway, which circled around to an unloading curb. Along the entire circle were lovely crystal birds: flamingos, swans, eagles, penguins, ostriches, birds big and small, of all variety and colors. Each had colored water inside, pink for the flamingos, black and white for the penguins (there must have been partitions inside to keep the colors separate) grey for the sparrows and so on. Occasionally a bird would sing, and when it did, water would spray from its mouth. I am quite certain the sounds were reproductions of genuine calls of each bird.

In the exact center of the unloading curb, the cab stopped. Slowly and deliberately, Mac did as he always did. He opened his door, stepped out, then marched around the back of the car to my door, which he opened while standing at the most rigid attention. I stepped out (I had never rebuckled myself) suddenly remembering my outrage, and turned to face him, about to give him the most vicious firing he could ever experience, but a hand reached forward and took mine.

"Olivia Salvadore?"

"Yes," I said, taken unawares.

"I'm Jacob Marson. Welcome to my home."

He kept my hand and led me toward the large, stately building behind the fountains.

# Chapter VII

## Reuben

*Charleston, West Virginia*

As soon as I hung up from my conversation with Nick, my phone buzzed. Tiffany.

*Well, it's going to happen at some point.* Setting my jaw, I punched *send* and put it to my ear. "Hello?"

"How was your night?" Her tone was as sweet as a lemon.

If I answered her question, I'd give her back the advantage. "Tiffany, what do you see in me?"

There was silence on the other end for a moment. Good. It was totally unexpected. "What are you talking about?"

"What is it about me that you care for?"

"Don't you mean *love*?" She had added ice to the

lemon.

"Okay, sure. What do you love in me?"

"Why are you asking this? Are you trying to break off our engagement?"

*Was I?* "No, no, it's just that I've been looking pretty hard at myself lately, and I'm not sure about–"

"Are you getting all humble on me all of a sudden? You know you're the biggest catch in Virginia. I don't know a girl that wouldn't *kill* to be in my shoes."

On top of the iced lemon, there was now a layer of bitterness that was almost overpowering. But I wasn't going to cave to just the tone of her voice. "This is important to me, Tiffany."

Her words came out in a rush, like she had it memorized. "You're the strongest, handsomest, fittest, smartest–"

"It's not like I don't like hearing all that stuff, but none of that counts." The words of my crazy passenger rang in my heart. *The idolater thinks appearance is important.*

"What do you mean none of that counts? Who have you been talking to?" Now the bitterness in her voice was blown away by fury.

And a sudden insight came to me. *Tiffany and I have something very important in common.*

But it was still too painful for me to push farther. "It's a really long story, Tiffany."

"I've got time." *Maybe she has the time, but the antenna of her heart isn't picking up any signal.*

"Umm, I'll tell you later, when the story's finished. Right now, tell me something else about me that you love."

Another pause. Too long a pause. "You're holding back a lot you're going to tell me later."

"Are you saying that because you can't think of anything important about me?"

"You're trying to pick a fight, aren't you?" The feeling of commonality was stronger yet. *We're both afraid of the same thing.*

"No, Tiffany. I really mean it."

"I don't want to talk when you're in this kind of mood." Click.

Classic case of projection. But what she was really saying struck me like a blow. *I don't want to talk about anything that really counts. I don't like things that really count.*

No, that wasn't quite right. *I'm afraid of things that really count.* Yes, I thought that statement was true, but still–

I couldn't go any further. It was easier to analyze Tiffany than it was to analyze myself, but I knew too well that stating her feelings was too close to stating my own. So I rang her back.

"Hello!" I could have been a porcupine salesman for all the warmth in her voice.

"Look, Tiffany, please don't be mad at me."

"What makes you think I'm mad at you?"

"Well, let's see. You just hung up on me, your voice

sounds like you've just gargled with kerosene, and– that was a tough question I wanted you to answer. The trouble is, I can't think of anything else about myself that's particularly remarkable."

"You're a really nice guy!"

"I hope that's true. And thank you." I wasn't being sarcastic.

Now I paused. "Can you think of anything else?"

"You give money to charities."

That was completely true, but she knew as well as I that I did it at least partly for tax purposes. Still I wasn't going to contradict her. And deep inside, I was hoping she had seen something that I'd overlooked. "More?"

"I love the way you smell!" She screamed it out in frustration, with weeping behind it. Then she hung up again.

Ouch. Really big ouch. *The idolater worships his shower...* Every time I was with Tiffany, even when I was working out, I had made sure I was freshly showered and plastered with deodorant and cologne. She didn't even know how I smelled. And it was possible *I* didn't know how I smelled either.

Suddenly, I wanted to get in my car and drive again. Was it my adventure urge, or was it a simple, basic terror of the answer to my fear? All I knew was, I wanted to drive. In my car, I could relax, in my car, I could cruise all day long, in my car, I could—what? Pick up another hitchhiker that would turn my life topsy turvy? Hide? Be anonymous?

It didn't matter. I was going to drive again, and I wasn't going to head for home. Tiffany seemed pathetic to me now, almost repugnant, and—but again, the similarity between us hit me like a blow between the eyes. If we were that much alike, then I considered myself pathetic, almost re–

Frantically, afraid my own ruthless thoughts would catch up with me, I undressed, showered, dressed back in the same clothes, then left. Within five minutes, I found a restaurant with a breakfast buffet, which would allow me to concentrate on my food, and keep me from having a chance to think while I was waiting for my order. I took too much, ate it all, and ended up with a bellyache.

But that was good. A bellyache was a distraction.

Then I got really inspired. My workout stuff was in the car, so I ducked down below the seats, got changed, then went on a run, bloated belly and all. My pace was way faster than I usually went, and my painful stomach protested mightily, but for once, I reveled in the pain. *Keep it up and don't quit.*

Five miles later, I touched the car again. *Thirty five minutes.* (I had a pedometer attached to my running clothes, allowing me to determine my distances fairly accurately) Most of my breakfast had contributed to the organic replenishing of the environment, and now I felt better, renewed. I would've liked another shower, but I was checked out of the hotel.

Sighing in resignation, I wiped my face with my

hand.  Then I unlocked my car and got in, knowing full well my sweaty back would soil the upholstered seat. Unpleasant insight was catching up to me, and the only way to keep it away was to move.  So I moved.

*I'll stay on 64 towards Saint Louis.  Then–*

I didn't have any idea what then.  All I knew was, I was going to continue in that direction.  Maybe I'd make it there, maybe I'd make it further.  However long my vision quest required, I would take.

*_____*

*Los Angeles, California*

I didn't know quite how, but somehow this man had arranged this whole thing.  Even though he was a stranger, and even though he had an extremely winning smile, I almost let him have it full force.  Except there was someone else that deserved my wrath more than he.

"Excuse me, sir," I said, pulling my arm away firmly. "But before I go with you, I have some business to attend to."

Mac stood where I had left him, by my car door, his shoulders slumped, his head down, as if he were aware of my imminent wrath.  "That was the most inexcus–" I began, but that's all the sound that came out.  Mac straightened up, reached up and pulled off his hat with one hand, then his shades and mustache with the other.

I gasped.  There in front of me, face to face, stood my father.

For a good minute, I did nothing but gape at him.  He stood as still as I, while Jacob Marson came forward and stood to my right and facing both of us.   A smile gradually formed itself on his face. "You would have fooled me," he said. "If you hadn't told me."

Fury was taking the place of surprise inside me. "How long?" I demanded.

"Since you were eleven," my father/Mac said.   "I started out on a whim, but when I saw how happy you were on our mall trips, I couldn't quit."

"All this time?"

He nodded.

In spite of myself, I couldn't find any anger.

*_____*

*Between Charleston, West Virginia and Lexington, Kentucky*

Running away from thoughts is a lot easier with actual running, but it is a good deal more difficult with driving, because although one travels much faster, the car is doing the work, while the driver just sits, needing something to think, to occupy one's mind.

Unless one goes fast. Which I did. 118.

It was not exactly prime time for speeding.   Eight o'clock in the morning, with every patrolman wide eyed and alert, a person is bound to get caught.   $720.00 worth of caught.

Something about getting a ticket has always incited a reflective mood, and even though I'd started my speed escapade knowing full well the risks, I was meticulous to go no faster than 64 the remainder of the morning. It had been irresponsible of me, and now it was time to pay penance.

And part of the penance had to be facing my feared fears. I sighed.

\*\*\*[2]

A man on the side of the road was standing by an ancient car that had smoke issuing voluminously from underneath the open hood. Even as I drove by, I could see the look of disgust on his face.

I pulled over. The man looked up at me, then back at his car. He was shaking his head in what looked like a combination of anger and resignation.

"Can I help?" I shouted out of my open window.

The man ignored me. He appeared to be about seventy-five years old.

*Probably deaf,* I thought, opening my door and stepping outside. *Plus, the cars going by are making a lot of noise.*

"Need some help?" I said, coming up and standing beside the old fellow. He was dressed in faded coveralls, which were noticeably spotless.

"I don't hear too good."

I leaned over and shouted in his ear. "Need some help?"

"Wouldn't mind a ride into town," he said. "I mighta' cracked the block on this old girl."

I shrugged. "Which direction is town?"

He pointed up the road, the same direction I had been

going. "What're you going to do?"

"It was just a piece of hose I put too much faith in," he said. "I gotta get another one."

I motioned to my car. "Climb in!" I shouted. "I'll get you there and back!"

He didn't speak, but got into the passengers seat. "Nice car," he said. "I had one once myself. Same year as this one."

For a moment, he stared at the console of my car. Then he held out his hand. "Jerry Davis," he said. "Forgot my manners there for a minute."

"Michael Marson!" I shouted back. "How much did your car cost you?"

He chuckled. "Nothin.' The fella thought it was wrecked, and just left it behind."

"You're a mechanic?"

"Yeah. And I drove a wrecker for my dad. I could fix anything." He hesitated a moment. "Still can."

"How's this one sound?"

"Pretty good," he said. "But I'd say you're running her a little rich." He leaned forward, concentrating. "Yes, you are. Pull over and I'll adjust it for you."

Wondering how he could hear my engine when he couldn't hear me, I nonetheless obeyed, grinning as I imagined what Eddie would say.

Jerry had the hood opened, and a screwdriver out so quickly, I barely had a chance to get out and stand beside him. "Start it up," he said.

I think he must have done some kind of magic

underneath the hood, but I'll never know, because before I had a chance to get out and watch, he was sitting next to me, wiping his hand off with a red handkerchief, which appeared to be as clean as his coveralls. He motioned his hand forward, so I pulled back onto the freeway. And shook my head in disbelief. The car was actually more responsive than it had been.

After leaning forward and listening for a moment, Jerry nodded in satisfaction and sat back in his seat. "That's more like it," he said.

I shook my head. "I've got a mechanic who–"

Jerry held up his hand. "He didn't grow up with 'em," he said.

We drove in silence for a while. "How long have you been married?" I asked, finally, leaning over to make sure Jerry heard.

Immediately, Jerry looked down at his coveralls. Then he laughed. "I keep telling her she spoils my image with her laundering," he said. "Fifty two years."

For several seconds, he stared straight ahead. "Fifty-two of the happiest years a feller could ever want."

"Got any kids?"

"Four. Three girls, one boy."

` "How about grandkids?" Older people always like to talk about things like that.

Jerry nodded. "Eighteen."

I raised my eyebrows. Jerry smiled. "Each girl has three and my boy has nine."

"Nine? They're all his?"

"Yep. He married a Mormon girl, and she got him to join her church."

"Are Mormons like Catholics?"

"Worse. He's got eighteen grandkids already."

I whistled. "I bet family reunions are wild."

"Oh, hey. You know, there's nothing that feels better than seeing absolute proof your family name's not going to die out anytime soon."

"I bet. How many of those nine kids are boys?"

Jerry grinned broadly. "Eight. I just barely figured out how to do it, but he couldn't figure out how to make *girls* until the last one. She's only eighteen."

"How many of his grandkids are–?"

"Divided right down the middle. Nine and nine."

"You know, your face lights up when you talk about it."

He stared at me for a moment. "Do you have a cell phone?" he said suddenly.

A little puzzled, but with only the slightest misgiving, I handed mine to him. He dialed a number. "Marge? Hey, I'm bringing someone over for lunch if it's okay." Pause. "A fellow that picked me up on the freeway." Pause. "Yes, you were right. But I'm not giving up on her. She took us on our first date and she's going to take us on our two thousandth." Pause. "I guarantee she won't. That's why I took her out today." Pause. "In about forty five minutes. I gotta stop by Bill's, and see if he can fit some hose for me first." Pause. "Homemade Reubens? Oh boy." He turned to me. "Do you like sour kraut?"

"I do in Reubens if its done right!" I shouted.

"Did you hear that, Marge?" Jerry said into the phone. Then he grinned. "Okay, I'll tell him. See you in forty five. You're beautiful."

He handed the phone back to me. "She says nobody's ever made a better Reuben than she does," he said. "You'll have to judge for yourself."

"Hey, thanks for the invite," I said. "You don't have to–"

"Yes, I do," he said. "You're a good man, but you need to see what a family can be like."

"How do you know–?"

"Nobody with a car like this has any kids," he said. "Or if he does, the kids aren't very happy."

"Oh." That was worth considering.

"Take this exit," Jerry said.

A moment later, "Left at the stop sign. Bill's place is the first store you come to."

We turned into the nearly full parking lot of a old building that appeared to be held together by a few loose nails and a lot of luck. I put the car in neutral and set the parking brake but Jerry shook his hand. "Better turn it off," he said. "This is my home away from home, and you'll want to see it, I think."

Shrugging, I turned off the car and walked into the dangerously sagging building with Jerry. "We tell Bill he needs to fix his place up, but he says it's part of his image," he said. "He might be right, but who wants that kind of image?"

I laughed, and we stepped through the threshold, passing from the twenty first century into an earlier time. Opposite to my expectations, the place was well lit with bright overhead lights (there were no windows). A wide bar ran along one side, going almost the entire length of the room, at least fifty feet. Along the first half of the bar, there were at least ten soda fountains spaced evenly, each displaying a different color of liquid. Behind the bar, there were waiters dressed in red and white uniforms with red and white striped hats.

On the customer side of the counter sat mostly men, but a few kids as well, sipping sodas and various other concoctions, all of them in huge glass mugs.

Jerry motioned to a pair of empty stools. "Order up," he said. "I can't get any auto parts until I (and any guest I happen to bring) have a soda."

"Does he take a debit card?" I said.

"What?"

"Does he take a debit card?"

"Can't hear you. Too much noise in here."

This time, I practically screamed. "Does he take a debit card?"

It was one of those instances where I spoke loud just at exactly the time when there was a lull in the noise. Everyone looked up at me.

"They only take them on the auto parts end. Cash only on the soda end. But don't sweat it," Jerry said. "I'll cover this end if you cover my hose with your card."

"Deal," I said. "What should I order?"

"You gotta be careful," Jerry said. "Just follow my lead and order what I do so you don't spoil your appetite. Can you eat a lot?"

"I can do heroics if I have to."

"Great. Then get what you want. I've got ten bucks on me."

"All right." I sat down and looked at the menu.

There was a huge selection of soda items, including many names I didn't recognize. "What's good?"

"Everything," he said. "You can't go wrong."

On impulse, I closed my eyes and put my finger on the menu page. Then I looked. "Indescribably Scrumptious." It was $1.50. "Is that okay?"

"Sure. But be prepared. These are thirty year old prices."

"Hey Jer! Who's your friend?" It was a deep, booming voice, that stopped the noise again.

"This is my friend Mike," Jerry said. "He gave me a ride today."

"Thanks for bringing our ace back, Mike," the man said. "We can't function without our senior mechanic."

"Yeah, right Phil," Jerry said. "You don't feel free to help yourself to Bailey's cookies without me there."

I raised my eyebrows. "My granddaughter," he said.

Phil gulped. "Well, her cookies are really good," he said.

"And you don't even have a car, Phil," another voice

chimed in.

"We can't have him starving to death," someone else said.

Everyone laughed, including Phil.  He was better insulated than most.

A moment later, I got my order.  It was in the same glass mugs as all the others, at least a quart, and it was *full*.  It had a butterscotch brownie suspended by toothpicks from the brim of the mug.  Under the still hot brownie, I could see a mixture of soda flavors, which combined made a color about the same as the brownie. Beneath the soda, I found as I worked my way down, were six scoops of ice cream, packed so tightly together they formed a layer that was almost soda proof.

Indescribably scrumptious was just that, and it was enough to be a meal.  *This is one of those food heroics times,* I thought as I ate the last bite of ice cream, realizing I was full.

While Jerry and I ate (his was a simple root beer float, but twice the size of any I'd seen before) we were included casually in the conversation around us.  They wanted to  know about me, but if I was reticent to talk about  something,  they  did  not  push,  and  the conversation drifted by.  If I wanted to participate, I was gladly included.

Once we had finished, we moved on down the counter to the Auto Parts portion.  There Jerry took ribbing about trusting in an antique water hose, but the one that waited on him (I found out it was Bill a little later) was very quick to dig through his old stores and find something that might work. Jerry looked it over, pronounced it "just what I was looking for," and we left. Several voices shouted goodbyes to me as well as Jerry.

"The dilapidation's a sham," I muttered, half to myself as we got back in the car. "But I agree with it."

"You're right," Jerry said. "Amazing you caught on that quick."

"How'd you hear me?" I said.

"I hear just fine." He gave me a small smile. "Deafness can be a useful tool sometimes."

"Do you mean tool or toy?" I said.

"Touche," he said. "How full are you?"

"Quite," I said. "You weren't exaggerating."

"No. Are you up to the heroics you boasted?"

"Yes. It wouldn't hurt my feelings to run a bit though."

"No time. It's been forty-three minutes. Turn left here."

I followed his instructions, and in a minute and a half, we had arrived.

It was of average size, about thirty years old. The walkway was lined with various flowers, with large, bright beautiful blooms. There was a front porch with a veranda that extended the width of the house. A charming porch swing moved gently in the midday breeze, inviting the hot, weary traveler to sit with the girl he likes best, with her knowing her parents are inside, probably right through the wall from the swing, trying to hear every word they say to each other.

Marge was in the kitchen when we arrived. "Go sit down," she said. "I hope you didn't let our guest get too full."

"Well, I'm afraid I did," Jerry said. "But he's a big guy, and can eat some more."

"Gerald Richard Davis!" She said it with gusto, but her heart wasn't in it. I had the feeling I was hearing more of a ritual than a reproach.

The table was covered with a cheerful checkered tablecloth, and six places were set with bowls and spoons. A moment after we sat down, Marge came out.

She perfectly fit the stereotype of a grandmother, with silver hair, sparkling eyes, wrinkly face, strong, veined hands, and a lively step. Her hair was tied in a neat bun, and I noticed her apron matched the tablecloth. "Hi," she said. "I'm Marge. Welcome."

I believed her.

"You did bring home a handsome one," Marge said, looking at me without embarrassment. What's his name?"

"Michael Marson," Jerry answered. "I would have gotten around to it."

"Half way through the meal, maybe," Marge said cheerfully.

She had already put a foil covered platter on the table. "You need to think big here, Michael," she said, pointing at the platter. "I've made three for you."

"Three!" A quick wave of panic passed through me.

"But I'll let you take one or two with you," Marge said, smiling broadly, including her acknowledgment of my distress in the smile.

"Thank you!" My gratitude was a little too heartfelt. I wasn't *that* fond of Reubens.

"Oh that's what you think," Marge said, as though she read my mind. You haven't had one of mine yet. But we'll have that taken care of–" She looked at her man-sized wrist watch– "in about two minutes, depending on who says grace."

Jerry said grace, and he did a fairly thorough job of it, asking blessings on every pertinent item in their life, including me. I think he took so long, because he wanted to let my *Indescribably Scrumptious* digest as much as possible before I had to put more in to be its companion. I actually think it helped a little, because when he finally let us go, my appetite was awakened—a tiny bit.

Marge must have known what he was doing too, because she did not even mention his long winded heavenly supplication. She simply uncovered the sandwich plate, then scooped one out with a spatula, onto my plate.

Inwardly I groaned. The sandwich was long, wide and deep.

But I had advertised myself as a hero. I bit into the sandwich.

At this point, my recent luck with cuisine ended. Marge's Reuben was, bite by bite, without relenting, as bad as I had anticipated the *Stink Bomb* to be. I don't mind sour kraut in small doses, and I'd always thought the idea of a Reuben was to surround the sour kraut with other tastes, so much it left only a hint of itself in the taste of the sandwich. But Marge's sour kraut drowned out any other taste, for a week at least. And I'd have an easier time calling it *bitter* kraut. *How would it taste if it weren't surrounded with the fixings of a Reuben sandwich* I wondered.

When the first taste of the *Ruin* in my hands assailed my nostrils and my taste buds, I gasped involuntarily. Then, realizing my faux pas, I managed to force out a "Wow!" and took another courageous bite. At the moment, it seemed like the bravest thing I had ever done.

It didn't help any that I was already full, and as I looked at the vast bulk of the badly fermented cabbage hiding in (under) the bed of bread, meat and cheese, I nearly despaired. The whole time, I felt Marge's smiling, expectant face on me. *I'm not going to let her know,* I thought, willing back my rising gorge with all my might. *To her, this is a great privilege she's giving me.*

But how could I do it? Even if it were delicious, it would be a chore to finish, and as it was, if I were to tell the perfect truth, I'd say it could have held it's own comfortably against the famous Chinese water torture.

But that thought gave me a happy idea. I had a friend that had spent two years in Japan, and the thought of Chinese as well as the pertinance of the memory brought it back to me.   My friend had lived with a group of three other men and he told me about the way someone devised of consuming the extra tasteless wheat cereal they had every morning.

Immediately, like a drowning man offered air, I implemented the plan.   *I'm going to yosh this thing down.*

*One two three, yosh!* I thought vehemently.   When I said the word *yosh* in my mind, I took a bite.   I had to chew and swallow what was already in there so fast, I didn't have as much time to taste the very close to *rotten* kraut I was forcing into my belly.   *One, two, three, yosh!   One, two, three, yosh! One, two, three, yosh!* Each bite, like a human garbage disposal, diminished the size of the torture.

I don't know if my lips were moving while I chanted a garbage devouring cadance, but it was the best I could do.   In something around three minutes, I had it finished.   The whole time, I could see Marge's nodding head, her face beaming with pleasure at my enjoyment of her creation.

And that look made it worth it.   Now that it was inside me, and the taste of the vileness fading, I realized I was no less comfortable than I'd been any other time I'd been this full.   So I smiled back at her, and told the most charitable lie I've ever told.

"I don't blame your boasting, Marge," I said.

Her smile became radiant.   Do you want your second

one now.?"

A feeling of panic almost blew my cover. "No thank you, but I'd sure be happy if you can find a plastic bag for me to take them along."

"I'm sure I can find one somewhere," Marge said, and disappeared into the kitchen.

"Shall we go get the car?" Jerry said.

I didn't feel much like moving, but I was afraid if I stayed, she'd appeal to my chivalry somehow and try to persuade me to eat another celebration of cabbage gone awry. "Sure," I said. "Let's go."

My stomach groaned when I stood, and a wave of postponed nausea passed over me, but I had accomplished the herculean task of chewing and swallowing the close-to-nonfood, and this was nothing in comparison. Marge came back in, still smiling hugely, and handed me a plastic bag that had to weigh twelve pounds. "For some reason, they keep really well," she said. "They'll last to the end of your trip."

I lied again, and thanked her. Then I hurried out to my car, carrying the sack with me. It was letting off an aroma that reminded me of my ordeal. I opened the trunk and carefully placed it inside. Then I got back in the car and started it up. Jerry was sitting in the passenger seat already. Without speaking, I drove out to the highway, not having any idea what to say. *Is it possible Jerry likes the Reubens his wife makes? I don't dare say anything, because I don't think I can successfully lie one more time.*

Without incident, we arrived back to the old jalopy, and Jerry had the new hose installed in no time. We added water, he turned the key, then listened a moment. "Block's okay," he said.

"Good work, Jerry," I said. "You're a great mechanic."

"Will you stay with us tonight?" he said suddenly.

"Um, thanks for the offer, but I really need to get on my–"

"No you don't, Mike," Jerry said. "I can tell a man that has to get somewhere. Why don't you want to stay with us?"

"Well, um, you know–"

"You know, my wife does just about everything perfectly," Jerry said. "She's been a great mom, a great community organizer, a faithful, witty, fun companion, she's loyal as the day is long, she writes great poetry, she loves me, she's a wonderful grandmother and great grandmother, her sewing is flawless, her conversation intelligent. On top of all that, she's beautiful."

I nodded. "You're just taking my word for it," Jerry said. "But you're smart to do it, because it's true."

He paused a long moment. "Did you notice anything missing in the list I just made?"

I dared to say it. "Cooking?"

"Right." He winked at me. "I've done a lot of traveling in my day, and I've never met a worse cook than she is. It's like all the ingredients in the world have combined to agree that anytime Marjorie Davis gets ahold of them, the resulting concoction will have a hard time making it as dog food."

In spite of myself, I nodded. "But you know what, Mike? She doesn't know."

I raised my eyebrows in surprise. "She doesn't have much of a sense of smell and taste, I think, because she likes her stuff just fine."

"Wow."

"Yeah, wow. You know why I took you to Bill's place first?"

"So you could fill me up on his stuff, and that way I'd have an excuse to not eat hers."

"You're a sharp kid. It works pretty well. If they throw up, it's Bill's fault, and mine for spoiling their appetite with too much sweet stuff."

"You've done this before?"

"I do it all the time. It's kind of my hobby. Sometimes it's a bicycle that breaks down, sometimes I'm just out for a walk and get tired, sometimes I fake a heart attack. Always near to lunch time, always to Bill's first. And you know what?"

"What?"

"Nobody's ever finished one of her sandwiches before. And you finished the worst one of all."

I breathed a sigh of relief. "I'm so glad to hear that. It's kind of been worrying me that I'm not going to get the smell out of my trunk if I keep her sandwiches in there any longer."

Jerry smiled. "Come with me, will ya? But leave

your badge of courage in the trunk for now."

He walked directly into the dense forest off the highway. To my surprise, after passing through two or three dense bushes, we were suddenly walking on a good trail that started out of nowhere.

"Couldn't have it seen from the road," Jerry said.

We followed it, deeper and deeper into the wood, for about five minutes. Then, beside a massive oak tree, Jerry stopped and pointed. A piece of cable arose from the ground, through a pulley attached to the tree, then looped back down to the ground. With some effort, Jerry pulled on the cable—and an entire section of ground raised up, revealing a deep, dark hole beneath. The cable was attached to a man hole cover, that had about four inches of soil atop it, and all kinds of indiginous plants growing in the soil. Before he had raised it up, it looked as innocent as any other piece of ground around. Jerry wrinkled his nose.

"Pretty pungent down there," he said. I dumped my last load just a week ago."

"This is where you throw your wife's cooking?"

"Yeah. It's the greatest secret I have. Please don't tell her. Or anybody."

I raised my right hand. "You have my word of honor, Jerry."

He looked at me carefully. "I believe you. You're a trustworthy man."

It was the greatest compliment anyone had ever paid me, and I found my eyes burning.

"When you leave us, you can dump it in there. Just make sure to take it out of the plastic first."

I nodded, feeling honored. It felt like he was offering me a burial place in the family's cemetery. "Thanks," I managed to croak out.

His car drove back to his house without difficulty, and I followed, with a few misgivings. *What's going to stop her from feeding me again?*

But my fears were groundless. By the time I got back, visitors had started to arrive. First of all, a neighbor woman, Dorothy, I believe, came over and asked Marge's advice about growing roses. (They were among the other lovely, big flowers I had seen when I came in) Before she was fairly finished, a couple more women came over, wanting to settle a dispute they had about a particular sewing technique. Using me as a model, Marge showed them how they both were close to the solution, but they needed to combine their ideas, not separate them. Both women left with happy expressions on their faces. *She's a genius in diplomacy.*

The parade of people continued. Next, a man in his mid forties came in, greeted Jerry and Marge as 'Dad' and 'Mom,' greeted me as though I were his long missing friend, asked his father a question about a 60's Chevy, then asked his mother a question about making pies. He wanted to make one for his wife's birthday.

For some reason, after that, I was reminded of a stream running merrily down a hill. Jerry Jr. left, promising to come back later. He was barely out the back door, when three more came in (nobody knocked) looking to be in their mid-twenties. One at a time, they asked the opinion of either their grandmother, their grandfather or both. Most amazingly, though fifty years separated them, all three seemed to regard the words of their progenitors as valuable. When they left, we had a break for about three minutes, while Jerry and Marge talked together, again not excluding me from their conversation. Then children came up, asking for a piece of candy (Jerry was the indulgent one, of course), a piece of yarn, a ½ inch socket wrench, a bit of advice about a teasing sibling. Through it all, Marge and Jerry sat smiling, love in their eyes for all their progeny.

I think sixteen people filed through that house. With each one, I had the impression that they were individually not just part of the family, but crucial to it. Even though I was an outsider, I could feel the love that was the foundation of the home, the intimate knowledge they had of each other and the stability of the relationship that had produced it all. In this homespun little podunctsville, I had found the desire of my heart I had never known before.

But I didn't have a chance to marvel. Even as I sat with mouth agape, four women showed up, each with at least one toddler, and deposited them on the living room floor, asking us if we would care for them while they made dinner. At that point, Marge got up, and said she needed to do her part, but I got inspired and started asking her advice for getting grease stains out of clothes. I could have sworn that the faces of the four woman and their father/father in law, expressed great gratitude. When Marge's back was turned, Jerry winked at me.

The women left us alone with five energetic, demanding toddlers. Jerry asked Marge to play the piano for the children, but that ploy almost failed, because Marge said the little ones wouldn't pay attention for more than three seconds. Again, I came to the rescue. I offered to dance while she played.

And it worked. She played, (her music was lively, rhythmic and energetic, the type of music that sets a pair of feet to dancing) I capered as hard as I could, to the point of breaking a good sweat. It had been long enough since my chewing and swallowing exercise (I cannot in good conscience call it a meal) that I was able to get a good workout without too much discomfort. Somewhat to my surprise, Marge's preparations appeared to have no trouble digesting. The children loved the bouncing and prancing, and "Do't gin!" at least a thousand times. Jerry taught them to wait their turn. At some point, we got them laughing.

It was the strangest feeling. Here I was, a successful engineer, playing with babies hundreds of miles from home, with no idea where I would be the next day. I couldn't think of a better time in my life.

Babies are a lot of work, and I can't say I enjoyed every minute of it, but I can't say I hated it either. It was a task I didn't envy their mothers, but it was a task that led to the peace I felt in that home, and thus it was worth it. If I knew that any labor of mine could lead to such a home as Jerry and Marge shared, it would be worth it a thousand times over.

We must have spent an hour playing, singing, dancing, clowning and enjoying. Marge's piano playing set the mood, my energy kept it going, and Jerry's wit and wisdom made it sacred.

To my absolute amazement, when the family started arriving, carrying various food dishes heaped high with some sort of feasting, I found myself hungry—a little. By the time the table was groaning under the weight of all the viands, and the family gathered round for grace, I was ready to eat again.

Did I feel bad for deceiving Marge? No. I watched her through the activities, and I saw she was too intelligent to be deceived by the ruse, especially since it had been practiced for decades. She was perfectly happy doing what she did well, and allowing others to do what they did well. The brilliant smile she flashed at me anytime she had the chance was not because I liked her cooking, but because I had been brave enough to pretend I did. And she didn't have to pretend too hard that it was true.

The food was good, home-cooked fare, and the conversation at the table simple, homespun love. Without needing to ask questions, I was able to learn all about a happy family. I won't forget it.

*_____*

*Los Angeles, California*

Somewhat in a daze, I walked into Jacob Marson's house, holding the right arm of my host, and the left arm of my—of Mac. Through all those years, he had been my faithful driver, never saying a word, only driving because it gave him a chance to see me smile. I squeezed his arm as we walked, but I don't know if he felt it. He had won this encounter hands down and I wasn't even contesting it.

Jacob Marson was speaking. "What do you feel about this arrangement we've made?"

It took me a full two minutes to build up my outrage. Something had become clear to me, something so basic and so vital to my soul that I *had* to cherish it, had to contemplate, had to feel the love that I now *knew* my father had for me. In spite of all my barbs of poison words, in spite of all my temper tantrums, in spite of every sabotaging effort I had made, he loved me. *I'm not one bit worthy, but he loves me anyway.*

So, for two minutes, I didn't answer Jacob Marson. I was resenting him breaking into my privacy, trying to get a reaction from me while I *needed* to think, to bask, to *rejoice,* at least for a little while.

When I answered him, I used my resentment to fuel my anger, until I could build up a head of steam. "What do you mean, how do I feel? How's someone supposed to feel when the control of their life is jerked away from them?"

It wasn't true, because I had a choice whether I'd

accept or reject, but it didn't matter. He didn't know me well enough to argue, even if he saw through my words. On the other hand, if he knew me, he'd know it was fruitless. So either way...

But he cheated. He ignored my answer. "Have you seen his picture?"

Now my anger was back up to speed. "Why should I answer if you ignore what I say anyway?"

His reply was immediate. "I wanted to have a conversation with you, and you answered my question with a question designed to *stop* conversation. So I tried a different question. And look at us. We're having a conversation."

"Is that how you define conversation? Does your *boy* do this well at communication?"

Michael's father stared at me for a moment. "You really want me to answer that, don't you?"

He had me, a little bit. If I answered affirmatively, of course I would be showing interest in something my code insisted I *not* show interest, and if I denied interest, it would beg the obvious question of why I asked in the first place.

But he had left me with no choice—unless I used his tactic.

"Where can this possibly lead?" It wasn't that great of a comeback question, because it almost implied the subject was worth discussing.

He caught it immediately. This man was a worthy opponent, the most challenging I had ever met. "To happiness. What do you think of him?"

It was like I was sabotaging my sabotage, because I actually answered him outright: "He's a pretty boy. Romeo, John Wayne and Apollo all rolled into one." I would've said 'Ken' too, but I'd already used it on my dad.

Marson raised an eyebrow, but did not answer.

"Pretty boys only like pretty girls."

"So he won't have a bit of trouble with you, then."

It was a good solid compliment, but I wasn't going to show how I felt when I heard it.

"Only skin deep," I thought a banal, superficial comeback might put him off course.

"Oh, come on, Olivia. Engage with me a little bit."

"What do you mean? What do you think I was doing?"

"Trying to put me off with a cliché. You can do better than that."

Fighting words. He had said almost exactly what I was thinking, and that was too close. "All right." I made my voice like ice. "I'll tell you what I *feel*." The fury was all the way up in me now, and I opened my mouth, about to let it loose.

Marson caught my hand and placed the gentlest of fingers over my lips.

"I know you can do anger, Olivia. But what good does it do?"

"I'll tell you what good it does!" I could feel it brimming over, about to become nothing but scream.

This man was coming closer to finding the real me than anyone ever had.

"No, Olivia, please don't." He was pleading with me. "You know nothing good comes out of your mouth when you're in your rages."

"How do you know so much about me?" Oops. I'd accidentally told him he was right. *Do I want him to win this battle? Maybe I do.*

"Your dad hasn't said anything, Olivia.  Not one word."

"Sure he hasn't."

Jacob Marson looked hard into my eyes. "I won't say it again.  If you choose to believe everyone in your life is a liar, that's your problem."

"You're an engineer, not a psychologist."

"My wife left me and my little boy when he was two. In some ways, it was the best thing she could have done."

For the first time in my memory, I recognized defeat. It was like I was in a game of chess and my opponent knew my moves before I made them, maybe two or three in advance.  I was going to lose this battle. Suddenly I felt weary, bereft of strength, bereft of desire to live.  What was the point of carrying on an existance when all I cared about was "winning" my interactions with men?

We were walking beside an inside fish pond, with large goldfish swimming about, making a moving pattern of color.  My knees began to buckle, I let go of my father's arm, staggered a few feet, and would have fallen into it, but Marson caught me by the waist. "Nice try, Olivia," he said before I started sobbing.

# *Chapter VIII*

## Potential

*Between Charleston, West Virginia and Lexington, Kentucky*

I had gotten up early the next day, but Jerry had been up already, reading from an ancient book that was called Plutarch's *Lives.*

"She usually sleeps 'til 7:30," Jerry said. "There's cold cereal in the cupboard and milk in the fridge."

"I've got to exercise first," I said. "Do you have anything that'd double as a pull up bar?"

"Down in the basement," Jerry said. "I haven't used it in awhile, but last time I checked it was still good."

He followed me down the stairs. "You're looking for something," he said as I opened the door at the bottom. "Light's on your right."

"Yeah, but I'm not sure what," I said, gratified to find not only a pull up bar, but a complete weight set, made from various sizes of cans filled with cement and labeled 10 through 100. I hefted each one individually and found it accurate, probably within half a pound. The whole set was homemade, including the dumbbells.

Jerry spotted me (I wasn't sure how much good he could do if I got in trouble) while I benched, mostly keeping quiet. There was a thoughtful expression on his face the whole while I combined lifting with various vigorous callesthetics, pull-ups, stretches and a final backward burnout of fifteen pushups, situps and squat thrusts, down to fourteen each, then thirteen, to one. It was always good for leaving me gasping at the end, thoroughly satisfied.

"You can stay here," he finally said. "I know five or six local girls that would love–"

He saw the expression on my face. "But Mike, that's the point. We're here on earth to be happy. Happiness doesn't lie in fame, notoriety, wealth, success or prestige. Those don't even help it along."

I was still recovering from my exertion, but I was listening. "You're on a Journey right now," Jerry said. "And you're at a crossroads. Here in Nonamesville, you've found a home where there's happiness. You've got what it takes to be happy—the willingness to sacrifice yourself for others. You're not going to find more happiness than we have anywhere else."

His eyes were fixed on me, and though the perpetual

twinkle was there, the set of his shoulders, the angle of his neck, the determination of his jaw showed his sincerity.  He was inviting me to be a part of his life.

I was struggling to dumbbell 80 pounds, but suddenly a surge of strength filled my muscles.  As if the weight were no more than a five pounder, I pumped it five or six times.

Jerry chuckled.  "Your arms like the idea," he said.

They did.  But did my mind?  "I like it here," I said.  "But I'm engaged to a woman in Richmond."

His shoulders slumped.  "Richmond?"

"Yeah.  I'm not sure we're going to make it, but I can't commit to anything else until–"

He lifted his hand.  "We only met yesterday," he said.  "And I don't know much about you except you have really good potential."

I wanted to ask specifically what he meant, but in a way, I liked having things a little bit unclear.  Lack of clarity meant the possibilities of more good qualities.

When I opened my mouth to speak, I found a great sob in my throat, so I shut my mouth.  Jerry paused, then cleared his throat.

"Look, Mike," he said.  "It's only something to think about.  You don't have--"

I held up my hand.  "No, Jerry," I said.  "I can't tell you how honored I am to have you say it to me, but I'm on a vision quest, and I can't stop–"

"What's that?"

"At the end of this journey I'm on, there's a rainbow,

and I'm going to find the pot of gold."

"What does that mean?"

I hesitated a moment. "Self understanding. The ability to love myself—and others. Commitment. Maybe even nobility."

"So you're looking for a vision of who you are."

"No. I'm looking for a vision of who I can be. It's nice to know someone besides me thinks I have potential."

Jerry held up his hand. "It's bigger than I am, then. I'm just a simple mechanic. But if you ever need a place to come back to, my door's wide open for you. And I don't say that to just anybody. In fact, you're the first one."

*_____*

*Los Angeles, California*

I can't exactly say why I started crying, because it seems quite complicated. First of all, I was losing. No, not just losing. Completely shut out. The frustration, the helpless anger, the fury—no, I didn't feel fury. I reserved fury for the people I knew best: my father, even though he had impressed me more on this day than he ever had before, my mother. This man, this stranger that held me by the waist, this father of my *intended*, was amazing, and even though I was the butt of his machinations, I couldn't help admiring him. No one had ever bested me so thoroughly.

But my defeat did not mean his victory. I was going to make him regret this as much as I could.

So I screamed. With all the power of my voice, with all the energy I could muster, I turned and faced him, and screamed.

He did let go of my waist, as I had intended, but then he proved himself my superior again. Barely a second after my scream began, he opened his mouth and screamed right back into my face, forcing me to smell the coffee and stale mints on his breath. It took me so much by surprise that I took an involuntary step backward. Then, not willing to give up an opportunity, I crumpled and deliberately fell into the pond. *He's not going to best me...*

But he did. He was almost in the water before I was. When I threw myself backward into the water, he did too. When I turned and put my head under water, he aped me. When I cried "help" with all my lung power, he did the same. When, in my frustration, I screeched even more shrilly, he screamed higher—*and in harmony.* With every scream thereafter, he screamed at just the right pitch that his voice made mine sound like a song.

The whole time, my father stood above us in the wide hallway, watching, a shell-shocked expression on his face. But when Jacob Marson harmonized with my hysteria, he smiled. When, in my helplessness, I continued, unable to think of anything else to do, he chuckled. As it continued, he threw his head back, and laughed. And laughed. Harder and harder, until he fell to his knees, holding his belly. Still he laughed.

My outrage at his mirth knew no bounds. I wanted to scream it out at him, but I was already screaming. There was nothing I could do but—start laughing.

No!! I wasn't going to *join* him! I tried to stifle it, but all that I was able to do was blow my running nose all over my blouse. Dad laughed harder, if it were possible. And I—joined him. It was the most ridiculous, the silliest, most pathetic time in my life.

It wasn't just a victory, it wasn't just a shutout, it was a *trouncing.* It was a *no contest.*

So I did something else I had never done. I gave up, and let myself laugh.

In a moment, Jacob Marson joined us. His laugh was loud and booming, like his scream, but it was also welcoming, inclusive.

And strangely, for me, almost shockingly, I suddenly felt the ephemeral something I sought every Saturday with my shopping. But it was not ephemeral. In the oddest way, though it felt delightful, it did not feel *foreign. This is the way it feels to be in a family. Joy. Only this time, it isn't just me pretending.*

*I don't think it's going to happen again, but as long as I'm here, and there's nothing I can do about it, I'm going to let it be. I'm going to enjoy this time, with all my might.* I laughed a little harder...

*_____*

*Between Charleston, West Virginia and Lexington*

About ten minutes out of Jerry's town, (somewhat curiously, I had never learned the name of it) my phone buzzed. Dad.

"Hey."

"Hey Mikey."

I could hear the distress in his voice. "What's the matter?"

"This feels so intrusive into your life!"

I paused for a moment. "It seemed like it at first, but because of your phone call, I've started on a quest that I think is going to do me good."

"What quest is that?"

I hesitated again. "The quest to understand myself. The quest to find real love, and to discover what is really important in my life. The quest to truly know the people and the features of my life."

"Really?"

"You know the one thing I can't shake?

"What's that?"

I hesitated a moment more. Then I spoke quietly. "It was hearing you give your word of honor, Dad."

***[3]

(To me, these conversations I'm putting in the fourth book are the best part of the story, so you're missing out if you don't go there and read it, but it's up to you)

Even as I pressed the button to end the call, I saw my next hitchhiker. Even from a distance, I could see it was a very old man, with a long white beard. *More in line with the way a prophet ought to look.*

I had already begun to slow my car. With great care, I eased over, stopping just in front of him, allowing him to take only a few steps to reach my door. With slow, measured paces, he approached my car, opened the door and got inside. He did not respond to my greeting, but simply nodded and pointed forward. I started out onto the highway again.

"Where're you headed?" I said, louder than usual, presuming some difficulty hearing.

He only shook his head and pointed up the road again. Shrugging, I turned back onto the highway. *I've been awful adept at attracting weirdos.*

But the man wasn't weird. He was just silent. For several moments, as we drove, he was content to look at the green scenery that flashed by us on either side.

It was lovely, but it was endless, non-distinctive loveliness. The man beside me gazed with wide eyes in rapt attention, admiring every hill, every gully, every wide-trunked tree. I'm sure he would have scrutinized every flower if we hadn't been going so fast.

I glanced at him several times as he stared out the window. He was dressed in faded overalls, with a threadbare shirt beneath. His hair spilled over his collar and trickled onto his ears. His head was bent forward like a boy watching a campfire, his eyes were focused keenly on whatever he saw.

An emotion and a thought flooded into my mind simultaneously. I felt a peculiar pang of longing, almost

an envy  of the old man's rapt attention, his ability to
engage himself so thoroughly.   At the same time, I
*knew,* with a thrill and a chill, that he was going to turn
the same intense scrutiny on me.

My palms were suddenly sweating.  Did I want this
silent man, who looked so much much like an ancient
prophet, to look into my face?  What would I do–?

He turned and looked at me.  No, he *stared* at me.
No, he *gazed* right into the depths of my heart.

It so happened, he caught me while I was stealing a
glance at him.  It felt awkward for a moment, and in that
moment, I tried to look away,  but I didn't succeed.
Unconsciously, I suppose, I took my foot off the
accelerator.

For maybe thirty seconds, he studied my face while
the car slowed down to almost nothing.   Somehow,
using my peripheral vision, I had managed to pull it
over onto the shoulder.

I don't exactly know why I wasn't uncomfortable.
As I think back on it, I believe it was probably—this is a
little difficult to express—there was no guile in his face.
He was absolutely harmless.

As a result, I felt absolute, total peace.   His
expression spoke no judgment, no reproach, no demand.
It was like I was one of the trees or the flowers he had
so diligently admired before he chose to give me his
attention.

While he was still looking at me, my phone buzzed.
Involuntarily, I glanced down. Tiffany. Great.

The man continued to look at me as I picked up the phone and punched the button. With him not saying anything, it didn't really seem inappropriate. "Hello." (With enthusiasm, a little feigned)

"Hello!" She sounded enthusiastic too, probably with some feigning of her own. "What's up?"

"Nothing much." Like I wasn't hundreds of miles away from home, driving a total stranger somewhere down the road. "I'm getting somewhere."

"Really? Like what?"

"Well, I found out I can be brave."

"I knew *that*."

"Oh yeah? When have you seen me be brave?"

Fairly long pause. "Well, anyone who's seen your arms–"

I didn't even bother to answer her directly. "And I have some potential to think of others before I think of myself. I never knew that about me until now."

"Good." She sounded genuinely happy. "How long–?"

"Look Tiff, cut me some slack in this. When it's all over, I'm going to be a better man than—no, I'm going to be a good man. The kind of man anyone could love."

"David Bruce asked me out today," she said suddenly, no expression in her voice.

It was an obvious gauntlet. Bruce was a thirty year old divorced man that ran a competitive engineering firm. He worked out at the same place I did, so I knew him fairly well, and he did have a decent build on him.

But—wait a minute.  What was really the matter with him?

With stunning clarity, I realized he was a lot like I had been when Tiffany last saw me.  But now–

"If it feels right to you, go out with him."  I had the feeling it wasn't the kind of answer she wanted, but it was what came out.  She had taken me by surprise.

"So it's okay for engaged people to go out with others?"  Was this still a test?

"Um, if someone wants to go out with someone else, they must not be terribly committed to the relationship," I said, a little heat still in my answer.

She hung up again.  The old man was still staring at me.  I became more acutely aware that his expression was completely without approval or disapproval, but at the same time with total and absolute interest.  He was a neutral spectator, as it were.

Less than a minute after she left me, Tiffany called back.  "I'm being unfair," she said.  "And I'm not going to be that way, even if it is the way you're treating me."

I opened my mouth to retort, but then I closed it again.  "Thank you," I said, keeping all sarcasm out of my voice.  "I'm really sorry, Tiffany.  It isn't fair to you at all."

And that was all it took.  I could hear the great intake of breath as my fiancée stifled a sob.  "What'd I do to deserve this?"  Her voice was barely understandable through her crying.

I had no answer, of course.  I had already discovered

this had much less to do about her than it had to do about me.

"Do you really love me, Tiffany?" I said.

"Of course I do!" Her reply was immediate.

"What's your definition of 'love?'"

"Michael!"

"No, I'm asking because I'm not sure. I thought I knew three days ago, but my answer now is so different, it bears no resem—"

"All right. I'm not sure I know." The weeping was gone, but the coldness in her tone did not hide the truth of her words.

"What's the point of being engaged if neither one of us knows what it is?"

"Maybe we'll find out if we commit ourselves and make some effort to discover it."

Oh. Good point. Or maybe not. "Tiffany, I'm getting the feeling from my journey that my love for someone else has more to do with my decision rather than their lovability."

"Well, grow up and make a decision to love me then!"

Good point again. "I think I love you as much as I love anyone besides my dad. But–"

"You love your dad more than you love me?"

"My feeling for you is so complex. I have physical feelings for you too, but–"

"Well, I hope so!"

"Yeah, but they don't count."

"What's that supposed to mean?"

"I mean, I'd have those same feelings for anyone as beautiful and–well-built as you are."

"*Is* there anyone else like that?"

"Well, maybe not, but it's nothing personal. I mean, I keep asking myself: How would I feel about her if she were just average looking, like most people?"

"How would I feel about *you* if you were just average looking, like most people?"

There. She'd said it. Or almost anyway. A wave of nausea passed through me, but I cleared my throat and voiced my fear, the one I had been running from for two days. No. The one I had been running from for most of my life. "That's right! How would I feel about myself if I weren't a handsome, muscular man with a great education, a great car and a prestigious, high-paying job? Who would I be?"

It was quiet on the other end for a long moment, but I knew she hadn't hung up. I became aware that the old man still looked at me, but he wasn't gazing. He was understanding me, and now, I saw empathy in his face. The car was completely stopped, somehow safely off the road.

"Who would I be if I weren't as—everything that I am?" Tiffany said, so quietly I barely heard her. Then she hung up again.

*She's going to go out with David Bruce.* I knew it. And I knew the reason why. *She wants to find out if there's more to her than what she sees in the mirror.*

*She's going to take my quest on herself.*

Suddenly the old man turned his head. He reached to his door handle and pulled on it. As the door opened and he stepped out, I felt a quick pang of loss. To my equally quick delight, he bent down, looked me in the eye once again, and deliberately nodded. Then he stood tall, his white beard blowing in the breeze of a passing semi, shut my car door, *and walked across the highway.* I watched him put out his thumb for a ride in the opposite direction.

*_____*

*Los Angeles, California*

Surreal. That's what it had been. I lay in my bed, staring at the ceiling, paralyzed by the conflicting thoughts that coursed through me. I had spent the last fifteen years of my life, buttressing myself against what had just happened. Enjoyable experiences always came with a price. Either a person has surrendered virtue, or truth or—all I had surrendered was pride, and when I let it go, the experience became truly enjoyable.

After our debacle in the pond, (eventually my father had joined us and we had had a water fight) we had all stood up, and wet clothes and all, continued our tour of the Marson home. It was, by Jacob Marson's own admission, at least ten times bigger than it needed to be, but it was spacious, lovely and in impeccable taste. Once again, Jacob Marson admitted that he had hired an expensive expert to create the perfect atmosphere, and that he well knew his own limitations. Interior Design was one of them, he said.

I wasn't convinced.  Jacob Marson was the most capable man I had ever met.  If his son were one tenth the man his father was...

Seemingly without my volition, my hand came up and slapped my face.  *I'm not going to let*—but I pushed the thought away.  I wasn't through remembering, and for the time being, enough of the magic remained with me that I could still feel some of it.

Our tour of the home had ended in the kitchen, where Jacob Marson made us lunch.  He told us he was serving us One-Eyed-Egyptian Sandwiches, and I was expecting some sort of exotic gourmet viand from Egypt, but all it turned out to be was a piece of bread with a hole torn out of the middle, and an egg fried in the hole.  Still, Jacob Marson served it with such aplomb, giving each of us two, that I surrendered my natural aversion to that much food at a time and ate them both.  I even squeezed out a happy face on one of them with ketchup.  They were good.

When we were finished eating, he walked us back to the taxi I had ridden in for so many years.  Somewhere, as we walked the long hallway, my father had managed to put on his mustache and hat, so when we got to the car, he was Mac again, and I was the child that rode to the mall.  Out of honor to my tradition, and out of deference to my father's great love for me, I fell back into the role I had played all my life, and I was an innocent child, while Mac, my beloved driver, drove me home. Once we arrived, I let Mac open my door as he always had, and I finished the ritual until I got to my room with the door safely locked. Then I lay on my bed and cried until I slept. After a half hour or so, I awoke and lay on my back, staring at the ceiling, thinking and remembering. I could feel the old, entrenched safeguards against vulnerability to others begin to settle back into place, driving back the pleasant thoughts, disallowing, transforming them into negativity. *How dare this total stranger intrude himself into our life, as if he had any real business with us? Is he trying to soften us up? Does he think we'll even consider marrying his pretty boy son?*

The old voice ranted away, and I let it go for awhile. It was familiar stuff, and the old bitterness was the real me, the me that would have the final say.

*It was fun to laugh for awhile.* I slapped myself again.

# Chapter IX

## KISAS

*Lexington, Kentucky*

I was sitting on the edge of my bed, thumbing through the Gideon Bible out of the bedside drawer. Two hours earlier, I had washed all my clothes in the hotel laundry, and now, clad only in one of the hotel bathrobes, I was trying to further my quest. A quick scan of the TV channels had showed nothing more than usual. If I had had my laptop, I would have tried to organize my thoughts in writing, but I didn't, so I thought I'd see if I could find some ancient wisdom. I didn't know my way around it very well, so I was opening the book at random, and reading the page that came to view.

On my third try, a few verses down the page, I saw

something that caught my attention. It was closer to the beginning of the volume, in a book called Deuteronomy, the tenth chapter, and I didn't understand it. *Circumcise therefore the foreskin of your heart, and be no more stiffnecked.*

"What in the world does *this* mean?" I mused aloud. "The heart doesn't have a fore–"

***4

My phone buzzed. To my gratification, it was Nick. Usually I was the one that called him.

"Hey Nick."

"I've figured out one of your problems." I didn't like the sound of that. It implied that I had multiple problems, which was undoubtedly true, but it was still painful to have it implied so blatantly.

"Oh yeah?"

"Yeah. You've got KISAS."

"What?"

"KISAS. Knight In Shining Armor Syndrome."

"What's that supposed to mean?"

"It means that when you see a DID (that means 'damsel in distress'), you feel an almost irresistible urge to hop on your white horse and go rescue her."

I thought about it a moment. "Maybe I do. What's it mean?"

"You're a sucker for needy dames. Tiffany might be needy, but not in any obvious way. This other girl is so bad off her old man has to line up her husband."

"Is that a bad quality?"

"Well, I'd say it was. For one thing, you'd have a hard time sticking with one because this world is loaded with DID's. and you'd be instantly attracted to every one that appeared in front of your face. As soon as you helped her solve her problems, she wouldn't be a DID anymore, and therefore most of her attractiveness would fade."

I didn't like what he was saying, but it had a painful ring of truth to it. Was it possible I had lost interest in my girlfriends the minute they no longer needed me?

"Okay, lets hypothetically say you might be on to something. What do I– what would a person with this condition do about it?"

"Tell me when you find out, and it'll help me too. You're the one on the quest and everything."

My first thought was to quip back some sarcasm, but I refrained. "Okay. I'll throw it into the mix of my thoughts. But you've got to go on a quest as soon as I'm done."

"Deal. And I mean it. It sounds like it hurts the same way a good run hurts."

"Yeah. Hey, but Nick."

"Yeah?"

"I don't think Tiffany's ever been a DID."

"And how interested in her have you ever been?"

Before I could answer, he asked another question. "And compared to her, how interested are you in this

California chick you've never met?"

"Yeah, but the mystery–"

"Sorry. Tiffany's got all kinds of mysteries about her if you were interested."

I thought about it. "I hate you."

"Hate's only love with anger. Talk to ya'."

He hung up. And I had KISAS.

*_____*

*Los Angeles, California*

It wasn't in my nature, but somehow I was able to keep my brief little hour of fun in my heart. Jacob Marson was so wise, and in spite of all the evil I had so vociferously accused him of, and all the trouble I continuously gave him, my father loved me. Like a person building a sea wall to protect her home from the relentless onslaughts of storm winds, rain and waves, I started laying down bricks in my mind and heart to protect this tiny part of me, so I would not, could not, lose it. Using a blank journal I had gotten on my twelfth birthday from my father, but had never written a single word in, I began a list of my bricks: I was allowing each one to be big.

Brick One. I need to be diversified, and therefore must have some positive qualities, as well as the others.

Brick Two. I have a right to be happy, just like anyone else. I've never been happier than in that time.

Brick Three. Just because it happened once it doesn't establish a precedent.

Brick Four. I don't need to tell anyone how important

it was to me.

Brick Five. Nobody has decreed I have to be unhappy.

Brick Six. It felt good to be vulnerable. (Would it be so bad to set a precedent?)

Brick Seven. For the first time in my life, I felt beautiful.

Brick Eight. I'm sick of never changing.

Brick Nine. I felt safe.

Brick Ten. I want it to happen with my husband.

It took all my effort to write the list. All my custom, all my very *identity* screamed out while I was writing, and I had to suppress impulse after impulse to keep from tearing the page out of my journal, but I didn't. As soon as I was finished writing, I shut the mostly blank record, then duct taped it closed and threw it (I wasn't tall enough to reach) onto the top shelf of my bookcase. It was relatively safe up there. I hoped I could leave it alone.

*_____*

*Between Lexington, Kentucky and Saint Louis, Missouri*

I had spent the entire day in Lexington. The first four or five hours, I had napped, and then spent several hours handling business back home, lining out the work for two weeks, making assignments to the various heavy equipment contractors, concrete workers, electricians, plumbers, metal contractors and anyone else that could possibly be involved in the projects, even if Murphy's Law were not the truest law in the universe and everything went forward without a hitch. As I was finishing my conversation with Casey, it occurred to me how I was taking it for granted she could implement the complicated instructions.

Casey was close to my father's age, never been married, about five foot even, probably three hundred pounds. Using Skype, I had interviewed all my candidates while I was still in California, and Casey was my last interviewee. Instantly I knew I had found my woman. She came across as a hyper-competent know-it-all, and I realized she would be hard to take sometimes, but I also could see something my father had told me: "When you meet a potential employee that is impeccably dressed, yet not attractive, and not flirtatious, count on them being really good workers."

"Why's that?" I had said.

"Because it means they're meticulous and pay attention to detail," he had said, smiling. "They are afraid anything out of place will reflect negatively on themselves, and they have a great fear of the confrontation such an error would entail."

As it turned out, he had been exactly right with Casey. She got to work early and left late, and she knew the office from top to bottom, remembering details I overlooked. She was at least forty percent of the reason why we were successful.

I had been right about her personality. She seemed affronted by anything she did not know, and read voraciously, books, magazines, newspapers and Internet articles. Nobody in our office could bring up anything that she didn't know more about. Casey was a walking, talking Wikipedia, and in that capacity, she came in very handy, but it was difficult to establish a relationship with her. Every time I'd tried to talk about anything that was remotely personal, she'd managed to display her knowledge about some obscure detail in my question.

As a result, nobody in the office knew anything about her. She worked long hours, did exactly what she was told, did not forget a single detail, and did not reveal anything about herself. So after years of working beside her, I knew no more about her than I did the first day I met her. She kept such a wall about her, I had never even found an opportunity to express my gratitude to her.

But as of this moment, that was going to end. "Casey," I said, interrupting her going over her list. "You are the most amazing office manager I have ever seen or heard of. It's mostly because of you that we're succeeding."

Casey continued her list, as though I hadn't spoken, but I heard an unmistakable tremor in her voice that lasted for two or three words, but then was gone. I nodded in satisfaction, glad she couldn't see me.

When she was finished, I let about three seconds elapse before I said. "When I get back, you and I are going to discuss your next raise."

"But I just–"

"It wasn't enough. If I were to double your salary, it

wouldn't be enough."

Now she took a few seconds to respond. "Well, is that it?" she finally said, but there was definite emotion in her voice. It was the first time I'd heard it.

"Yes," I said. "Call me in a couple days to keep me posted."

"I *will*," she said, emphatically.

I couldn't keep the smile from my face as I hung up. "Another manifestation of KISAS," I murmured. "I wonder how long she's been a DID. What's the matter with me?"

I shook my head as I chuckled. "But at least this time, I'm not going to break up when I get her rescued."

Because of my naps, I felt fresh when the evening came. Sometimes, a night drive was quite relaxing, even invigorating, and, I admitted, usually free of hitchhikers. I had quite enough to think about without the added burden of another message. So, at 10:00 P.M., I set out.

When I found my last motel, I had made sure I was within walking distance of a lube and oil place that would service the Corvette that day. I had noticed it had passed the three thousand mile mark since the last oil change, and I wasn't going to let a little cross country journey keep me from taking care of my car.

The tank was full, the oil was fresh, the lube thorough, and my machine seemed to purr down the road. Jerry's adjustment was giving her an extra 1.8 miles per gallon.

Just for the sheer joy of it, in an obscure section of road, when I could see no cars either ahead or behind me, I took the old girl up to one hundred twenty. Only for five minutes. This time, I encountered the officer after my speeding, when I had slowed down to one mile over the speed limit. He didn't bat a blinker as I drove by.

For three hours, I drove, enjoying the brilliance of the night sky, enjoying the coolness of the air, enjoying the smoothness of the road as my Vette ate up the miles. It was calming beyond belief to be able to drive with only the headlights of oncoming cars to distract me.

*My greatest fear,* I thought. *I have discovered my greatest fear, and I feel freed.*

I rubbed my chin. It kind of bothered me that Tiffany and I shared nearly the same fear. Even in the first days of our association, I'd considered myself a somewhat deeper person than she. Was it possible I appeared as shallow to others as she appeared to me? The thought was intolerable.

***5

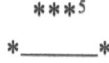

*Los Angeles, California*

I found, almost to my chagrin, that I was unable to keep the part of me I had hidden in an old journal completely out of my subsequent life. At odd times, I was finding myself smiling as I remembered the play of lights above the pool where I had taken my ad hoc bath at Jacob Marson's place. Sometimes, when I was flipping through the stations on the radio, I would think of Jacob Marson harmonizing with my screaming, and the smile would leak out again. At first, the vigilant part of my other side protested, almost vehemently, over the intrusion into it's sacred control of my moods, but eventually it became almost lax in what it was willing to allow.

And something else happened. I started having Vanessa make me two One-Eyed-Egyptian Sandwiches for my breakfast every day, and I was able to finish them and not throw them back up. Somehow my father found out what I was eating, and he joined with me. During that time of the day, I was able to let myself be like I had been the first time I had them at Jacob Marson's house. It quickly became a ritual for both of us, one we would go to great lengths to avoid missing: our daily chance to be happy together. I couldn't maintain it for the rest of the day, but during that breakfast half hour, which soon worked its way up to an entire hour, I was fun, and I adored my father. And during that hour, I started opening my heart to the possibility of Jacob Marson's son—my unknown suitor.

# *Chapter X*

## Angel

*Between Louisville Kentucky and St. Louis, Missouri*

It was after two in the morning that I saw him. The hitchhiker broke out of the dense forest on the right of the freeway, and dashed right in front of me, so I had to hit my brakes to avoid hitting him. As soon as he cleared my car, he put out his thumb. Though I only glimpsed his eyes as I passed by him, they appeared desperate.

I shouldn't really have even been driving at this hour, much less picking up hitchhikers, but in the split second I saw him, I made my judgment of him:  *He's safe, but whoever's chasing him isn't.*

So I screeched my brakes and stopped, right in the middle of the road. Other than me, it was empty.

He was about fifty feet from the car when I stopped, but he appeared at the side window in less than a second. Just in time, I reached over and lifted the lock, allowing him to open the door and tumble inside.

*I hope I'm not helping someone run from the police,* I thought as I pressed down the accelerator, "laying scratch" for fifty feet. I heard a dull 'boom' off to my left and behind me as we got going.

My new passenger was still sprawled in the seat, face first, the top of his head touching the floor. "12 gauge," he said. Loaded with slug."

We were going over seventy by now. "Thanks for picking me up," he said, maneuvering himself around to a sitting position, even as he was speaking. "I know she wasn't going to shoot me, but I wasn't going to take any chances."

"Who–?" I began, but my newest guest interrupted me.

"Last time she threw a hunting knife at me, and the time before, she shot rocks at me with a sling shot. I'm just glad I don't have anything more than the shotgun in my arsenal."

"This has happened to you before?"

The man laughed ruefully. In the darkness I couldn't see anything but shadows, but he appeared to be short, between five four and five six, and medium build, maybe even stocky. "About once a month lately," he said. "But I can't tell when it's going to happen."

"Your wife?" I said, holding my hand to my face to

hide my grin, even though I think he could hear it in my voice.

"Yeah. My sweetheart." Interestingly enough, I could hear no anger or irony in his voice.

"How long have you been married?"

"Eighteen years tomorrow," he said. "We're going to the Derby for our anniversary."

"What? Aren't you worried–?"

"Naw. It's out of her system for a month or so now."

"Are you sure about that?"

"Oh yeah. She won't mention it, and she'll get mad if I do. It's just how she is."

"Should I turn around then?" I was being sarcastic, of course.

"Sure," he said. "But we might want to wait a little before you take me back. Just to make sure she's fired both barrels."

I signaled into the passing lane, then slowed and turned into the median. I hadn't seen any signs that told me I couldn't. Once we got to the other side of the road, I pulled over and stopped.

"Look man, this is the weirdest thing I've ever come across. Would you mind telling me a little bit about it?"

"I guess so." His voice sounded just the slightest bit put out.

I didn't say anything, and in a moment, he started talking again. "She loves me, I know she does," he said. "But she can't tell me."

"Why not?"

He shrugged. "I dunno. Even when we were dating, she never told me. But she has to."

"Why's that?"

Now his voice was defensive. "We've got three children. Why would she stay with me through all the tough times if she didn't love me?"

"Beats me."

"She's beautiful. Five foot two, eyes of blue, all that. Lots of other men look at her."

"I bet."

"She flirts with them, but she always comes home to me."

"I still don't get it—what's your name?"

"Dan," he said. "Dan Cranston."

"Mike," I said, reaching out and shaking his hand. It was small, but the grip was like iron. "Why's she get so mad she tries to kill you once a month? And why do you keep on going back to it?"

"I love her," he answered simply, the defensiveness gone from his voice. "Sometimes I hate her too, but mostly I love her."

He hesitated a moment. "I love her, and I'm not going to leave my kids behind."

"So she—what's her name?"

"Alexis."

"So Alexis is beautiful, but she has a really bad temper that only manifests itself once a month?"

"No, she's mad most of the time, but it boils over once a month. The thing is, the best times are right after she's boiled over."

"Dan, that's crazy. This gal's homocidal. I'm sure there's some kind of medication–"

"We've tried it. This guarantees me a good time on our anniversary. Penance for this is going to last two or three days."

"And then she starts getting mad again?"

"Yeah."

"What's going to stop her from going out and buying a cannon or a bazooka for next time she *boils over*?"

"I took away her credit card. She might figure out a way though."

"Do you have any idea why she's so mad all the time?"

"I really don't. I work three jobs, and I make really good money at them, but no matter what I do, it's not enough."

Dan was quiet for a moment. "You know what I think sometimes? It might be she's mad at me for being short."

I couldn't hear any emotion in his voice, but there was a definite ring of conviction in his statement.

"Hmmm. Why'd she marry you then?"

"That's the thing about her. She always does stuff she doesn't like to do."

"She sabotages herself?"

Dan considered a moment. "I'd say yes. I've even caught her holding a lit match under her arm. It was almost like she wanted to burn herself."

I bit my lip. "How'd you two get together?" It was a deliberate attempt to change the subject, but I had an uncanny feeling his answer was going to bring everything home.  Everything else on this strange journey had.

"It's kind of a weird story.  Her father told my dad he'd like me to marry her."

Dan began supplying explanation and background, but I barely heard him.  While he told something about his qualities of being a hard worker and ambitious, I was feeling so breathless and sick I couldn't pay decent attention.  *He's come to prophesy to me.*

For several minutes, I breathed deeply, trying to shake the nausea, the breathlessness.  About the time Dan finished his narrative, I had recovered enough to ask another question.  "What was her childhood like?" With pure conviction, I knew this was my chance to get to know Olivia...

*_____*

*Los Angeles, California*

With a dull 'snap' the rubber band sprang back against my wrist for the eighty second time.  I could feel the exquisite sting, finally, in full force, suffering sufficient to atone for my daily violation of my standard, my allowance of enjoyment with my father, when I deserved nothing but suffering.  Suffering like now.  Just for good measure, I snapped myself again, even though that guaranteed I would have to snap at least eighty-five times the next day.

The rubber band had been the idea of Dr. Langley, the second psychologist my father had taken me to. It was the only good thing he came up with, but it was worth it. Because of him, I was no longer acquiring scars on my arms from cutting. The pain was a little different, but the suffering was sufficient to prove again my existence as I felt myself becoming less and less real. If I administered the snap enough times until I felt a fulness of pain, it satisfied the urge.

My cutting had started at age twelve, but after Langley's suggestion, it ended in less than a year. It had taken the life of my mother when she was thirty-three, not because she had tried to kill herself, but because she had what the doctors called an AVM, or arterial-venous malformation. Apparently she had administered the exact same pressure, with the knife she always used, but had chosen a new, previously unused site for her activity.

I didn't know anything about it until I caught her one day, just three weeks before I turned twelve. She had tried to explain it away, saying something ridiculous like she was testing the sharpness of the blade, but I knew immediately she was lying. Even while she lied to me, I could see the parallel scars all the way up her arm, some of them still red, angry appearing.

"Your knife gets dull a lot?" I had said, mock innocence in my voice.

When my mother looked up at me, I could see no sign of embarrassment in her face. "This is part of your heritage," she said, her voice hoarse, but otherwise without expression.

"What's that supposed to mean?" I said, roughly, to keep the terror out of my voice.

"We deserve to be punished." Her voice was flat, but her face reflected the hatred I felt in my heart.

"I hope he rots in the deepest hell," I said.. My mother nodded.

On my birthday, I had started cutting. It satisfied my need for self punishment, and my need to feel *real.*

My father had not been pleased. He hadn't said anything when I had blood oozing onto my sleeve one morning, but that afternoon, he had picked me up from school and taken me to my first counselor, number One. (Twelve years later, I was working my way through Thirty two.)

Less than a week after I had begun, my mother had caught me in the very act. She had watched me for some period, standing behind and to my right, so I had not been able to see her. Finally, I had heard her sigh, but when I turned around, all I could see was the door of my room closing.

Eight days later, my mother had died. I knew it was just a coincidence that her death came so soon after I adopted her habit, but still–

I pulled the rubber band back as far as I could stretch it without breaking, and–

Suddenly, the pressure vanished. I looked up, startled, to see my father standing beside me, a pair of scissors in his hand.

It had been my favorite rubber band. I opened my mouth to give some kind of a scathing rebuke, but he put his hand on my arm. "I've heard it all before," he said.

"Oh, sure. The exact same words?"

"No, not the exact same words, but the same message. Misplaced hatred, relentless anger. Totally predictable."

"I'm not predictable!"

"That's true. At breakfast."

"Don't tell me you know what I'm going to say all the rest of the time." I was throwing all my vituperation into my speech, but it wasn't coming out like it had before my day with Jacob Marson. My heart wasn't in it. It was like my breakfasts with my father were influencing the remainder of the day.

"Not exactly, but really close. I was with your mother for thirteen years, you know."

"You can't compare me to her!"

"Why not?"

"Because we're two different people, that's why."

My father sat down at the edge of my bed. "I need you to understand something, Olivia.

"What's that?"

"You and your mother have both been brilliant."

"Then why did we both end up such basket cases?"

He ignored my interjection. "That means you've known exactly the right words to say that would hurt me the worst.   You've been with me longer than your mother, so you probably know better, but she was good at it.  And it's not fair."

"What's not fair?  Aren't you strong enough?"  I had almost all my mockery in my voice.

"I've spent all my time trying to prove I was, but lately, during our breakfasts, I've come to realize something.  I've been protecting myself from the two people I loved best.  I've been afraid it would hurt more if I showed pain.

"But that's wrong.  By taking away your ability to see my pain, I've been missing something.  And I'm going to tell you.  When  you say your nasty things to me, it hurts.  Olivia, you're my daughter, the person I love best in the world.  When you speak all the hatred in your heart, it hurts me. *What've I done to deserve this?*  I've been kind–"

"It's not you, it's your sex," I said.

"Well, it isn't my fault that I'm a man.  And you're making an assumption that all men are the same as the demon that attacked my sweetheart."

"Do you mean my mother or me?"

My father looked down for a moment.  "You," he said.

"Why not my mother?"

"She never let me call her that."  I thought I could see tears in his eyes.

One might think, at age twenty-four that something as basic as what I discovered at that moment might have occurred to me earlier, but it had not. *My father loved my mother.* I had been seeing him as the enemy for so long, I had never ascribed any virtuous qualities to him —consciously. Until our experience in the taxi.

"You *loved* her?" I said. "I never saw her say anything even decent to you."

"When she was in a good mood, she was incredible. So much that I was willing to wait until the next time."

He looked up, and I could see glistening in the corners of his eyes. I had never loved him like I did at that moment. "You didn't have anything to do with her death," he said. "You were her only reason to get up in the morning."

"Yeah, right," I said. "Less than two weeks after I ape her nasty habit, she's gone. Coincidence? I don't think so."

"Coincidence," my father said. "Do you know when I finally found out about her father?"

"When?" For some reason, I was feeling very anxious.

"The day she died."

I was flabbergasted. For several moments, all I could do was breathe fast and look at the floor. "What do you mean?" I finally said. "How could you not have known–?"

"He was the friendliest, most personable guy I've ever met," my father said. "I liked him until I found out. Even then, it was hard to think differently about him."

"How'd you discover it?" In spite of myself, I was interested.

"Your mother was cursing me for something or other, I don't remember, but she was more angry than usual. Maybe she saw a dent in the car fender or something. I protested any knowledge, and she said, 'Well you're guilty anyway!'

"'Of what?' I demanded.

"'All you care about is sex! Just like the old man!'

"'What old man?'

"'The rutting old goat. The one that can't go for a day without.'

"I don't have any idea whom you're talking about!"

"The one that would have been Olivia's father if he hadn't been in Hawaii when I conceived.'

"I knew only one person who'd been in Hawaii when you were conceived. 'You're not talking about your father.'

"It was a statement, because I thought her father was about as good a man as I had met. The fact that she very rarely spoke of him had puzzled me, but I'd never even asked about it. I was doing everything I could to keep her from getting angry. And any question I asked her made her angry."

There were tears in my father's eyes again. "It was then your mother chose to tell me about your grandfather. I don't know why she waited so long, and why she let the same thing happen to you. I wanted to ask her, but I decided to wait rather than risk her anger."

The sorrow and emotion in my father's expression and voice were unbearable to me. "I never knew you were such a wimp," I said, standing up to go to the bathroom. My hand defied my control and gave a slight squeeze to my father's shoulder as I walked by him.

*_____*

*Between Louisville, Kentucky and Saint Louis, Missouri*

I sat for probably an hour listening to Dan describe his wife. Since I knew nothing about Olivia, (except that her father had thought it necessary to arrange for someone to marry her) I did not *know* whether what he told me applied to Olivia, but I continued to have the chilling idea it did. I felt such a conviction, I even took my notepad out of my pocket and wrote down the qualities of Dan's wife. At some point, I would see how they matched up to Olivia...

1. DW (Dan's wife) was almost always angry, except for brief periods when she was delightful.

2. DW was highly intelligent, and her words were bitingly pertinent and inflammatory.

3. DW was terrified of (real or imagined) abandonment.

4. DW hated all men, yet flirted outrageously with them.

5. DW never forgot a (real or imagined) offense.

6. DW carried grudges forever.

7. DW went to extreme lengths to sabotage anything good in her life.

8. DW was almost always almost suicidal.

9. DW could put on a front of extreme affability.

10. DW's associates shared her emotions while they were with her.

11. DW was a black widow.

12. DW had constant identity problems.    She questioned every aspect of her life.

13. DW had constant fears of losing reality.

14. DW's feelings about others were totally polar. There appeared to be no gray areas in her mind. They were either wonderful or awful.  Sometimes the same person could be good one day and bad the next.

15. DW was obsessed with feelings of emptiness and boredom.

16. DW had been horribly mistreated as a child.

When Dan finally finished his description of his wife, I read my list back to him.  "Yep, sounds just like her," he said.  "But you forgot to put down that she's the worst cook in the world."

(I hadn't forgotten, but simply disagreed.  I had already met that woman)  While Dan spoke, a police car pulled up behind us.  A moment later, the officer appeared at my door.  I rolled down my window.

"Everything okay?" he said.

Dan leaned over.  "Everything's great, Len.  This guy gave me a ride when Lexi was trying to shoot me."

The officer nodded.  "How'd you wind up on this side of the road facing this way?"

"He's taking me back," Dan said.  "I just got done

telling him all about her."

"Makes sense," the policeman said. "Think you'll ever leave her, Dan?"

"Naw. Unless she accidentally succeeds sometime."

"I wish I completely believed that. I was coming by to check on you. It was about time for something to happen."

"Yeah. But now everything's okay until next month. But thanks anyway."

"At some point Dan..."

"I know. But I probably won't."

"Thought so." He looked at me. "Thanks for stopping, sir. It's illegal to cross the median, you know."

"Oh. Yes, sir." *Is he going to give me a ticket?*

"Can't give you a ticket because you were sent from God to save my brother's life. What would happen to me if I gave a ticket to an angel? Just obey the law from now on."

"Yes sir. What do I do after I let Dan off?"

"There's an overpass less than a mile up the road from there. Use it."

I nodded. I was going to use the overpass and we both knew it.

"Still going to the Derby for your anniversary, Dan?"

"Yeah. Can you come?"

"Think so. Last time I asked, Peg didn't have anything. Call me."

He was gone. I pulled the car onto the freeway

again, until Dan told me to stop.

"Hey, thanks for the ride, Mike. Would you mind borrowing me that list you made? I'd like to make a copy of it."

"Sure. What for?"

"It kinda helps to have her figured out on paper."

I snorted, handing him the list. About five minutes later, I heard a knock at my window. Dan handed me my notepad.

"Thanks. This helps me a little. Maybe you *are* an angel."

I snorted again, waved and left him behind, heading back toward Louisville. But only for a little less than a mile...

*_____*

*Los Angeles, California*

I went to bed that night, not only remembering, but *feeling* my father's tears. *He loved my mother, and in spite of everything I've done to him, he loves me. What's the matter with him? How could anyone find me lovable?*

At midnight, unable to sleep, I stood in front of my bathroom mirror and looked at myself again. "You've gotten fatter," I said. (No more than two pounds, but I was an expert.)

"No," I answered. "I've added some needed weight."

"You've begun the road to fatness."

"No. I've begun the road to better health."

"You've started being a pig."

"I'm on a quest to be beautiful." (At that comment, I suppressed a desire to slap myself)

"You'll never succeed."

"Yes I will.  I think I already am, a little." (This time, my hand came up to the level of my chest, but I forced it down.)

"Why try?  It's hopeless."

"I'm on a quest to be positive." (I kept my hand from moving)

"You have no right."

"Everyone has a right."

My eyes filled with tears.  "*We* don't."

"Oh yes we do."

"Says who?"

"Dad."

"What's he know?  He's just a man."

"He's Jacob Marson's best friend."

"The father of our pretty boy fiancé?"

"Yes.  He's going to be part of my life."

"*Our* life."

"No, *my* life.  You're part of me."

"How *dare* you?"

"How dare me what?"

"Usurp control of us."

"I'm not in control of me?"

"No.  We are."

"Who's we?

"We are the whole person!"

"Me and who else?"

Suddenly, it seemed the other side quit responding. I smiled. A victory. Not a permanent one, but a victory nonetheless, and I wasn't going to forget it. The sides had changed, and that was going to last...

# Chapter XI

## Change

*Between Louisville, Kentucky and Saint Louis, Missouri*
(I wonder if the Louis of 'Louisville' and the Louis of 'Saint Louis' was the same person)

I had a grin plastered to my face for ten miles after I turned around. *Len the policeman wondered if I might be an angel. I was wondering the same thing about Dan.*

*Is it possible...?* I rubbed my chin. *Could we both be? Could I be an unwitting messenger from God? Could He orchestrate the universe so both Dan and me received exactly what we needed from each other?*

Wow, deep question. How could I ever know the answer to it?

When the smile faded, I was suddenly sleepy. Really

sleepy.  Fortunately for me, I was smart enough to recognize it immediately.  I hated to pull over at the side of the road, when a town with a hotel was probably only a few miles away, but I hated more to fall asleep and wreck the car and maybe me.

My seat didn't really go back, but it didn't matter.  As I thought about how uncomfortable I was, and how unlikely I'd catch anything but a few snatches of fitful misery, I fell asleep.

It was daylight when I heard a knock at my window.  It was Len the policeman again.  "Smart idea," he said.  "I've seen too many accidents happen because people thought they'd go a mile more to the town."

I stretched.  "How far to the town?  I wouldn't mind finishing my nap in a bed."

Len grinned.  "A mile.  Go to the Blue Bonnet, and tell the woman at the desk I sent you.  She won't give you a discount, but she'll give you a pretty smile."

"Sounds good," I said.  "I'm tired enough to pay ten times the regular cost."

"Can I tell her that?"

"I'd rather you didn't."

The woman at the desk had the name 'Peg' on the front of her dress, and she had a nice smile, that did get pretty when I mentioned her husband.  "Doesn't he look good in his uniform?" she said.

"To tell the honest truth, Peg, I like to go fast in my car.  *No* policeman in uniform looks good to me."

Now her smile got downright radiant.  "I like to go

fast too, but I get professional courtesy," she said.

She didn't give me a discount, but her smile had been enormously cheering. *What would it be like to awaken to that smile every day?* (Not matter how hard she tried, or what she was doing, Tiffany's smile always looked like a pose. I'm not sure she had a real one in her)

\*\*\*[6]

I don't know if it was the bed, the friendliness of the desk receptionist, or the peace of heart I was finding, but I slept well in the room they gave me. A rest like I couldn't remember.

When I awoke, I lay in bed for a quarter hour, savoring the utter relaxation I was feeling. Did this mean I was finished with my quest? *Is this the peace that comes with the completion of an ultimately challenging task, a sign that my mind was complete, that my understanding has reached its nadir?*

Maybe. But if I stop now, what do I do? Go back to Tiffany?

It didn't feel like I knew her anymore.

*But why? I've talked with her in the last day or two.*

As if in answer to my thought, my phone buzzed. I knew it was Tiffany before I even looked at it. That was the way this adventure was moving.

"You went out with Bruce." I didn't even bother to say hello.

There was a pause on the other end. "He's a lot like you," she finally said, very quietly.

"Not true," I said.

"What?"

"If you're talking about the me you knew when I left, *I'm* not like him. If you're talking about the me I've become, you don't know that one. Therefore, you're not qualified to make that statement." I was speaking in a light tone, almost whimsical, but I meant every word. I think Tiffany sensed it.

"Okay, let me modify that." Her voice was strangely without expression. "David Bruce is a lot like the man you were when I last saw you."

Something about her speech tipped me off. "And you didn't like him."

Longer pause. "No." More hesitation. "What does that mean?"

"It means you've changed too. You wouldn't like the old me if you were to go out with him."

"But I'm just sitting here at home. Why would I have changed?"

I thought about her question. But I knew the answer before I thought. "Because you've asked yourself the ultimate question."

"And didn't have any kind of answer!"

"Right. But asking the question is the most important thing. Once it's been asked, we humans with normal egos *have* to find an answer, because we have to find an identity."

"But we'll be deeper than we were before."

"Right.  And you know what, Tiffany?  I ran away from the question for two hundred miles."

"Well, what's your answer?"

"First of all, let me state the question:  If I were to take away my good looks and good body–"

"Make that *great* looks and *great* body."

"Whatever.  If I were to take away my appearance, my great job and education, my car, my house, my cabin, maybe my social grace, my girlfriend, (Tiffany didn't correct me and insist I say 'fiancée') all the material parts of me, who or what would I be?  How's that sound?"

"Fit's me to a 't,'" Tiffany said.  "What's your answer?"

"You've just answered a question I was asking myself.  First of all, I *am* discovering things about me that I could use in my definition, but what I know about me isn't enough to define the non-material part.  My quest is still going on."

"What're some of the things you're learning about you?"  I noticed the defensiveness and impatience she had exhibited earlier were gone.  Now she was inquisitive, really wanting to know, like she really cared, or something.

"It doesn't sound like much, Tiffany."

"S'okay.  I just want to hear a little more.  Maybe to give me a little direction."

"All right.  I told you about being brave, and thinking

of others."

I paused. "All right. I've got KISAS."

"Michael!"

"It stands for Knight in Shining Armor Syndrome. I have a need to help DID's."

"DID's?"

"Damsels in distress."

"Is that good or bad?"

"Well, it ends up blocking intimacy, because the only women naturally attractive to me are ones that need my help. So it's bad."

"I didn't seem like a DID, did I?"

"Um, no, you didn't."

"Do I now?"

"No, even though I can see several ways that you are."

"Like what?"

"First of all, let me finish my list. I've learned I relate well to children, I've learned I have compassion, I've learned I can learn to love people." (This was more a wish than a reality, because I was beginning to think I loved Olivia, even though I'd never met her. I was just *imagining* myself loving her) "I've learned I can face my fears, I've learned I can face a different future from what I planned, I've learned I love scrutinizing myself, I've learned I can be a deep person."

"Wow!"

"You know what, Tiffany? I agree. I might have said 'wow' over my bench press or my success in landing high dollar contracts, but I like my 'wow' a lot better now."

"So do I, Michael," Tiffany said.

"You know what's amazing, Tiffany?"

"What?"

"Here we were, supposed to be engaged, and I'm enjoying this conversation more than any I've ever had with you."

"Same here.  Does that mean we're not engaged anymore?"

"Well, with you going out with Bruce and everything–"

She must have heard the embarrassment in my voice. "I agree.  That was just kind of fun making you uncomfortable."

I laughed in relief.  "Now that I know you were teasing me, I admit, it was fun."  I paused a moment. "You know what, Tiffany?"

"Do I want to?"

"I don't know, because maybe I'm saying this for the first time.  I—like you."

"That sounds really good.  I like you too.  If we keep it up, I might fall in love with you.  The *now* you."

"I might really like that.  Talk to you later."  I meant it.

*_____*

*Los Angeles, California*

My father was sitting at the breakfast table, playing his harmonica.  He wasn't terribly good, but I was singing along just the same, *Oh Suzanna* as best as I could remember. It was one of the delightful, totally random activities we had stumbled across in our morning meetings, and we both enjoyed it tremendously. He had been practicing in the non-breakfast times, and was a lot better than it had been.

It was a major identity shift. Up to this time, my code had not permitted me to enjoy another's company for any significant period. Now, day after day, like a love sick puppy, I was running up to my master and lying down with my legs in the air, wanting my emotional belly scratched.

All the old activities hadn't been able to sabotage my morning meetings. Nausea, hives, aching joints, mouth sores, and even hiccups had been tried, but to no avail. The part of me that had loved laughing in the pond with Jacob Marson and my father stood stubbornly resolute, insisting on my meetings with my father.

He told me stories from his childhood, stories of his summer camps, stories of his college days. During our time apart, he even made notes of all his experiences with Jacob Marson, because he knew I enjoyed them the most. He never mentioned my overwhelming crush on his best friend, and I was grateful, because I would have had to deny it if he had said anything, and I was keeping a policy of not lying during the morning meeting.

On this day, when my father finished playing, he chuckled. "That reminds me of a story Jacob told me."

Of course, I was all ears. "Well, it was kind of my

story too, at first."

My father looked up at the clock. "But it's 8:59, and this is at least a ten minute story."

"That clock's fast," I said, without looking up. "Tell me the abbreviated version."

"Too good of a story," my father said. "It'll have to wait 'til tomorrow."

He was teasing me, but he was technically right. I'd experimented once with extending the time, but my penance had lasted so long I'd missed my session with my cosmetologist. That time, it had been only two minutes overtime, because of some apple strudel my father had brought out at the end of our visit, and I had chosen not to resist. This time, though, a *ten plus minute* Jacob Marson story, dangling out there for me to grasp.

"Is it funny?"

"I think so, but I'm not sure how you'll take–"

"Time's up," I said. The rules more important, and even though I was breaking my own personal ones, by talking to him at all, if I didn't constrain myself somehow, I would lose all control of my life.

I got up to leave. The clock now showed 9:01. It wasn't a bit fast, actually. "It better be good," I muttered as I walked toward my room. Even that was breaking my code a little, because I really wasn't supposed to be remotely civil to him after 9:00.

Following my pattern that was as much a part of the routine as the One-Eyed-Egyptian Sandwiches, I went and stood in front of the mirror, and let the one part of me castigate the other part. The castigation was getting worse day by day, but I had been around it so much, I was able to hear it out and still continue the offense.

"Man lover," I said to my image, pronouncing the words as if I were swearing. *I am swearing.*

But now my reflection didn't take it as peacefully as before. "What of it? How would we populate the world if some of us didn't love men?"

"You call that love? That's all we're going to get from them."

"Not all men are like that."

"You're in love with a man the same age as your *father.*"

"I'm in love with his son."

"You've never met his son. You love *him.*"

"So do you!"

"No, I'm a protector of the old ways."

"You're having fun too."

My expression grew hideous. "You don't deserve to be happy. You're guilty!"

"You had to fall back to that one. That meant I was winning!"

"How can you win when you're in love with a man?"

"We're happier and we know it."

"One hour out of a day!"

"That's better than no hours!"

"Well, it better stop?"

"Why?"

"I said it already.  We're guilty!"

"Who says?"

"You're saying we're not?"

"I'm saying we were only a little girl."

"We seduced him."

"How?"

Tears formed in the eyes of the person in the mirror, but I knew they were mine.  "I don't know."

"I do."  My voice was soft now.

"How?"  It sounded like the question of a little child.

"He was a devil."

"Why would God let a devil harm a little child?"

"I don't know.  I'll ask Him when I see Him."

"We're never going to see God.  We're not–"

I held up my hand.  "Looping."

"Well, God's a *man*, anyway."

"So is Jacob Marson.  And so is his son."

I was winning.

# Chapter XII

## Confession

*Between Louisville, Kentucky and St. Louis, Missouri*

I stayed at the restful hotel for three days. There was a small restaurant less than fifty feet from my room that had really good fried chicken and some kind of salad dressing they called 'the pride of the heartland' that I couldn't get enough of. A dilapidated old gym down the road had ancient versions of the equipment I used to work out, so I made due with that in the evenings, and spent two days on my cell phone, borrowing the hotel computer as I caught up at work. Casey had done perfectly well with the assignments I had given her, and as before, I complimented her. It was still a little awkward, but I could tell she was touched, enough to stroke the KISAS in me.

The drive I had felt earlier was not as strong. I wasn't convinced I knew myself as well as I could, but who did? Hadn't I gained more insight into myself than most people had?

During the busiest parts of the evenings, Peg waitressed at the restaurant, and I kind of enjoyed watching her charm all her customers. Through the years, I had had a lot of women flirt with me, and it didn't exactly seem like that, coming from Peg. Her smile was genuine, really interested in the lucky recipient of her smile. But she hauled in the tips like crazy. *If she's faking, she's the best I've ever seen.*

I didn't believe she was faking it. I wanted her smile to be real.

On my third evening, I was sitting at one of the tables with Len, Peg's policeman husband. He was in street clothes, cheerfully eating a generous part of the chicken breast I was buying. We were both watching his wife as she took the order of a sixtyish year old man that was very particular about the way his steak was cooked. I had the impression he wasn't usually a heavy tipper. In fact, I was thinking the people who waited on him probably were lucky to get anything at all.

Somehow, Peg had already learned his name: "Wow, Gene, you really know your steak, don't you? How'd you get to be such an expert?"

Len was watching my expression. "She's like that with everyone," he said. "And she means it."

"Don't you ever, uh–"

"Get jealous? I used to. Like crazy. There's so many guys that think she's got something for them and everything."

"But she doesn't?"

"Well, Mike, I think she does. But it isn't just for the guys. She's the same with all the women too."

"It's nothing personal?"

"I think it *is* personal. She loves all of you."

"But she loves you better than anyone?"

Len winced, nodding slowly. "I couldn't take it at first, you know."

"What?"

"It was so, well, *vulnerable.* She told me everything about herself, I mean *everything,* stuff I never wanted to know, and she seemed to want me to tell everything about me. I tried a little, but I couldn't, Or at least I didn't think I could. Every time I was with her, I felt like she was wanting me to be as open as she had been, and I—I just couldn't stand to have her know everything I'd done. I was trying to leave it all in the past."

Len shook his head. "In the first three months of our marriage, I had three affairs on her."

I stared at him. *For someone that has trouble telling everything about himself, he's doing a pretty good job now.*

He was watching me, and he smiled. "I'm a lot better at it than I used to be. But in the line of work I'm in, a guy gets used to lots of liars."

"Why, when you were feeling a need to tell her

everything, did you do stuff that made it even harder?"

"It's weird.  After our times of physical intimacy was when Peg was the most open about—everything.  That was the time she expected it most of me.  So I avoided it—and found it somewhere else."

Did you tell Peg about the affairs?"

He nodded grimly.  "It nearly cost me the most precious thing I had, but I had to.  With every affair, I hated myself and wanted things to be right with her all the more, until—well, I decided the only way out was to kill myself."

I cleared my throat.  "Um, why didn't you?"

"For the same reason.  I love her too much.  I knew if I killed myself I'd lose her too, and lose the opportunity to be with her."

"How'd you manage to tell her?"

"I just told her.  I knew she was going to cry, and I couldn't stand that, but I still told her, one morning as I mixed up some orange juice.  I wasn't looking at her, and I wasn't even in the same room."

"What happened?"

Len's voice had started quivering.  *Does he tell everyone this much?*

"Ordinarily, I don't tell people about this," Len said. "But it kind of feels like you're on a special quest, and this is one of the most amazing things you'll ever hear."

His voice faltered, and he put his face in his hand for a moment.  In spite of his hand's shadow, I could see tears glistening in his eyes.  "She came into the kitchen and stood right in front of me, and I could see she was crying like crazy. 'What?' she said.

"I knew she'd heard me, but I started to tell her again anyway. This wasn't any time for me to act proud."

Len shook his head. "And do you know what she did next? She put her hands over her ears and said 'what?' again. And when I started telling my shameful story a third time, she said it again. It took me four tries to realize she was telling me she chose to act like nothing had happened."

"Wow."

"Yeah, wow. How much chance do you think there is that I'll ever do something like that again?"

I shook my head, a feeling of breathlessness in me. "Zilch."

"Right," Len said. "Why am I so lucky? I'm not any better than my brother, and look what he got."

I shook my head, holding out my hands. "I wish I knew that answer."

Len bit his lip. "I've come up with something, but I don't know if it has any chance of being the truth."

***7

(Read the fourth book to connect the disconnect)


Len shook his head. "I know the things in this world have no lasting importance, but it's kind of hard to look at your lovely blue Vette and pronounce it worthless."

"Let's look at it this way. How much value will it have to me when I die?"

Len nodded. "Still, you of all people have got to know what I'm talking about."

"Of course I do. But that's part of the problem."

"It is?"

"Yes. Because I know perfectly well the price that thing would fetch at an auction with the right people there, it's hard to turn away from it."

"How much would it sell for?"

"Sorry, I'm not going to indulge you."

"I could find out what you've insured it for if I pulled you over."

"Yeah, you could. But isn't it more fun to just imagine?"

Len shrugged. "Maybe. But I'd like to do more than imagine what it's like to drive it."

"Let's go."

"Really?"

"Sure. I've always wanted to know how fast cops go when they're off duty."

*_____*

*Los Angeles, California*

I was approaching a crisis. Up to now, they had always heralded change, but now, I could feel my very essence threatened. *Who am I? Am I guilty, or do I care about guilt? Do I believe in happiness, or is it just an illusion I try to comfort myself with? Am I going to let my father into my life, or am I going back where I did everything to keep him out?   Do I believe myself capable of a real, enriching relationship with a husband, or is this my way of talking myself into letting him down my trapdoor, into my web, so I can eat him at my leisure?*

These weren't just questions, these were questions that *demanded* an answer.  And all I had to answer them was my behavior up to that point.  That wasn't terribly encouraging.

But it was the fact that it *wasn't* encouraging that gave me any hope at all.  Up until that time, I had considered myself a confirmed man-hater, justified in my thinking, justified in anything I could do to complicate the life of any man.  Happiness was not something I considered possible for me.  In truth, I believed it a fantasy one could read about, but not a reality one could actually experience.  In many ways, I had despised people who sought for it.  Weaklings, dupes.

God to me had been an adversary, my enemy, if He were real.  If He existed, I hated Him.  How could He sit there in heaven or wherever he sat, looking down on the world, claiming to love everyone in it, and allow the things that had happened to my mother and me?  How could He let men like my mother's father live until he was eighty-five and keep him virile the entire time?

But all that was changing now.  I was feeling things, on a daily basis, that I had thought mere fairy tales.  I was discovering how I liked to smile, I was discovering how I liked to imagine, to dream, I was finding pleasure again and again. My mother had found nothing but despair, until she perished of it, but the inner voice that seemed to tell me it was inevitable for me too, was growing softer and softer.

It might seem all this was brought about by my visit with Jacob Marson. Certainly he was introduced into my life at a time when I could feel the swirls of change brushing against my cheek, but he was only a player, perhaps even a catalyst. But *I have a father who loves me. He grieves for me, he even weeps with me, but in spite of everything I've been through, in spite of the fact that he knows my deepest, ugliest secret, in spite of the incredibly awful way I've treated him, he loves me.*

And if he can love me, why can't God feel the same way? I don't know if I can explain how an all-powerful, all-knowing Being could let it happen, but I can see how He might grieve, and still love me. In spite of all the curses I've sent up to Him.

But the part of me that had dominated my life up to then, the me that had run my soul with such bitterness and hatred and sarcasm wasn't going to let it all just happen. It had kept us alive, kept us surviving when another voice wanted to call us into the sweet oblivion of death. I owed it my allegience–

But why was I fragmenting myself? I was the one, the only one in charge of me!

*No, I am.*

*I am.* I made the statement firmly in my mind. *There isn't another. I'm in charge of all of me, and I'm going to pull everything together.*

*No you're not. You aren't in charge of this part over here. You never will be.*

*Oh yes I am. I refuse to let myself fragment again.*

Up until that time, it had not been such an argument. The part that had dominated all along held sway, and though the other part was still in there, it hadn't had much reason to disagree.

But I hadn't known the depths of my father's love at that time. Now I did.

*Of course he loves you. He doesn't have anything else to do.*

*Oh, yes–*

No. I wasn't going to argue. Argument kept the nasty thing alive. I was in charge of me, but if I used the weapons of former times, I would lose. Maybe the only way I could win was to put down my weapons.

# Chapter XIII

## Choices

*Between Louisville, Kentucky and St. Louis, Missouri*

One hundred eighty. It was three o' clock in the morning, and Len was driving my car down a straight stretch of freeway, pegging the speedometer. I wanted to watch the expression on his face as he drove, I wanted to exult in the speed we had attained (I'd never gotten above one twenty-five) but all I could do was watch the road. I wasn't going to reach out and jerk the steering wheel if something went wrong or anything, but I couldn't look away. My heart seemed to match the car's speed, beat for beat.

As Len the peace officer slowed down to one hundred miles per hour, I had an insight. Suddenly I understood about all the thrill seeking in life, the wing suit flyers, the rock climbers, the bungee jumpers, the snowmobilers, the bull riders, the combat soldiers, the drag racers. At the heights of adrenalin, when we produce in bucketfuls, it seemed like the activity wasn't just the coolest, most exciting thing in the world, it seemed like it was the *only* thing in the world. Engaged in activities that were designed to flirt with death, intimacy became impossible, but the activity seemed to take its place, filling the universe.

But it was never satisfying. It was a lure, pulling mankind further and further out to greater levels of speed, of height, of danger, up to the place where we came as close as a brush against the death we sought to avoid. But even that was not enough. The eventuality was all that would satisfy us.

Once we got down to sixty-five, Len steered the car for a while. "If someone had offered me that for my pay check," I would have done it," he said. "And even now, I don't know how I'm going to to feel about it."

"You know what?" he said, suddenly pulling over to the side of the road. "When I got up to the top, for some reason, I tried to think of my wife. I couldn't even remember her name."

He was speaking slowly now, and there was great regret in his voice. "Almost like I was being offered a choice," he said. "Am I going to take the thrill, the exciting chase, the dangerous bandit, the hot cars, or am I going to take my Peg?" Len reached out and opened his door. "You know how I feel about that."

Now he shrugged, and undid his seatbelt, then stood. "I'm going home now," he said. "Someone'll give me a ride."

"What're you talking about, Len?" I was suddenly realizing he had become a good friend.

"Naw, Mike. I've gotten you closer to Saint Louis, haven't I?"

"Yeah, but nobody's even on the road. Who's going to to stop at this hour?"

"Then I'll walk. I'm choosing the slow way. This is going to be symbolic of the sacrifice I'm making right now."

"You take your wife over the thrill of the chase." It wasn't a question. "What're you going to do now?"

"I always wanted to be a school counselor," Len said. "Peg makes enough to get us by until I can get the education I need."

He leaned back into the car and gave the interior one last look. "I'm hoping you find what you're looking for," he said. "And I hope, when I see you again, we'll both be the men we want to be." Then he shut my car door and disappeared into the night.

\*_____\*

*Los Angeles, California*

It was Friday night when he brought it up. He must've known I was changing, because he broached the subject at a time when I traditionally was at my worst. "Do you want to go to *Sea World* tomorrow?"

I had never liked the water. I got so seasick, I got so

cold, my clothes chafed so much. I didn't go swimming, I wouldn't even go on drives overlooking the ocean. When I was a little girl, and a boy had thrown a water balloon at me, I had jumped on his back and pulled his hair so hard it had made him cry. When I was out jogging, and I had to go by working sprinklers, I would brave the middle of the road rather than taking a chance of the cold water on me.

But in the pond in Jacob Marson's house, I remembered no fear. If it had not been for that experience, I would have told my father he was crazy and cataloged the memory of him asking me as a dead giveaway that he was nothing more than a calloused old man that was going senile. He had been with me in the pond, and he had seen me laugh.

"Okay," I said, secretly enjoying the look of gratification on his face.

He surprised me again. "Thank you for accepting." He reached out and hugged me. I thought I could hear emotion in his voice.

"Why does this mean so much to you, Dad?"

"Well, there's something there that I did a long time ago. It was an amazingly powerful experience for me, and I'm hoping I can give you the same thing."

"What–?"

He held up his hand. "Nope. I don't want you getting any expectations ahead of time. It will spoil it."

I admit, I made him pay for his presumption the next day. We got up and into the car at ten minutes to eight.

That meant we were going to miss our morning time. It was unforgivable. I was making snappy, sarcastic comments about everything I could think of, from the nip of the morning air, to the tuft of hair that blew up from over his main bald spot.

He did as he always did, and ignored all my meannesses. I had sat on the back right, as had been my custom all those Saturday mornings, but at eight o'clock exactly, he pulled the car over. "Olivia, will you come and sit up here by me?" he said. "I owe you a story, and I don't think you'll be able to hear me back there."

What he was asking me to do was to disrupt *two* rituals. Usually we ate breakfast together during this hour, and now we were traveling. On Saturday mornings, when I rode in the car, it was my taxi, and I rode in the back, on the passenger side.

But, he was asking me to come closer so I could hear a Jacob Marson story, one that sounded better than usual, and talking about him was part of our morning breakfast hour. So, without a word, but only a very subtle groan of complaint, I got out of the back and into the front. As soon as I was buckled in, my father handed me a paper towel wrapped package, along with two packets of mayonaisse. And I knew everything was going to be fine.

As I bit into my first mayo daubed One Eyed Egyptian Sandwich, a conviction of security passed through me, not as powerful as it did at home, but still there. "I'm ready for my story, Daddy," I said. It was something I had said back when I was a very little girl, before the monster visited.

I could see by my father's expression that he was especially pleased. And I realized, with a shock, that I enjoyed being the one that had pleased him.

"Well," he said, lifting his hands off the wheel and cracking his knuckles, (we hadn't pulled back on the road yet) "During the last part of our sophomore year, Jacob wrote a fifty two verse saga."

"What?"

"That's right. Fifty two verses. It was called *The Tale of Sir Brenowaite,* and it was a story about a knight who sets out to kill an invincible dragon."

My father chuckled. "It wasn't bad. In fact, at the time, I thought it was really good."

"Do you remember any of it?"

"Well, maybe. Let me think for a minute."

He started to chant, but I held up my hand. *"Sing* please."

For a moment, while he was pulling back on to the road, my father was quiet, but after a moment, just as our speed had matched the traffic around us, he started singing:

Sir Brenowaite the Brave began
Bedecked in armor hard and bright
Astride his steed Rehoadan
A-questing for the dragon Blight.

"Where did the music come from?"

My father's face suddenly flushed. "That's where I come in."

"You?" I had spoken louder than I wanted.

"Well, yes. I used to play the piano."

"You did? Were you any good?"

"I thought so. My parents had me take lessons my entire childhood."

"Why didn't I know about this?"

My father fidgeted. "I used to play a little when you were really small, but your mother didn't like it. She said it gave her a headache."

"She's been gone for twelve years, Dad!"

He nodded wistfully. "Yeah, and I'm sorry. I thought it would probably give you a headache too."

"You've been playing the harmonica badly when you could have been playing the piano well?"

"The piano's in the parlor, where we never go. The harmonica's in the dining room, in my shirt pocket."

"All right, I guess. I'd like to hear you play. All this time, I thought the piano was just there because it was the chique thing to have in a home."

"Well, I'm not as good as a Steinway Grand."

"Let's have our meetings in there."

"It's a deal."

"So you wrote music for the entire saga?"

"Yes. Jacob and I worked it all out. I was quite pleased with myself."

"Sing some more."

"All right.

His head was balder than three eggs
His mustache spread across his face
His arms were thicker than your legs
His fists were harder than his mace.

Walter had begged him not to go
His friends beseeched him with their tears
The dragon was a fearsome foe
His claws like knives, his teeth like spears.

"Does the whole thing rhyme like that?  With one-three, two-four pattern?"

"Yes.  That was one of the things that impressed me about it, and gave me motivation to set it to music.  In the story, Brenowaite and Rehoadan set forth in the winter, through the deep snow, but they falter and almost perish at the base of the dragon's mountain.  An angel, disguised as a pilgrim, comes to them and gives them food and warmth, enough to finish their journey.  They make it to the dragon's nest, where he lies asleep, but Brenowaite realizes it is impossible for his sword to pierce the dragon's invincible scales."

"What does he do?"

"Well, the dragon is snoring so loudly, it almost drives Brenowaite crazy.  So he blocks the opening to the lair with huge chunks of ice, to muffles the sound.  Then he has an idea.  He awakens the dragon with a taunt, then tricks the monster into trying to destroy him with his fire.  The dragon's fire turns the ice blocking the hole into steam, and eventually Blight suffocates. His deadly fire is his own bane, according to the saga."

"Wow."

"Then Brenowaite breaks through the wall of nearly melted ice, and goes into the cave.  He finds the seven Great Treasures, the most precious of which is Sarah's Flower, the princess imprisoned in ice by the dragon for a hundred years."

"It sort of does sound good, Dad."

"I think it is.  The dragon's treasure is enormous, and Brenowaite uses it to requite everything the dragon plundered, but there's a huge amount more.  Brenowaite uses it to build Stonehenge, a university for knights.  It is, in it's time, the greatest treasure trove of learning in the world.  In fact,

The ancient school doth yet abide
Her scholar knights the very best
Her gates are strong but will swing wide
To those whose hearts can pass the test.

Then come, brave knight to Brenowaite's school
Study in mighty Stonehenge' hall
Come learn the ancient knightly rule
Come dream beneath her pillars tall.

"Wow, Dad."

"I know. I guess I still believe it's pretty good."

"I'd kinda' like to hear the whole thing."

My father laughed. "That is, unfortunately, what Jacob thought everyone would think."

"What do you mean?"

"A little community near our college was putting on a barbarian feast to raise some money for their soccer team. Jacob was friends with one of the city councilmen, who told him about the event. He signed us up to perform the saga at the feast."

I saw him turn red again. "When he called me all excited about our "first booking," as he called it, I got a little weak in the knees. It was one thing to write music for my own amusement, but to perform it in front of paying customers—that was an entirely different beast.

"So, I told him I couldn't. At least I was honest, and told him why."

"Because you were chicken," I said.

"More or less. He was disappointed, but he was confident enough to do it alone."

My father laughed again. "After some deep soul searching, Jacob decided that since he wasn't the only act at the feast, it wouldn't be fair to subject his audience to 52 verses. So he shortened the thing down to 32 verses, and had me record the music.

Then he went to the show. I got to see him in the costume he put together, and I gotta admit, he looked pretty cool—for a medieval bard. He had these green tights he found somewhere, as well as a doublet and a jaunty hat, and he did a little prancing about for me. I almost regretted my cowardice. Almost."

My father laughed vigorously. "It's kind of funny, but it's kind of sad too. Jacob told me about it the next day, and he didn't think it a bit funny, even though I've heard him tell it several times since then, and he laughs now. He had to perform twice. The first time, he got up and started to sing. The audience was polite enough, but they tried to applaud when the music changed the first time, thinking it was over. That happened five times before it really was finished, and Jacob said at the end he thought they clapped mainly because they were relieved he was finally done."

"That doesn't sound that bad," I said.

"No, and that would have been tolerable if that's all there was. The second performance started at 8:00, and the audience was comprised mostly of a group of men from a local hunting lodge who had entertained themselves with an excessive amount of hooch before they got to the feast, so they were at least half wasted when he started. This time, he made sure the audience was prepped as to the number of verses they had to endure, (he didn't put it that way) so he thought things were fine. Jacob always was an optimist.

"Things seemed to be going okay, except at about verse twenty, one of the cleverest of the hunting lodge contingency suddenly realized he didn't have a convenient place to stow his chicken bone. So he threw it—at Jacob. His fellow lushes thought that was a fine idea, so they followed his example. Jacob told me he saw twenty or thirty chicken's worth of bones flying at him. He was able to fend most of them off with his hands, but a few hit him. At least, he told me, most of his pelters had had the decency to eat the chicken off them."

I laughed—in spite of myself.

"It sort of sounds humorous now, but Jacob told me it was one of the worst moments of his life. He wanted to run off the stage and go bury his head somewhere, but like the true man he is, he finished the last verse. The barrage of bones had ceased, only because his audience had run out of chicken. (Thirty two verses gives a man a lot of eating time) Jacob said it felt like they were rejecting our work, and even though they were having fun, acting like true barbarians, it was like they were rejecting *him*."

"I bet he never tried something like that again."

"Well, this story gives you a chance to know him better. Jacob turned around, and three weeks after he had been boned (I think it's the barbarian way of booing) he had finished writing a play with the same title, *The Tale of Sir Brenowaite,* using the saga as a background. He wrote songs for it, and some members of the cast and other talented community people and I wrote music for it. He talked the local arts council into producing it, and he directed it. They performed it six times, and at the end of the final performance (which was the best attended) they got a well-deserved standing ovation at the end.  It was excellent, as good as any other musical I've seen in San Francisco."

"Really?"

"The interesting thing about it is, a man with the confidence and drive Jacob has, was still so completely intimidated, almost incapacitated by a bunch of drunks."

"But he wasn't."

No, but it was close.  The only thing that kept him on stage was his unwillingness to accept defeat."

"I think I've discovered that same quality in him."

My father smiled.  "I guess you did.  You also found out how clever he is, and how well he thinks on his feet."

"The question is, does his son have any of the same qualities as his father?"

"It just depends on how true heredity is.  I do know he set up and runs a branch of Jacob's engineering firm in Richmond, Virginia."

"He's ambitious anyway."

"At least.  I just hope there's more to him than that."

"How far do apples fall from the tree?"  But then I bit my lip.  *Which tree?  The father or the mother?*

# Chapter XIV

## Arch

*St. Louis, Missouri*

For some reason, I wasn't sleepy when I let Len off, so I finished the drive to Saint Louis, checked into a hotel and fell into bed. I had kept myself awake the remainder of the way by listening to an all night talk show host wannabe trying to convince his (undoubtedly a bit eccentric, or at least desperate for communication) audience that the moon was hollow and there was a civilization living inside it. If I needed proof that I was driving too tired, I confess that by the time I reached my hotel, I was half convinced.

When I awakened, I was back on my quest again. It was somewhat of a delayed reaction, but I was profoundly moved at what Len had done. His whole life as a policemen had to some extent revolved around fast cars and daily adventure of one kind or another. To many, his work might have even seemed glamorous.

And I saw him give it up. I was positive he was going to carry through with his resolution and not look back. When I met him again, (and I was determined I would) he would be a school counselor, or well on his way to being one. It had taken a drive in a machine he had dreamed about driving, at a speed he had dreamed about doing, to help him see how hollow it was to him. *How many people have that kind of honesty with themselves? He's a man that has come to know himself, and is willing to risk rejection, failure and embarrassment for the sake of his conclusion. I was a catalyst, or at least my car was. Maybe, since the day of its creation, that's the most important thing that has happened because of its existence.*

It was a good thought, and it strengthened me, gave me just a little greater sense of importance. *I might be an insignificant little pea in a big pod, but I can make a difference with some of my fellow peas.*

Once I had cleaned up, I called the office, and we problem-solved a few minor crises. Casey had, as always, carried out all of my instructions and pushed everything forward. I complimented her, as I had been, but this time she answered me. "It's easy to follow instructions when you have a boss you love."

It's possible she heard my great gulp on the other end. *What do I do with this one? Is it possible she's coming on to me?*

No, it wasn't possible, I decided. She was twice my age and then some, almost as old as my father. So I was going to take it as a super compliment. I was touched anyway. "That's the nicest thing I've heard in two weeks. I really appreciate you saying that."

"Well, it's true," she said, almost snappily, and I could tell she was embarrassed again. "When will you call again?"

"Probably in a couple days," I said. "All the operations we're putting in motion should last that long, if not longer."

"I think so. I'm looking forward to hearing from you."

As I hung up the phone, I shook my head. My relationship with my office manager had changed so much since I last saw her that–

On a whim, I dialed Bart Oglesby's number. He was a cost analysis specialist, and my best friend in the office.

"Hey, Bart."

"Mike! Man, do I feel privileged. I thought you only talked to Casey."

"Sorry. I'm on an incredible quest."

"Yeah, I know."

"What? How?"

"I ate at the Plug and Chug last night. Nick remembered me from the time you took me there."

"Oh."

"What's up?"

"Is everything going as well as Casey says it's going?"

"Mike, what have you said to her?"

"Whaddya' mean?"

"Casey's actually listening to us now.   She still knows everything, but now she acting like we know something."

"Cool."

"And she's becoming like– office glue.  She's acting like she cares about all of us.  It just feels different coming to work.  Like joining a team you've always loved."

"What do you think–?"

"Cynthia asked her what was going on, and she said, "We've got a great boss. I'm just following his orders."

"Um, Bart, you don't think she has uh, like *feelings* for me or anything, do you?"

"Why do you ask that?"

"Well, because I just started complimenting her.  I mean, she's deserved it like crazy all along, and I finally decided I was going to tell her.  Ordinarily she makes it so hard–"

"I don't know if she has a crush on you or anything, but if she did, I wouldn't be too surprised."

"Great."

"Hey, but Mike?"

"Yeah?"

"Whatever you've been saying, keep it up."

"I appreciate your concern."

"Anytime."

"Hey, Bart. I think you do a great job, too."

"Hey, Mike. Roses are red, violets are blue, sugar is sweet and Mikey is coo.'"

"Wow, I'm touched."

"I'm *impressed*. I just made up poetry."

"Top quality stuff, too. See ya,' Bart."

"That's all?"

"That's it. Casey gets all the rest."

"All right. Be that way. Glad it's her, not me."

"Me too."

As I hung up the phone, I wasn't completely happy with the call. It had been lighthearted, but it didn't exactly match the level of communication I was trying to reach—in every interaction. I dialed Bart's number again.

"Quit buggin' me!"

"Look Bart, I want you to know I meant it about you doing a great job. We would be in a lot worse shape without you."

"All right. Thanks, and I mean it, but what's got into you? I just do my job."

"And it's worthy of appreciation. But your friendship is worth more to me."

"Why're you getting all mushy?"

"It's part of my quest. I guess I'm trying to get away from superficiality."

"But it's all some of us expect—*and* want."

"I know. But I'm trying this out."

"I'm not sure I'm going to like the new you."

"I'm not either. But I am sure I didn't like the old me."

"What was the matter with him?"

"He was shallow as a settling pond."

"Talking about yourself in the third person? Not healthy."

"Yeah. I'm just trying to make a real change, and that means leaving the past behind."

"All of your past?"

"I'm getting there."

"What's left?"

"My car, my job."

"*Tiffany's* gone?"

"Kind of. We sort of have an understanding that we're broken up."

"I'm getting in line!"

"Better hurry. She's already gone out with David Bruce."

"Bruce? That pompous–"

"Before you get too far in your description, you better hear what she said about him."

"What's that?"

"He reminded her a lot of me."

"Oh. Well, David Bruce is an okay guy, I guess."

"And that's all I was, before my quest. So I'm going to see it through, so on the other end I'm more than just okay."

"All right. I'll be interested to see how it turns out."

"You might want to do it yourself."

"Doubt it. But we'll see. Talk to you, man."

"See ya.'"

Hanging up felt better this time. Real communication had not only occurred, it had been the rule, not the exception.

It was difficult to do, but it felt right. Gritting my teeth in determination, I dialed the phone again. And waited.

Five and a half rings later, I was about to hang up the phone, but I heard my dad's 'hello.' I put the phone back to my ear. "Hey Dad." He was breathing hard. "Sorry to interrupt your workout."

"S'okay. What's up?"

"I want you to tell me about Mom."

"Right now?"

"I'd prefer it. But I can wait if it's too inconvenient."

"Naw, I'll just change workouts. Whaddya want to know?"

"Well, first of all, let me get my list out and you can tell me how close it is."

"List?"

"Yeah. Here, listen to it..."

When I was finish reading the list to him, he was quiet for at least half a minute. "Where did you get that?" he finally said.

"I picked up a hitchhiker who described his wife to me."

"Mike, you've got to be careful.  You never know when you'll pick up someone bad."

"His wife was threatening him with a gun."

"But you didn't know that when you picked him up."

"No, I stopped when he ran in front of my car, signaling frantically."

"What time of day was it, Mikey?"

"You don't want to know."

"You're just cruising for trouble."

I paused for a moment before replying.  "Maybe so, Dad, but it's been uncanny.  Every single person I've picked up has taught me something."

"Well, that's only because you've been looking to be taught."

"That's true, I suppose.  But if it is, do you know what it means?"

"Are you deliberately bending the subject away from my rebuke?"

"I don't think so.  But think about what it means if everyone I've met can teach me."

"I dunno.  Probably that you've been trying really hard."

"That's probably true, but it means something more. It means every single person I meet, young or old, stupid or brilliant, male or female, dirty or clean, literate or illiterate can all be my teachers."

"Well, yes, but–"

"No Dad.  I don't have any more for them than they have for me.  Even if I have education and money, they have life experiences I have never known, and if I will hear their perspective, it will give me understanding in a way I could not have known without them."

Now my father was quiet a long time. "That's very good, son," he finally said. "I really like that."

Another long pause. "As far as I can tell, your mother is still alive," he said, and now there was a curious flatness in his expression.

"She is?" My gut twisted. "I thought she was in an car accident."

"Her car was," my father said, his voice still flat. "But she wasn't in the car."

"How do you know this?" I was having trouble getting the words out.

"It was a bottle of perfume. Her favorite kind, very expensive, about one hundred fifty per bottle. I found it in the burned wreckage of her car, along with remnants of bone, so charred it was impossible to determine the identity, or even the species of the deceased person. Since it was her car, and since she was never seen again after the accident, we all assumed it was Mercy that had died."

"What does the perfume–?"

"Think about it, son. At the temperature it would take to combust *bone,* how would an alcohol based perfume bottle stay intact?"

"So she carried the perfume with her everywhere?"

"Yep. She must have realized that I would have suspected something if the perfume wasn't with her."

"When did you find this?"

"A few days ago. I'd always thought that there was something a little odd about her death. After I met— well, I met someone a little while ago that reminded me of her. So I–"

"Hey, Dad, please level with me. It was Olivia you met."

"What makes you so sure about that?"

"Why do you think I was pumping Dan for info on his wife?"

"Oh. Okay, I wasn't giving you enough credit. Anyway, I went out to the site, to see if I could find a remnant of bone that could be checked for DNA. That technology wasn't around when it happened."

"And you found the perfume bottle."

"Yeah. And as soon as I found it, I thought, "wow, of course she would have had it with her." Only about a minute later it occurred to me that it wouldn't have survived."

"So where do you think she is?"

"No idea, son. But apparently she doesn't want anything to do with us, or she would have contacted us."

My heart was beating faster. A lot faster. "Not necessarily, Dad. Maybe she's embarrassed and not sure we'll accept her."

He paused a moment. "Maybe. For your sake, I hope so. I'm not sure I could stand her now that I've been away from her for so long."

"The DW description's right on?"

"It's uncanny. The only difference is, she never had any open aggression to me. She just did her best to ruin me financially, without quite doing the job."

"And Olivia's just the same?"

"Mostly."

"That's what you wanted to tell me the other day, wasn't it?"

"Yeah."

We were both quiet for a few moments. I spoke first. "You know, Dad, it's kind of ironic. Even if I never get to meet my mother in my conscious memory, if I decide to come all the way to LA, I get to meet her."

"Hmmm."

"You know what's funny. Just thinking that makes her more desirable."

"Great. Look son, you don't know what you're getting into–"

"But she doesn't know what *she's* getting into. And I'm not the man that started on this journey."

"I can tell. You've deepened, son. I'm—very pleased."

"Thanks, Dad. But the process isn't over yet. And if whatever's working on me is going to work on Olivia, she might be changing too."

"Well, as a matter of fact, you could be right. Her father tells me my interaction with her the other day has made a difference so far."

A chill of conviction went through me. "What

happened?"

"I'll tell you later, but my phone's beeping. My battery's about gone."

"All right. Thanks, Dad."

"Thank *you*, son. I can't tell you how much you've made my day."

"It's good to hear." (I said it like I meant it) "I love you, Dad."

"I love you too, Mikey."

One more call. I dialed Nick's number. "Can't talk, bro. In the middle of noon rush."

"It's only—never mind. Time zone."

"Right. Looking forward to talking to you later. Half hour okay?"

"Sure. I don't have much of a schedule." But he had already hung up after my 'sure.'

Even as I realized my conversation with Nick was finished, I decided on one more. I dialed my father's number again.

"Sorry to bug you, Dad. Can you give me Iago's number?"

My dad hesitated a moment. "This is probably a good idea, son. No one can give you straighter stuff than he can."

A moment later, with trembling hands, I was dialing the number. After three rings, he answered. His voice was tenor range, without a trace of an accent. "Hello."

"Mr. Salvadore? This is Michael Marson."

(Pause) "Hello!"

"Um, are you free to talk?"

"Just a minute."

(Nearly 30 second pause) "Hello, Michael. How are you today?" His voice was warm and welcoming.

"I'm really well, sir. I wanted to introduce myself."

"Call me Iago, or Salvy. As the son of your father, you're my friend."

"I'm more familiar with Salvy, if that's okay. But it doesn't sound very dignified."

"Salvy is fine. I can't afford to worry about dignity."

"I'm on a quest right now, Salvy. No, I'm sorry. It doesn't work. I'm on a quest right now, Iago. Has my father told you about it?"

"No. But he did say you might come here."

"At this rate, I think I will. I've been able to keep the business going over the phone."

"I don't think she's ready to see you yet, Michael."

"Mikey. I'm not ready to see her yet either, but what do you mean?"

"It's tempting to deceive you, but considering the stakes, I cannot. My daughter is learning how to be a wonderful person. She has far to go, but she is making progress."

"I'm glad to hear that. The man you will meet when I get there is not the man you requested to marry your daughter."

"Is that good or bad?"

"I don't know, but I think good. I am gaining insight and better ability to have meaningful relationships than

I ever have before."

"That sounds good to me. I just hope when you meet my Olivia, you can see her with eyes of patience and a belief in the ability to progress."

I chuckled. "I have some hope I can do that already. But when I meet you, I hope to be even more sure of that."

"Um, Micha—Mikey, Olivia's looking at me and wondering what I'm doing."

"Tell her the truth. But I'll see you, probably in less than a week. I'm glad to speak with you, sir." (The 'sir' had just slipped out)

"Same here. Goodbye."

"Bye."

I hung up, but reluctantly. Iago Salvadore's voice was nothing unusual, but he had been so genteel, so welcoming, so dignified. *He's a friend worth keeping. No wonder my dad's stayed in touch with him.*

He spoke of his daughter so gently. If he were my father-in-law...

The hotel had an exercise room, and I was able to get an excellent workout on the treadmill, the elliptical, and the universal. The bench maxed out at 220, but with a lot of reps, it got me breathing hard and feeling it. It wouldn't have hurt my feelings to go to a public gym and really lift, but I felt my quest was too pressing. Besides, I wasn't certain power lifting was going to be part of the new person I was becoming. I was just finishing my 12 mph sprint on the treadmill when my phone buzzed. Nick. It had been an hour.

"Hey Mike. Saw your friend the other day."

"Yeah. He told me."

"Haven't talked to you in a while."

"And a lot's happened. Wanna hear it?"

"Yes. Let me see if Bev can handle things now."

"Well, it's gonna take a while."

"All right. Hang on a minute."

Less than that later, he was back. "I'm ready."

"All right. Here goes."

"It took me about a half hour to tell Nick all my adventures he hadn't yet heard. For an additional hour, we processed everything I had seen, all my adventures, from the first hitchhiker that loved my car so much to the last one who had become what felt like my good friend. I told him about my recent conversations with my father, with Iago Salvadore, with Casey, with Bart and with Tiffany. When I finished, he synthesized it all with one sentence: "This thing's for real."

"Yes, it is," I said. "Every lesson's been painful, but each one is like lifting a greater weight. I'm getting stronger and stronger, but in the way that counts because, for the first time, I'm allowing myself to see me clearly."

I took a deep breath. "Nick, this is the strangest thing. One would think this is the most irresponsible thing imaginable, driving across the country, leaving my job, picking up hitchhikers, sleeping on the side of the road, but it feels *right*."

Nick seemed to ignore my declaration. "So you and Tiffany aren't engaged anymore?"

"No, we're not. And it's a good thing."

"Um, Mike, do you you think you would mind if I asked her out?"

"What!!?"

"Well, my little romance didn't work out, and, well, she sounds more interesting to me now."

I laughed, but I felt a little dizzy. "Nick, she didn't even like your restaurant!"

"Yeah, I know. So what do I have to lose?"

I shrugged. "Nothing, I guess. Go for it."

"I've got an idea I'm gonna try, if she'll have anything to do with me."

"Let me know."

"I will." Nick sounded more animated than usual.

"I'm hoping for you, pal."

"No you're not."

"I'm not hoping for you?"

"You've never called me 'pal' before."

"Oh." I hesitated a moment. "All right. It's just weird." I paused again. "No. I'm really okay with it."

"All right. We'll talk to you."

"Yeah. Thanks for giving me so much insight."

"Thank you for listening. You make my life more worthwhile. It's for guys like you that I've taken on a sandwich shop."

"Cool. Let me know when you have something to tell."

"Let *me* know. See ya."

I was done with phone calls for a while, and felt like getting out of the hotel, but I didn't want to drive yet. I had heard of the Gateway Arch, so I got directions and drove through downtown St. Louis to the Mississippi River. I could see the Arch towering above me, six hundred feet above the ground.

While I waited for my turn to ride the unusual elevator to the top, I read the pamphlet. The Arch was supposed to represent the Gateway to the West, the starting point for the pioneers who forged their ways into the wilderness, settling the vast lands between the Mississippi and the Pacific Ocean. How incredibly different it was today, where I could, with no more effort than it took to push down my accelerator and hold on to the steering wheel, traverse the distance that less than a hundred fifty years earlier, had cost such extraordinary labor and life.

It was a beautiful, clear day, about 85 degrees, humid, but with a slight breeze that mitigated the heat. My turn came, and I rode the elevator with about 11 others to the top. With somewhat of a sense of awe, I stepped out at the top, looking down at the spectacle before me.

I could see for miles, the broad band of silver blue that was the river, stretching forever in both directions. I could see forest and farmland, city and country, riverboats and endless cars. The west, the east, the north and the south disappeared in haze far away from where I stood.    I felt a strange feeling for a few moments that I was on the top of the world, a place like heaven, or Mount Olympus of the ancient Greeks.

A longing seized me, as I pondered the millions of people below me, to know them all, to find with each of them the intimacy I was bringing to my life and the people I knew.    I was filled with love for the earth below me, a love that included not only the land itself, but the people that lived on it.

Next to me, a man and his wife were standing, seeming to admire the view with as much feeling as I was.    They were in their late twenties to early thirties, and they had three children.    Both held a child, a boy and a girl, about three years old and wiggling, apparently twins.    The third child, a little boy about six, was hugging his mother's legs so hard she was having a hard time keeping her balance.

They were dressed cleanly, but not stylishly, in clothes that looked like they had already seen a lot of action.    The couple stood close together, unmoving except for the shifting the woman made to keep her balance, their shoulders touching, as if transfixed, speaking softly, pointing out landmarks to each other.    I thought they probably lived locally, and were splurging on the price of elevator tickets for their whole family. The twins wouldn't have cost much, if anything, but the older boy, who paid attention only to his mother's leg, would have been an sacrifice if they were as poor as they looked.

For just an instant, the boy looked up. By the expression on his face, I could see he was a special needs child. Something about the way he looked at me, like I was only a part of his surroundings, no different than the ceiling above us or the floor below.

The couple continued to exult in the sights they were seeing, but I could see the little boy was escalating in his agitation. He pulled back and forth, banging his head against his mother, causing her weight shifts to become more extreme.

But she didn't notice. The view, which their family had paid dearly to obtain, took the forefront of her mind, and she continued to gaze, pressed hard now against her husband. *This is something they have planned for a long time.*

But their son didn't care about the family plans. He wanted something he wasn't getting. Suddenly, in the midst of another leg butt, he jerked backward, throwing himself on the Plexiglas window we gazed through.

And he started to scream. Not a civilized scream, like a woman in mortal danger or even of a spoiled child, but the highest, shrillest screech, the granddaddy of all shrieks, making fingernails on a chalkboard sound like Beethoven's Ninth in comparison.

The two parents were helpless. In the crowded narrow room atop Gateway Arch, they could not put their rambunctious twins down, (I wondered if they couldn't afford strollers) to try to console the boy, and their soft pleading voices had about as much chance to be heard as a mouse squeak in a roaring stadium. Almost immediately, people all around started glaring in resentment, and one ultra compassionate jerk (who happened to be right beside me, so I heard him) came up with the brilliant remark "If you can't control your kids you shouldn't be up here."

I actually think I was ready to elbow this guy hard in the ribs, but before I got my armed cocked and ready, I saw the woman's face. If ever there was a DID, I was seeing her.

So I don't get as much credit as one might think. The DID (admittedly she was not in a white gown, and her clothes were tattered) needed me. I scooped the little boy in my arms.

I don't know quite what I was expecting, but I was surprised. The little fellow (he couldn't have weighed more than thirty-five pounds) quit his screaming as suddenly as he had begun. He looked me in the face with no expression on his face, in a stare so strong it seemed he had quit blinking.

Both the man and the DID breathed their thanks. Somewhat reluctantly, it seemed, they began shuffling toward the elevator, apparently feeling cheated by their circumstances.

"If you want to stay longer, go ahead," I said, even though the boy's stare was unnerving. "He's not heavy."

Their thanks this time was profuse. While I held their older child, they continued their scrutiny of the panorama, and Junior stared at me. I had no idea what he was thinking.

I held him a half hour. Somewhere close to the end of that time, I felt something warm against my skin and realized the child I held had at least an occasional problem with his continence.

*Oh, well. I can wash everything.*

When the man and DID finally decided they were finished, it still seemed they moved with reluctance to the elevator. I followed, immediately behind, wanting to make sure my charge didn't protest a separation. We got into the elevator, which after a half a minute wait began to clank its way down.

I was still holding tight to the boy, when I noticed him bringing his head close to my chest. Somewhat surprised, I held him yet tighter—and he vomited down my shirt.

For some reason, it was not totally unexpected. I thought I had detected a strong vein of distrust and dislike in his stare, and this was a logical way to express it. I simply held him closer, trying my best to keep his donation off the elevator floor.

The descent couldn't have taken longer than the ascent, but it seemed like an eon more. When finally we got to the bottom, the parents thanked me again, and offered to take their son, but I told them I would carry him wherever they wanted to go. As it turned out, they were going to their car, ready after their adventure to go home and relish it.

Only when I had placed my rider onto his car booster

seat, did his mother see the state of my shirt. "Did Emil do that?" she said, somewhat unnecessarily, I thought. Usually grown-ups that had the inclination to vomit stayed home so they could do it in privacy.

"Well, yeah," I said. "But it'll all wash out."

Tears appeared in the former DID's eyes. "Thank you so much, (my brave knight)" she said. (I supplied what was in the parentheses) "I had prayed we'd be able to stay as long as we wanted. Emil doesn't like to be in public places."

"It's my pleasure," I said, and in spite of the slime and the smell, I meant it.

"God bless you," my former DID said. "You're His angel."

Speechless, I backed away, feeling my face flushing.

"Thank you, sir," the man said, taking my soiled hand. "Will you allow my wife to clean your clothes, and then will you eat with us?"

"I really–" I began, about to say "gotta' get going," but it wasn't true. I altered the ending of my sentence: "would be honored."

Both husband and wife appeared surprised and gratified at my acceptance. Using a burp cloth, the woman sponged the worst of the vomit off me, then I got into my car and followed them to their home, which happened to be in a suburb town of St. Louis called Shrewsbury. Their house was very modest, appearing to be about eighty years old.

They found me a pair of too large shorts and a too

tight t-shirt to wear while Abby (my former DID) laundered my clothes, at the same time beginning their evening meal.

It was simple fare, macaroni and cheese, with hot dog slices, and they had to have me sit on a sturdy coffee table, because they didn't have any more chairs. Surprisingly, it was fairly peaceful. The twins, subjected to an afternoon of activity, succumbed to the lure of sleep, and Emil, once at home, acted almost normal. He was very interested in details of my clothing, and found the foil of a gum wrapper in one of my socks.

As it turned out, it was a delightful time. I participated in Abby and Maurice's animated reliving of their experience up in the Arch. Both made reference to my rescuing their outing, both simply accepting that I was sent from heaven to help them.

How could I contradict them? I didn't know how things like that worked out. All I knew was I was there because I had had a whim to see the Arch. *Could that whim have come from above?*

When my clothes were freshly laundered and I was dressed in them again, I realized once again, I did not want to leave. The love in that home, the peace, the life satisfaction they both had was so inviting, the love they bore their children and me was so lovely, I had to exert my will to take my leave. I could not do any better than they had done.

But my life was not theirs, and there was no room for

me.  It was seven o'clock, and I thought I could reach Columbia in less than two hours.  So as the shadows grew long and then the night became dark, I drove, pondering.  Having KISAS was not always a negative thing.  That day, I had made a difference in the lives of a whole family, and had helped to give them something to relish in the days and maybe years to come.  With Casey, it was helping too, without doing real harm, as far as I knew.  It simply appeared to  depend on the attitude of the KISA.

*_____*

*Between Los Angeles, California and San Diego, California.*

"Who was that?" I asked my father as soon as he came back to the car from his phone call.  He had pulled off onto a side street and had stepped outside to speak to this person, whoever it was, but I had a suspicion.

"I'm not sure I want to tell you," he said.

"Let me guess," I said.  "It was Michael Marson."

My father was a horrible liar.  His face turned immediately crimson.  "Why do you say that?" he said, but his voice quavered as he did.

"Because he's unpredictable to you, an unknown.  You wouldn't get out of your car to talk to someone in your business, you wouldn't do it to any friends, and I'm certain you don't have a girlfriend."

He paused for a moment.  "All right, it was he."

"Why is he more important to you than I am?"

"You just said it, Olivia.  He is an unknown, and

until today, I had not talked to him before."

"Why did he talk to you, rather than me?"

"Because he knows nothing about you, and I am the one that made the request of his father."

"Is he considering–?" I felt so trapped, having people talk to me as though I were a commodity or something, but the question had just slipped out. *I have to watch myself more carefully.*

"Yes, he is," my father said. "In fact, he's driving across the country."

"Why would he come? He knows nothing about me."

"But he knows his father loves your father. He knows his father trusts your father."

"But what does my father have to do with me?"

"I reared you, Olivia, to believe as I believe, to–"

"Yeah, but you know how well that's worked. I've taken after my mother!"

"We're still working on you, Sweetheart."

His answer was so gentle and full of love that I backed down. It was part of our morning hour, even if the surroundings were different than before. I could feel the seed of anger inside me as before, the outrage that others would have the gall to speak of me without my input, but for the time being I held my peace. *Why didn't he call* **me?**

When we arrived at Sea World, my father took me immediately to one of the pools where the dolphins swam. I don't know if he had to pay for the privilege, but after a few moments of negotiation, which I did not watch, he said, "Come here Olivia. There's someone here I would like you to meet."

I stepped forward, tentatively, seeing nobody next to my father, until I saw he had his hand over the edge of the pool wall. His hand rested on the back of a dolphin.

"Uh," I said. "I don't want to touch it."

"His name is Skip," my father said. "Come and meet him, or you'll hurt his feelings."

"Sure I'll hurt his feelings," I muttered, but drew closer. The creature sat completely still in the water, without any sign of wanting to swim away, allowing my father to touch him.

Very gingerly, I reached out my hand and touched the thing on the head. It was rougher than I might have expected, even though it was still wet. That was unremarkable enough, but there was something strange. I had the uncanny feeling I was touching the head of a child. This dolphin was not only alive, it was sentient.

And I felt perfectly conflicting emotions. The one part of me wanted to snatch my hand away, to recoil as though I were feeling an alien from Barsoom, but the other part, the part that was cooperating with my father during the morning hour and loving the cooperation *felt the unconditional love of the dolphin for me.* More correctly, I felt the love that Skip had for me.

What had I done to earn the love of this creature? I had done nothing. I had simply followed my father's request, but even if I had not, Skip would have loved me.  *He loves me because I am, not because I am worthy.*

*No!*  The voice inside seemed desperate.  *The dolphin has been trained to believe that humans are good because they bring food.  It's nothing more than that.*

I gritted my teeth and ignored the other voice.  *The dolphin loves me because I am, not because I am worthy.  Through this animal, this extraordinary animal, I have learned how God feels about me.*  Still gingerly, I stroked the rough grey head.

# Chapter XV

## Stud

*Between Columbia, Missouri and Kansas City, Missouri*

It was 9:00 A.M., the next day. I had arrived in Columbia without complication, rented a hotel room, slept through the night, awakened, worked out in the hotel facility, cleaned up and got back on the road without complication. It felt odd, and I wondered if this was a sign my quest was nearly over.

At 9:05, I saw him. He was dressed in shorts and a tank top, with a cigar in his mouth, about 32 years old. There was something in his stance that was distasteful, but I had no reason to avoid him, and I had given rides to people much more repulsive than he.

So I pulled over. He came up, threw away his cigar

stub, and got in the car as comfortably as if it were his. "Nice ride," he said, plopping himself down on the seat.

He was clean shaven except for a carefully tended wisp of a goatee on the point of his chin. His hair was blond, cropped short, his eyes were blue, heavy lidded, somewhat lazy looking. His physique was impressive, more so than mine at my very best. His biceps bulged out from massive shoulders, his neck was wider than his head, thighs and calves were extremely cut, with each line of muscle prominent, as clearly as though he had been sculpted. His feet were bare except for a pair of flipflops.

While I looked him over, he scanned me. "You do a bit of body building too, I see," he said.

"Just lifting," I said. Somehow I didn't really like the idea of associating with him.

"Whaddya bench?"

"Four hundred, at my best." I didn't like the guy, but I still had the foolish desire to impress him.

"No, c'mon." He whistled. "That's a ton."

He looked me up and down again. "I'm going to a competition in KC. You wanna come?"

"What sorta' competition?"

"Mr. Stud U.S.A."

Against my will, I snorted . "What's that?"

My passenger looked instantly affronted. "Hey, it's a big deal. There's about two hundred guys in it from all across the country."

"What sort of stuff are they judging on?"  I was

interested in spite of myself.

He grinned. "Lotsa chicks gonna be there too."

"What sorta stuff–?" I said it even louder.

He didn't quit grinning. "Oh, you know. Overall strength. Physique, looks, strength, smarts, that kind of thing."

*You're out then.* But I didn't say it. "Huh."

"Costs three fifty each to enter, but I go every year, and I get a hundred off for bringing someone."

"Oh. Okay." I shrugged.

"You game?"

"I don't think so, but I'll have a look"

"Good enough."

"What's first prize."

"Movie contract and one hundred grand."

"Wow."

"Yeah, wow."

So we talked as I drove, about lifting weights, beautiful women, hot cars, wild music, good drinks, professional sports, action movies, all the typical "male bonding" stuff. Only I didn't feel any bond. *Is this the kind of thing I used to entertain myself with?*

I managed to think the thought, but I was still engaged in the conversation, and to my shame, must admit I enjoyed the visit, and even liked my passenger by the time we got to our destination. His name was Terrence Carter, from Jefferson City, Missouri, and he was a welder by trade. I knew enough about his business to ask a couple intelligent questions, but he was not really interested. It turned out he had been attending the contest every year for the past five years, and had come in third the year before. I started really doubting the legitimacy of the contest.

When we got to Kansas City, he directed me to an exit, and we drove into a downtown maze. He had me park in a parking garage, and we went upstairs to an expansive office. There we met others, all of them roughly resembling Terrence, all heading the same way we were. By the time we got to the office, a line had formed, starting at a desk inside, through the door and spilling into a hallway. I'd say there were about seventy -five of us. All of them seemed to walk the same, as if they were trying to remind the world what studs they were, but in reality proclaiming pretty loudly that strength and looks do not bring emotional security.

I don't know how it happened, but I suddenly found myself filling out papers for the woman at the desk, who was dressed in an outfit that exaggerated her feminine features. In spite of her outfit, she was quite professional, taking my name, nickname, my profession, measuring my height, weight, my waist, my chest and my arms. Then she skilfully typed my opening statement, which I had written on a small slip of paper given to us at the beginning of the line. She was exceedingly efficient, and the whole process took only five minutes. I felt like an idiot, but I didn't stop.

A moment later, feeling rather foolish, I had selected my costume for the next day, a very unimaginative leather kilt. I went with the herd of men to some kind of assembly hall in the building that had balconied seating, with a capacity of about 2000. There was a temporary stage set up, and there women clad in about half what the desk woman had worn showed us the various stations, where we would be interviewed and exactly what sort of strength tests might be given. Each of us would have to do three of a possible twelve.

I looked through the list of events, and none of them were too far from my areas of workout concentration, even though I'd probably do best in something that came closest to approximating the bench press.

The whole thing looked fun, if nothing else. There were some fairly impressive specimens of muscularity, but as far as I could tell, I didn't see any fairly impressive specimens of intelligence.    (Hopefully anyone that saw me *would* see that)

That evening, as I did a light workout in my hotel exercise room, I was actually nervous. *What's the matter with me?    It's not like this is important or anything.*

But it didn't help. I had trouble sleeping too.

The next day, I got up and showered but did not shave. I decided I was going to try for the rugged look. By some chance, I arrived at the building just as Terrence did, and we signed in at the same desk where we had started the day before. From there we went into the dressing room, where I donned my kilt, and he put on his (totally cliché) leopard skin. As we left, two women, wearing only skimpy swim suits, beckoned to us. I went over, several steps behind Terrence, who went with alacrity. They were oilers, and both had a paper covered table in front of them.

Terrence climbed on the table. I hesitated.

"Let's get you oiled," the attendant said. She was about twenty years old, with dyed blond hair, too much make up and a body that looked surgically enhanced. Her smile was frozen in place.

I looked over at Terrence's table. His oiler was already at work, her hands gloved in plastic, kneading the oil into his shoulders. She seemed about as enthusiastic as my attendant.

Terrence's face was turned toward me, and showed an expression of ecstasy. *It's amazing how differently two people perceive the same event.*

"Uh, no thanks," I said.

The girl looked shocked. "Everyone gets oiled.

"Yeah, well I don't. I don't think real men need oil."

For the first time, the girl smiled a little. I thought I could see her give the smallest of nods. "Can I quote you on that?" she said, so quietly I could barely hear.

"Sure. My name's Michael Marson." It was probably blasphemy in this population, speaking against oil, and I know it was supposed to accentuate the muscle definition, but like I had told Terrence, I wasn't a body builder, so I hadn't worked on my definition. Leaving it off would differentiate me from the other contestants, but I could use it to my advantage. Besides, it kind of gave me the creeps.

When the event started at 11:00 A.M., I peered out from backstage to see if anyone cared enough about Mr. Stud U.S.A. to show up to the contest. As it turned out, the place was packed, mostly with fiftyish year old women, give or take ten years, looking like older and wrinklier versions of oiler girls. The only difference was, they were interested in us.

*They've found nothing meaningful in their lives, so they're willing to settle for fantasies about real relationships with gorgeous men, who are the very opposite of meaningful.*

On the heels of that thought came the obvious addendum: *And here I am in the middle of them. And what's worse, in spite of what I know and believe, I'm going to enjoy their attention.*

With that, I actually turned around, to go back to the locker room, don my regular clothes, and leave. Shamefully enough, the only thing that kept me from doing it was the thought *They're not going to refund my three fifty.*

Three hundred fifty lousy bucks! For that, I betrayed myself. For one (somewhat lavish) night out, for the price of one cheap laptop, for the cost of my cell phone, I sold my soul, I betrayed myself to my vanity. (I wonder how much thirty pieces of silver is in today's money)

I was the thirty-first contestant to appear before the audience. Four or five people before me, I had rushed back to the locker room, ripped off the kilt and put on my jeans. It would mean I would not show off my legs, but in my case, they might have looked better left to the imagination.

The spotlight was bright in my eyes, blinding me to the audience when it was my turn, so I couldn't see the reaction my strategy was gleaning. I walked to the front without the strut the remainder of my fellows had taken, having decided I could not compete with them in physique or "pretty boyness." I had to seduce my spectators with what I knew they wanted.

There were some whistles when I stood on the dais, but everyone before me had had a few. Did I have more than they?

I remember the words they said. They were words I had given them, but the last ones were unexpected: "Michael Marson, Vice President and Branch Manager of Marson, Inc., an engineering firm. He likes long walks in the moonlight with his lady, fitness, reading and discussing good books, slow dancing, fixing things around the home and finding the bright side of everything. He says real men don't need oil."

As I said, the last statement took me by surprise, but not unpleasantly. By singling myself out as the only one not slathered in baby oil, I would impress myself in everyone's mind: They would remember my appearance and the words I had used to describe myself.

When my introduction was over, there was a collective sigh from the women in the audience. I felt kind of slimy, for I had appealed to exactly what they had missed in their relationships: the intimacy, or at least pseudo intimacy they craved.

For the remainder of the competition, every time I participated in any event, I received a cheer. As a result, every performance was singled out, brought to the judges' attention. I'm certain, in the parts of the contest that involved subjective judging, such as the overall appearance, I was viewed with a less critical eye than my fellows. Not once did I flex my muscles and preen in front of the camera. I tried my best to ignore it, to walk as though it wasn't there. Until I was being interviewed. Then I gazed earnestly at it and answered the questions articulately, (which were along the lines of things like "What would you do if you were attacked by a bear?") with some thoughtfulness, as though they were carefully crafted, engaging all my knowledge, ingenuity and know how. With that particular question, I said something like. "Well, first of all, I'd make sure all my loved ones were safe. I'd wave my arms and shout at him, I'd take off my shirt and wave it in his face until they got to a place where I knew he couldn't get to them. Then I'd take my fist and jam it down his throat. I've heard bears don't feel like attacking when there's a hand down their gullet." As far as I could tell, the next most articulate answer to the question was something like. "I'd just hit him on the nose so hard he'd fall down unconscious. Then I'd put a stick through him and roast him for dinner."

The premise of the contest was that a true stud was well rounded, able to improvise. One of the stations involved the wiring of a two way switch. I hadn't exactly done it before, but my father had showed me the rudiments of wiring, and I was able to figure it out. Only two of my fellows, both of them electricians, passed that particular obstacle.

I realized immediately that the traditional appeal of the contest was not to find the most manly of the men, but to find the caricature of manliness that involved posturing, grunting, flexing, much the same activity that two male animals exhibit when fighting over a female. Traditionally, they were not interested in the actual thought, research and intelligence that had kept our species alive and thriving through the ages of the world.

But that's what I gave them. There were men there that had musculature so perfectly defined, they could have been the poster children of anatomy textbooks. There were men there strong enough to compete in any contest of strength anywhere, with great jaws and prominent foreheads indicative of massive steroid use.

In the end, they picked out the six most "studly" men, divided them into pairs, and had them engage in battle, one defending his woman and one attacking to steal the woman. The attacker had ten minutes to bring the woman over to his side of the fighting area, and the defender had to keep her on his side for the ten minutes. The attacker had two chances because it was considered easier to be a defender.

I was one of the six, pitted as the attacker of a man about six feet ten inches tall, with a physique that would have made Hercules ashamed, probably the best body of the program. He had tattoos of two cobras on his biceps, which, when he flexed, appeared like they were undulating forward, and were, I must admit, completely intimidating. His face was covered with a black beard that reached in scraggly wisps about to his mid chest, and his hair was long and braided, like a Viking. His eyes were like lumps of unlit coal. The woman, a dark skinned beauty with soft eyes like a doe, clung to his arm, looking at me as I approached like I were a hideous monster of some kind.

When I got within about twenty feet, Snake Arms put one hand on the girl and thrust her away, roaring out something like, "How do you expect me to fight for you when you hold on to me?" which was a legitimate question, but poised poorly, in my opinion. Then he hefted a huge club, about six feet long, that was nothing but a tree branch with a knot on one end. It must have weighed forty pounds. This he swung over his head and called out, "Just try to get my girl, pretty boy!"

It was too long to be practical, but it was definitely something that needed avoiding. There had been some kind of statement we signed in the beginning that was a disclaimer for any injury, and now I saw why. I can vaguely remember the people in the audience, screaming out some kind of worthless advice, but it was somehow invigorating.

The way I saw it, I had three tasks. First of all, I had to stay away from the swinging death club, and second, I had to neutralize him, one way or another. Third, I had to get the girl.

I decided to start with the last while I was working on the first two. "Come away with me, lovely woman," I called out to her while I dodged the swinging branch. In the meantime, I scooped up two fist-sized stones that were part of the scenery, while rolling under a blow aimed at my head. The first one, I threw at my opponent, hitting him in the left side of the chest.

I hadn't thrown with everything I had, but it connected solidly, and for a moment, slowed him down. After he processed the pain, he became angry, and his swinging became more vicious. That helped me a little, because though a landed blow would have done some serious damage, every swing took a little longer to recover from than the ones before.

I threw the other stone then picked up two more. "You've already seen how roughly he's going to treat you," I called out. "I treat my women gently and with great respect."

"Don't listen to *him!*" my opponent screamed out. "He's a smooth talking liar."

"I'll be kind to you, and I'll protect you from people like *him*" I called out as I continued avoiding the club. I threw another stone. This one was aimed for the face. Snake Arms had to duck, but because he was so intent on braining me with the club, the rock beaned him at the top of the left temple. This time, it actually stopped him for a moment. He shook his head, lowered his club for a moment and rubbed his head. When he drew his hand away, there was blood on it. For several moments, he stared at his hand in disbelief.

And then I realized two things. First of all, his club waving was mainly an intimidation ploy, and he had expected me to cow away and thus lose all credibility. Second, since I didn't know that, I was being set up to fail.

The crowd was going wild, and it was powerful music to me. I knew now that Snake Arms was most likely not going to back down to this upstart who came in trying to change the time honored system. When he stood up this time, he was not going to be playing any more.

But he wasn't quite ready to stand. He was gathering his strength, distilling his anger. I had a few seconds maybe. "Why stay with a brute when you can have a gentleman?" I said to the woman, blowing her a kiss. *She's not going to come to me until she knows it's safe. And it won't be safe for her until she knows her brute won't come at her for revenge.*

"Hey, are you an employee?" I said to my opponent. He looked up, startled. In that instant, I rushed forward and untied the sash that held his gladiator type tunic secured in the middle. He put out his hands to defend his face again, thinking I was going for that, so I was actually able to yank the thing off him and come away with it.

It had been totally unexpected. His tunic fell open, revealing nothing but white briefs underneath. He looked down, and his eyes went wide. This was obviously more than he had bargained for. He pulled his tunic together, looking wildly around for something else he could use to keep himself within his standard of modesty.

It was funny, in a way. Here was a guy that had undoubtedly appeared before thousands of people in nothing more than a Speedo, but he couldn't allow them to see his underwear, which actually covered more.

The girl ran over to my side of our mini arena. I caught her in my arms and gave her a kiss. I had won. Four minutes and thirty-seven seconds, according to the clock above our station.

The audience was cheering so loud I couldn't hear the words Snake Arms was saying, but I'm pretty sure that was a good thing.

I stood, breathing hard, flushed with pleasure. I had not only won, I had won a contest I had been set up to lose.

The woman I had enticed to my side still stood next to me. To the great delight of the audience, I kissed her again, then we both bowed. She walked away then, but I saw her look back at me. It might have been just my fancy, but I thought I saw longing in her gaze.

The remainder of the contest pitted the three winners of the last event against each other in an interview. We were supposed to respond to questions such as why we were most deserving of the award of Mr Stud U.S.A., what was our definition of studhood, how we would use our victory to promote fitness and physical strength in the world. At least, those were the questions they asked my two fellow interviewees, and what I was expecting for me.

They almost surprised me. Not quite, though. The interviewer, another beautiful woman, appeared comfortable with the questions and answers she was receiving. She did not even look at her paper during the first two interviews, but after she had asked the second man his second question, I saw her look down, and saw her lips move as she read what was there.

So I had the time that it took the man to give the remainder of his answer to prepare for something wholly different from the other's two's questions. *No matter what they ask, honesty and sincerity are the only way to answer. No matter what...*

He finished speaking, having given an answer that had to have been given a thousand times before. I saw the woman look up from the paper, then look down one last time. As she did, I caught sight of her name badge. *Janice.*

"Mr Marson," she said. "If you win this contest, you're going to have thousands of women in love with you. How're you going to decide which one you will favor with your attention?"

I drew a deep breath. "Let me speak completely

frankly, Janice. No one can possibly be in love with me after this."

My answer obviously flustered her, but she rose gamely to the occasion. "What do you mean, Mr. Marson?" she said, turning to look briefly at the audience. I could see she had an ear bud. *Someone's coaching her.* "All those women out there are already in love with you." A great cheer arose as she spoke.

I turned and looked at the audience. "I am honored by your attention," I said, bowing slightly. "But let me tell you my definition of love."

A great quiet came over the assembled people. *This may be casting my pearls before swine,* I thought as I began. *But they deserve to hear it too.*

"Love means I am willing to make her things my things," I said. "It means I am willing to give all my attention to her agendas, it means when she speaks, I give as much attention to what she says as she is giving."

Some clapping broke out in the audience, but it was soon shushed. "It means I am willing to give myself, every part of myself for her. It means–"

"What you're saying sounds great, Mr Marson," Janice said. "But–" she paused to get the remainder of the sentence from her "bug–" "No one in real life is like that. Not even you."

I looked Janice deeply in the eyes. "Maybe not," I said. "But if I give it all my effort, all my energy, all my focus, I can improve every day of my life. Every day, I can become more and more what I believe the woman I love deserves."

A sympathetic sigh came up from the audience.

"You're very good, Mr. Marson," Janice said. I could tell by her expression that she was not sharing the feeling she was expressing. "My next question is, how did you find this contest? We don't seem to operate on the same plane."

"A friend told me," I said. "A new friend."

"What new friend?" she asked, but now I could see her interest.

"Terrence Carter. He's one of the contestants."

"How did you meet him?"

"I picked him up," I said. "He needed a ride."

"He was hitchhiking?"

"Yes."

"So how many hitchhikers you pick up become your friends?"

I shrugged. "As many as will let me, I guess."

"Wow, Mr. Marson. "You're a real Boy Scout, aren't you?"

"I'm on a quest to be a better man," I said.

"Is this contest part of that?"

"Maybe," I said. "But, to be completely honest, I didn't come here thinking that."

"What did you think when you came?"

"I thought it would be a fun competition. And I was right. But it's taught me something too."

"Oh, and what is that?"

"I realized how much we all crave intimacy."

"You didn't know *that?*" This question came directly from Janice.

"I don't mean sexual intimacy, although that's probably true most of the time." An appreciative laugh came from the audience. "I mean true intimacy, the willingness to let another see in to the depths of our soul, not holding anything back. If everyone had it, no marriage would ever fail."

"Is it desirable?"

"Yes, it is. Can you imagine looking into the face of the one you love and knowing there was nothing in them that was hidden from you?"

Tears appeared in Janice's eyes. "I'd like that more than anything," she said. Then a pained expression appeared in her face as she received her chastisement.

"Take it out, Janice," I said, very quietly.

"They'll fire me," she said, with equal softness.

"You'll find a better job," I said. "If you can't, I'll give you one—if you're willing to move to Virginia."

She smiled and took the bug out of her ear. "Are there other men like you?" she said, again in her interviewing voice.

"Yes there are," I said, with more confidence than I felt. "And I think more men would be that way if they just knew what to do."

"How are they going to learn it?"

I paused for a moment. "I'm going to write a book," I said. "Telling about my own quest."

"When are you going to write it?"

"As soon as I finish the quest."  I suspect in two months.  It'll take me six months to finish the book."

"What will it's title be?"

I hesitated a moment.  "I Worshiped my Car," I said.  "I kind of made an idol of it."

"An idol?'

I took a deep breath.  "It's kind of complicated, and I don't know the complete answer, but let me give you this much.  Would it be understandable for a man to be attracted to you, Janice?"

Her answer was immediate.  "Yes."

"Why?"

Now her face flushed pink.  "Because I'm an attractive woman."

"Yes you are.  And if a man were to admire your body, what parts would he be admiring?"

The pink in her face grew brighter.  Without speaking she pointed to her legs– and so on, ending with her face.

"Is that anything personal?" I said.

"What do you mean?"

"I mean, does his admiration of your body have anything to do with your soul?"

She hesitated a long moment, and tears appeared in her eyes again.  "No," she answered.

"I am calling that admiration, without any knowledge or even care of the person behind it, 'idolatry.' Kind of like the Greek guy who made a statue and then worshiped it. Does that make sense?"

"Yes," Janice said. "Yes it does." She bit her lip for a moment. "Is there any value to it in a relationship?"

Now I hesitated a moment. "In the beginning, yes," I said. "It makes a good introduction."

"Nothing more than that?" She was pleading with me to give her beauty more meaning.

"Well, yes, it comes in handy day to day too," I said, smiling. "I would say it starts the day out more easily."

"Nothing more?"

"It depends on the person you are with. In a true relationship, appearance is only the beginning."

Janice nodded sadly. "I've let my body become his idol." She put her head down. "Mine too."

"What?" I asked the question.

"Do you know how much time I spend every day making myself pretty? Do you know why I do it?" There was a strange expression on her face, one that was engaged in our conversation, no longer even aware of our audience. It was like the world of cameras in a great auditorium had shrunk to one that included just her and me.

"Why?"

"Because I'm afraid I'd be nothing if I'm not pretty." Janice started weeping.

I could not help myself. I stood up, gripped Janice by the shoulders and kissed her cheek. "That was very brave of you to say it," I whispered. "Thank you."

I sat back down. "When I began my quest, I felt the

same way about myself."

*_____*

*San Diego, California*

I had experienced what my father wanted me to experience, and it was profound. *Unconditional love exists. And since a creature like a dolphin can have it, I can assume the Creator of the dolphin can also have it.* The thought eased my mind, brought peace to my soul, feeling like cold water in a blazing sun.

And it stayed with me through the day. We toured Sea World, me holding to my father's arm, watching three shows, feeding the sea lions, enjoying the beauty of the creatures. It was a wonderful time, with me able to hold back all the fury more easily because of the depth of feeling and understanding my father had given me. I felt great love for him, great admiration of him, great gratitude for him.

But things in my mind were hanging back, biding their time. I knew they were there, and as we walked back to the car, I spoke of them. "I'm not going to be the same tomorrow," I said. "I'm not even sure I'll make it through breakfast."

My father put his arm around me. "It's okay," he said. "I'll be ready for the change. Let's just keep it out of today if we can. It's going to be a special memory."

So we did. He drove me home, with me back in my accustomed spot, using all my power to keep the feeling of a Saturday at the mall. I got safely into my room before I let the floods loose and let the outrage have its say. "No breakfast niceness tomorrow." I murmured.

But at eight o' clock the next day, I was at the table, as usual. My father was there too, but he said nothing more than "I've got a You Tube video I'd like to watch together."

It was a Polynesian film called "Johnny Lingo," about a shrewd trader who paid an unheard of eight cows for Mahana, a girl everyone thought was ugly. As I watched, I wondered *How many cows would Michael Marson give for me. Or would he give just the horns and tail Mahana's father thought her worth?*

After the film, my father stood up. "I'm going to Church," he said. "I hope you liked the film."

I nodded curtly but said nothing. I started to seethe as soon as he closed the door.

*How dare he do any of this? How dare he try to change me so blatantly? Does he think there's something wrong with me?* But most of all, more forcefully, I heard the words rattling around in my mind: *How does he dare speak to the man in my presence? He's negotiating my happiness without me. What makes him think he knows my mind?*

The outraged part of me raged like normal, but it was all familiar stuff, nothing original.

*You're like a broken record.* It really wasn't proper for the opposing side to speak, after so long a silence from the negative side. The outraged part gasped (or whatever the mental equivalent of a gasp is).

*How dare you interrupt us?*

*So now I've become the bad guy?*  I knew the drill perfectly, and the other half knew it.  No reply.

*C'mon, let's have it out.  Can't you think of anything original?*

*It's been good enough for us up to now.*

*It has?*

*Yes.*

*Well, it's not good enough now.  You've got to find something new, or I'm not going to listen.*

*Fine then.     Why does Marson talk to our father rather than to us.  Does he want to marry him?*

*Because I have a reputation of being an unreasonable, spoiled, impossible woman.*

I thought a moment more.  *Because he's being old fashioned, continuing with the precedent my father set when he started negotiations with his father.*

A storm of outrage tried to start with that one, but it was just rehash, so I quashed it.

*Give us more of a chance.*

*You have all day in there.*

*Yes, but we need your conscious thought.*

*Since when?  And who's we?*

*The same we that's always been there.*

*There's more than one of you?*

*No!  You and me.*

*You were talking to me as if there was more than one of you.*

*No.  Just you and me.*

It was not true, but I stopped thinking.  I was going

to banish them away. They did not love me, but I could not let them see. I would play along, as close to the way I ever did, but I was going to leave them behind. They had nothing to do with my happiness.

But how would I hide me from something inside of me? Was it possible they knew my plans?

It didn't matter. Whether they knew or not, I was going to cast them off. No matter what, they weren't going to want to leave, so when I got rid of them, I would have to force them out.

How was I going to do it? I would know when the time came.

\*_____\*

*Kansas City*

In spite of their efforts to sabotage me, I won the contest. The audience was the final judge, and they made it so painfully clear who they wanted that it was embarrassing.

To my surprise, the sponsors of the contest were extremely gracious in their presentation of the prize. I found out why when they presented me with the check.

"In the interview with Janice Weiss," the announcer said. "Our TV ratings tripled any previous high. Michael Marson has taken this contest to a new level. Will you come back again next year to judge this contest?"

"Sure," I said. "I'd be delighted."

Another great cheer went up from the crowd. "We'd like now to present our bonus award," the announcer said. "As winner of the Mr. Stud U.S.A. Contest, Michael Marson has earned the privilege of a Hollywood contract. Presenting this honor is Richard Trenton, booking agent."

A smallish man, wearing dark glasses and an overcoat stepped forward. He handed me a piece of paper, then backed away, ignoring all the clapping.

I looked down at the paper. On it were written a few simple words: *You might have potential. Meet me in my hotel room in one hour.* Underneath was scrawled the name of the hotel and the room number.

Somewhat dazed, I accepted the check, the handshakes, endless hugs, countless scraps of paper with names, phone numbers and email addresses, and finally, a note from Janice Weiss. *You've made a difference in my life,* it said. *They didn't fire me, and they might even want to promote me, but I'm not doing this anymore. I'm going to make more of my life than just the way I look. Thank you so much.*

*Love, Janice*

On the elevator to Richard Trenton's room, I read the note. I had two minutes to spare, but I needed them to get my composure back after reading what she had written. At that moment, I felt more of a man than ever I had before.

"Come in!" Trenton's voice sounded as soon as I knocked. It was exactly an hour.

Richard Trenton was sitting at a desk, but he stood up as soon as he saw me. "I am very happy you came,

Mr. Marson," he said. "Your performance today was—most impressive."

"Pardon me, sir, but I didn't consider it a performance per se." I said.

Trenton waved his hand. "Even if you believe everything you said, which I doubt, it was still a performance. Those women there– well, you just took them by storm. If you had asked them to dance around on broken glass barefoot, they would have done it."

"Well, I figured they'd want the same stuff I've been seeking myself," I said.

"Yes, yes, I know. You're totally sincere." His manner was brusk and no nonsense, as well as a little insulting.

He spun in his chair and pushed a button on his desk. In a moment, I saw myself and Janice at our interview, face to face, involved in what looked like earnest conversation. "What do you see in this couple here?" Trenton asked.

I knew immediately what he was saying. "They look like they love each other."

"Right. You're quick in the head too. Do you love that woman?"

"Well, uh, how could I? I just–"

"Right. But to anyone that sees you two speaking, it looks like you're about to start your honeymoon. Does she love you?"

"No. Not enough time."

"But she thinks she does. And from the way you've

started to look at things, this is probably as close to love as she's ever been."

"You're quick in the head too."

He looked up and smirked at me for about half a second. It was, I decided, as close to mirth as he ever came. "You're an effective actor," he said. "You become immediately comfortable in the situations you find yourself."

"Oh. Is that good?"

"Why would I bother telling you if it weren't good? Every other Bozo I've had to deal with here was good for a cameo shot in a beach scene. The only reason I come to this thing is because my sister lives in Independence."

For a moment, he looked me up and down. "You have the real stuff. Do you have a card? Here's mine."

It was the most unimaginative collection of name, phone number and email address I'd ever seen. Not even a title. I handed him mine, which wasn't a whole lot more, except it did list my title.

"Save your imagination for the work, eh?" In his expressionless way, he sounded pleased.

"Yeah. My results speak for themselves."

"I'll be calling you within a week. If you don't hear from me in seven days, call."

That was it. I was dismissed. But what a dismissal! A Hollywood agent thought I might have what it took! And presumably with a part that would give me a chance to convey something.

It sounded too good to be true. I looked him up on my Smartphone:

*Richard Trenton. Hollywood Booking Agent.* It was the second entry in Google.

So I read the article on him. It was actually his life history, with a list of the films he had booked actors, with major and minor parts into. It went on for three pages. And I had heard of a lot of them.

Just to make sure, I looked up one of the films, and scrolled down through the credits. His name was listed again. Finally, I looked up all the references to him, until I found one that had a picture. It was the same man I had talked to a half hour earlier.

I remember walking aimlessly around the town, wanting desperately to tell someone, but realizing I was too embarrassed to tell anyone. Why, with the quest I was on, would I enter a bodybuilding contest?

Just to make sure, I went through the list in my head. Nick? No. Tiffany? No, maybe not quite as emphatic. Bart? Maybe, but if I told him, he'd tell Nick, and I'd— Dad? No way. Casey? Maybe, but it wouldn't be satisfying enough. Iago Salvadore? Not in a million years.

It just didn't fit my quest, who I was trying to become. It actually didn't fit anyone I ever wanted to be.

But I had to tell someone. I found myself walking into a bar.

In all truth, I frequented them less than once a year,

because I thought people started getting obnoxious when they'd had a few. Only when a band or comedian I wanted to hear was performing at a bar or club would I go.

In this case, I was desperate. How often does a man win the Mr. Stud USA contest or find out he has what it takes to be on the silver screen?

A thought, a rebuke, was simmering in the back of my mind, but I pushed it aside. *Bartenders are usually good at listening.* I shouted inside my head, trying to damp out the other voice.

It didn't work. *Justifying one foolish thing with something more foo–*

But I didn't even allow the voice to finish. I was in the joint, the bar pushing against my belly.

"How can I help you, friend?" The bartender a young man, about my age, with a clear eye and a smiling face. He had the build of a bouncer, about the same as mine. His smile looked real, even though I didn't believe it.

"I just want to talk."

"I'm good for that. No business besides you."

I gulped. "All right. I'll have a Sprite."

He poured me the drink. "Talk to me."

"S'alright, man. Talk to me."

"I just got a big time Hollywood agent to take me on."

"Really?" The bartender looked me up and down. "How'd you do that?"

"Well, I just won a contest and–"

"What contest?"

"Um, Mr. Stud U.S.A."

"You're kidding me! *You* won that?"

"Well, somebody's gotta win."

"Yeah, but you're not that—I mean, the guys that win that are usually *huge!"*

"I'm okay."

"Yeah, but 'okay' doesn't win that contest."

"It did for me."

The bartender (he had the name 'Tom' monogrammed on his shirt) eyed me more critically.

"I don't believe it."

"Do I look like the kind of guy that would come into a bar and start bragging about stuff like this?"

"No, but why would you come in and tell a *bartender* you don't know news like that?"

I looked him in the eye for several seconds. Then I looked down. "I'd rather not say."

He was staring quizzically at me. "You're ashamed of it."

"Maybe."

"Why would you be ashamed at something like *that?* I mean, I'd give anything to win that contest."

"Never mind." I turned to leave.

"No, wait!"

I turned back.

"You and I are about the same build. What do you have that I don't?"

"Well, we're more than just our builds, you know."

"Of course, but not for that contest."

"How much do you want to know?"

"Like I said, I'd give *anything* to win that."

"All right. I know what women like to hear."

"Sure. So do I. So does everyone. It's never won me a contest."

Now I stared back at him. "You've been in it, haven't you?"

"What makes you think that?"

"Well, you know a lot about it, and you're not being terribly gracious in congratulating me."

He smiled ruefully. "Well, you're not buying drinks that make much money."

"So I'm getting the real you."

"Touche. All right. Yeah, I competed three years ago. I was a lot bigger then. And I didn't come close."

"Well, maybe they're looking for different stuff nowadays."

"No, they're not. Not that I know of. What'd you do?"

"I told you." For a moment, I stared at him. "All right. You leveled with me. I'll do the same."

I became quiet inside. "I've been on a quest to find out what really has meaning in life."

"Oh, that sounds like–"

"I've started to find it. And I used what I've learned to capture everyone's heart."

Tom stared at me for a few moments. "Considering that you say you won, you must have had something pretty amazing to say."

I reached into my billfold and took out the check, unfolded it, then held it in front of Tom's face.

He stared at it for a moment. "Okay, talk to me."

I was in a *bar*, talking to a *bartender.*    But he had earnestly asked me, without guile, and—I kind of felt sorry for him.  *Is it possible to have KISAS about a man?*

"I just said that everyone craves true intimacy."

"You're not kidding.  You wouldn't believe how many girls have led me to think something was going on and actu–"

"I mean the vulnerability to let someone see the depths of your soul."

"What do you mean?"

"I mean, let everything be open.  No secrets."

"I can't do that."

"It's why you're in a bar, Tom."

"What're you talking about?"

"I can tell you're an intelligent man, and–"

"What're you talking about?  I flunked out of college."

I shook my head.  "I know smarts when I see 'em."

"Oh yeah?  Why can't I pass a chemistry test?"

"You do okay in everything else?"

"Yeah.  It's just that chemistry—"

"Why were you taking it?"

"It's a requirement."

"For what?"

"Medical school."

"Oh, *medical school.* Always a good idea when you're dumb."

"Well, I don't think I'm dumb or anything. I'm just not smart enough to be a doctor."

"You do okay in math, including algebra?"

"Yep."

"And physics, biology, history and all that?"

"Yeah. It's just when I get to chemistry..."

"That's nonsense, you know."

"What?"

"If you can do all that other stuff, you can do chemistry. It's just a combination of that other. Do you want to be a doctor?"

"It's been a family tradition for years."

"So you feel you don't have a choice."

"Well, right. Every time my *daddy* sees me, he's ashamed."

"Do you have any siblings?"

"Nope."

"Do you want to be a doctor?"

"I don't think so. My dad had such awful hours, and I can't count the number of times he had to leave in the middle of a birthday or a graduation or something."

"Any idea what you do want to do?"

"Hey, I'm the bartender. Aren't I supposed to talk about *your* problems?"

"Yeah, but like you said, nobody's here to see."

"Okay." Pause. "I'd like to be something like an

architect."

"So be an architect."

"What would my parents think if I went to school for something other than medicine?"

"Wouldn't they rather you go to school for something rather than nothing at all?"

Pause again. "I guess so."

He looked at me for a moment. "You know, you'd be a good bartender."

"I thought about it during college, but I was able to get by on the money I had coming in."

"I bet you could bring in a hundred a night in tips."

"You think so?"

"Yeah. If my boss didn't come in at every weird time possible, I'd let you try."

"Well, I'm flattered."

"But you're not good enough to get a smile from the ice queen."

"What?"

"Bella Cherie. I don't know her last name. She comes in here every day at–" he looked at his watch.– she'll be here in ten minutes."

"Why's she come here every day?"

"Nobody knows. Some say her dad drank himself to death in this bar (it's been here forty years, you know) and she comes here in honor of him."

"Kind of a strange way to honor him, isn't it?"

"Tell me about it. But she comes here every day, no matter what else is going on."

"And she never smiles?"

"Who knows? Never in here.It's almost like she hates the place and hates us."

I leaned forward. "So you think I can't make her smile."

"I'm willing to wager my entire paycheck. What about that against your latest check?" He snorted.

"One hundred grand against how much? A few hundred bucks? And I don't even know how much of a challenge this is."

"It's about one percent of what you have in your billfold. But with your sorry looking body, you just won Stud U.S.A. You've got to be a super charmer."

"I'm a *sincere* charmer."

"All right Mr. Sincerity U.S.A. Here she comes. You win, I buy you the most expensive bottle of booze I got here. You lose, you buy me tickets to the next Chiefs game."

I stuck out my hand. "Deal. What're the rules?"

"No rules. Whatever you think of doing is cool."

"I looked up and through the windows I saw the woman. And gasped. If the illumination of the early street lights was accurate, she was beautiful, spectacularly so, rivaling and maybe surpassing Tiffany. "Wow." I said it softly enough for only Tom to hear.

"Yeah, wow. But I tell you, she's made of ice."

"Okay, game's on."

I stood up and went to sit at one of the tables. As I sat down, she came through the door. She glanced at me once, and then sat at a table two away from me. I could see her profile, as she scanned through the menu written on a board behind the bar. I'm certain she was aware of my scrutiny, but she made no sign.

"I stood up and came up to the bar. "Hey, Tom," I said, winking. "Do you happen to know this woman that just came in?"

Tom winked back. "Oh, sure." As far as I could tell, she had not paid the slightest attention to either of us.

"Bella Cherie, this is–" His eyes widened as he realized he didn't know my name.

"Michael Marson." I stepped toward her and reached out my hand. She hesitated, then held out hers, but did not allow me a full grip.

I didn't want it. Bowing low, I brought her hand to my lips and kissed it. For just an instant, her expression showed surprise, but then her eyes narrowed. "What about you makes associating with you worth my time?"

"Since you're sitting in a *bar*, the chance to meet someone new, with fresh perspective, from a different part of the country, with a desire to converse on subjects other than inanity, makes your associating with me worth your time more than what you were doing."

A ghost of a smile appeared on her face. "What was I doing?"

"Staring at a menu to decide what drink you want."

Now her smile disappeared. Somehow, I didn't think the pittance she had given me was sufficient to win the wager. "It so happens that my choice of drink is very important to me."

"More important than new knowledge, new perspective?" I was exerting all my effort, and so far, losing the wager.

"When someone's been through what I've been through, the drink takes precedence over everything." Her face showed great bitterness.

It was a start. Emotion of any kind was the beginning of a breakthrough.

"What have you been through?"

"Why should I tell you? You're a total stranger!"

"That's true. But who could be safer?"

She stared at me for a long moment. "If I tell you, you won't be a stranger anymore."

"And I have a feeling in your life, you've made everyone a stranger."

A sudden anger sprang up in her eyes. "What right do you have to say a thing like that?"

"Just making an observation. The way a person acts toward one is usually the way they act toward everyone."

"Oh, is that right, Mr. Therapist? And I suppose you really care about me too."

"I do, in a way."

"If you care about me so much, buy me a drink."

This was a test of some sort, but I didn't have any clue what was expected. I swallowed hard. "All right. Tom, get Bella Cherie the drink of her choice. On me."

"Make it two, Tom!" Bella Cherie said. "My usual."

She turned to me and smiled brilliantly, only for an instant. "I won't have you taking advantage of me." I was certain Tom hadn't seen it.

I'm not a drinker. My father's brother had stayed with us for a while until he died of liver cirrhosis, and he had done a great job of keeping me away from it. But this was a situation where I felt trapped into it.

Looking back, I can see what I was doing. I had compromised myself by coming into the bar in the first place, I had compromised myself by accepting a wager to manipulate the feelings of another person, and now I was excusing my taking a drink by telling myself I was trapped. If I had already wounded myself with the two compromises, several more if I counted all my efforts to compete in the contest I had just won, I was killing myself now.

Tom delivered the mud-colored drinks with a smirk on his face. I paid in cash and a two dollar tip. "Thank you, sir," he said.

"That's 'Mike' to you," I answered, looking with dismay at the glass in front of me.

Bella Cherie downed her glass in one gulp. "What's the matter?" she said, no trace of her smile left. "Can't compete with me?"

I wish I had been honest and told her I she was obviously a pro and I was a hopeless amateur in that category, but to my shame, I grimly took the drink and downed it. The stuff burned all the way down.

"We need more over here, Tom," Bella Cherie said,

and my heart filled full of dread. She smiled sweetly at me. This time, I was sure Tom saw it.

He was grinning as he came up. "Can't beat you," he said. This time he poured us both doubles, maybe triples. I paid again, but this time left no tip. He was enjoying my discomfort too much.

"Bottom's up," Bella Cherie said. As before, she downed her drink with one tip of her head. I followed woodenly. Whatever I was drinking tasted somewhere between vomit and papaya juice. (The only papaya I had ever eaten was nothing to order twice) In just a few minutes, the alcohol was going to take effect, and I was going to become worthless.

"That's better," Bella Cherie said. "What were you saying?"

"I was saying I think you have trouble having any loved ones in your life."

"Are you willing to do anything about it?"

"What?"

"Will you love me?"

"How—I don't know–"

"I thought so," Bella Cherie said. "You're just like all the rest."

"No I'm not!" I said it louder than I should have. The booze was taking it's effect.

"Oh, yeah?" How can I know that's true?"

A feeling of hopelessness settled on me. I was on my way to becoming drunk, in a strange town, with no way to find my way to my hotel room. I tried to stand. My legs buckled. I sat back down.

"I'm a fool," I said. I could hear the slur beginning in my voice.

Bella Cherie came up and put her arm around me. "Why are you a fool?" Her voice was suddenly very gentle.

"I–can't handle alchol. I should've shaid shomesing, but I's tryin' to be—I's 'fraid of bing a wimp."

Bella Cherie laughed, and pressed herself against me. "You *don't* handle your booze, do you?" She looked up at Tom. "I'm taking this one home, Tommy boy. I like him."

She grasped me under my arm and pulled upward. "C'mon, Michael," she said. "I better get you out to my car before you're completely gone."

Somewhere in my befogged brain, I realized I was going into a situation that might be dangerous, but part of my impaired faculties thought at least I was going to a place where I might be safe while I slept off my drunk. I went with her. As I was leaving, Tom tucked a dark green bottle under my arm. "I don't know what you'll do with it," he said.

I think I remember Bella Cherie guiding me out the door. Someone whose face I never saw came up and helped her pack me into the back seat of some kind of a limo. My impression was that it was a Cadillac.

I have no idea how far we drove, but I vaguely remember stopping a few times, because I lunged forward every time and fell on the floor the third time.

Bella Cherie laughed. "I should've buckled you in," she said, but she left me on the floor. "You're safer down there than you are on the seat." The driver of the car did not bother laughing.

It may have been ten minutes, it may have been an hour. At any rate, all I know was I was feeling quite nauseous by the time I arrived at wherever it was we stopped for good. She opened my door for me, and I think I crawled forward and fell out the door onto some kind of lawn. I remember breathing in some kind of fresh fragrance, like green grass, and it helped to calm my stomach. Bella Cherie and I think the driver of the limo pulled me to my feet again, and led me somewhere, but I don't remember any more.

*_____*

*Los Angeles, California*

I had won a major victory. The amazing thing about it was, it was not over my father, or any man. It was over myself. I was a different person inside, now that I had drawn the line between myself and whomever or whatever it was that engaged me in the constant dialogue. They had lost power over me, and I felt lighter, more powerful, even happier.

*I am not obliged to act in any way to any given situation. I am free, I am my own woman. I will not allow anger to foil my happiness. I am happy with my father. I am going to be happy with my father.*

Oh, they were still there inside me. I could feel them, but they were lying low. They would come forward again, they would try to catch me in an unguarded moment and seize control, but I knew them too well. I would not let myself be unguarded.

The next morning, when my father came down to our daily meeting, I could see the wariness in his expression. I greeted him with a smile.

"I got over it," I said simply.

He stared at me for a moment, then relaxed. "What would you like to do today?" he asked.

"Daddy, today's Monday. What are you going to do after our breakfast hour?"

He shrugged. "Just go to work," he said.

"Well, then, this is what I vote for. Let's spend our hour with you playing the piano and me singing."

His eyes widened. "All right, but be prepared. I haven't touched it in—"

"After that, I'd like to go to work with you."

His mouth fell open. "You would?"

"I can't believe I've been your daughter all my life, and have never cared about where you work."

I saw tears form in my father's eyes. My heart melted. I ran to him, put my arms around him, and sobbed into his shoulder. "Daddy, I'm so sorry I've been so horrible to you. I—I don't really feel confident to promise you it's going to be better, but I'm hoping it's going to be better."

"It's been better," he said. His voice was husky with emotion. "And this is worth more to me than all the money I've made in my life."

We spent the day visiting each of my father's restaurants. I found, as I watched this man I had seen all my life, that he was extremely competent. I could tell the way the managers spoke to him, not in fear, but in earnestness, that they trusted and even loved him. He knew every aspect of his business so well, he was so innovative in his solutions.

*Is this my father? If I had known that this man I thought the greatest buffoon in the world is this talented, this efficient, this revered, could I have treated him as awfully as I have?*

At the last restaurant we visited, the manager came up to my father and indicated he needed to speak to him privately. My father said nothing about me joining them, but he beckoned to me when I would have hung back. The manager, Henry Ketton, looked nervously up at me before he began, but my father waved his hand. "You can trust her the same as you trust me," he said.

*Will I ever be willing to betray this trust?* I asked myself. *No.*

Henry drew a deep breath. "Wilma Kingsley has stolen about nine hundred dollars from the till," he said.

"Are you sure?" my father said.

"Yes, sir. I've back checked all the receipts. The money disappeared during her shift, and at the time it happened, there was none other that could have had access to it."

I saw the pain and concern in my father's face. "We've never had this kind of trouble from her before, have we?"

"No sir. Up to now, she's been an ideal employee. She works hard and everyone likes her. If you remember, she was employee of the month three months ago.

My father rubbed his chin. "There would have to be something extraordinary in her life to bring her to this then. What would you like me to do?"

"I have to let her go, of course," Henry said. "That's my job."

"Have her come see me as soon as you're done with her," my father said.

Henry took out his handkerchief and wiped his brow. "She should be here in a few minutes." He glanced up as someone passed by his window. "Um, here she is."

Glancing once at my father, as if an appeal for help, Henry got up. "I'll use the Assistant Manager's office," he said. "You can see her in here."

My father rose in his turn. "No, use your own office," he said. "You'll be more comfortable. I'll use the other one."

"Thank you, Iago," Henry said, and it sounded like he meant it.

"Would you like me to tell her you'd like to talk to her?" my father said.

Relief flooded Henry's face. "Yes Sir!"

"She doesn't know me, does she?"

"I don't see how she could," Henry said.

I followed my father out to the lobby. A fortyish

looking woman was just taking her coat off at the
reception counter. The name 'Wilma' was embroidered
on her dress.   With my omniscience gained from
Henry's report, I thought she looked anxious.

Without speaking, my father approached the counter.
Wilma immediately took the stance of a receptionist
welcoming a customer.  A genuine appearing smile lit
her face. "Welcome!" she said.

My father shook his head. "Mr. Ketton would like to
see you in his office," he said.  I thought his voice was
full of compassion.

Immediately, Wilma's countenance fell.  I saw tears
spring into her eyes as she took her coat and began to
leave.   My father gently took her arm.   Without
speaking, he turned her in the direction of Henry's
office, then opened the door for her. With halting steps,
she went inside.

My father came up and took my arm.   "Now,
Sweetheart," he said. "I need your help. Henry is going
to tell her to come see me once he has fired her. You
can see she isn't going to want to come. But do what
you can to encourage her."

A pang of nervousness went through me. "What if I
can't–"

"It's up to her whether she comes or not.  If she
doesn't come, it's her choice.  You can't control that."
With that, he turned and strode into the office.

I was instantly angry. *If she doesn't go in there, it's
my fault.  How dare he–?*

But I allowed a rational thought to come to my consciousness. *He's trusting me with something very important.*

*Yes, but if I fail–*

*Can I fail at this? After all, it will be her choice.*

*Her choice? If you can't–*

*Wait a minute. The last time you spoke, it was in the first person, and now it's in the second person.*

*What does that have to do with–?*

*It has everything to do with it. If you're not me, then I don't have to pay any attention to all the doubt you're trying to weigh me down with.*

*I **am** you.*

*Then why are we having this conversation?* Gritting my teeth, I took my place outside Henry's door.

A moment later, Wilma emerged, weeping profusely, almost blinded by her tears. And, in my nervousness, I did the thing that came the most naturally. I put my arms around her and hugged her.

It was almost too easy. She sobbed for a few moments, her body shaking. She could not have known who I was, but in the extremity of her emotion, she was willing to take whomever offered her any kind of comfort. When she was finished, just like Daddy, I took her arm, and led her into the Assistant Manager's office.

My father smiled at me when we came in. Though he said nothing, his expression said *Well done, Olivia. I knew I could count on you.*

I smiled back at him, and I meant it.

# *Chapter XVI*

## Corruption

*Kansas City, Missouri*

I woke up in a bed the size of a normal sized bedroom. My head was pounding so hard, at first I thought the drummer of some heavy metal band was using me for the drum. I had no idea where I was or *when* I was.

The bedroom where the Goliath bed resided was about as big as an ordinary house. As far as I could tell, it was empty, except for the fool that lay in the bed.

A raucous jangling nearly vibrated my teeth loose. It sounded familiar. Only after it had rung three or four times, did I realize it was my cell phone. I fumbled around, my mind still adjusting to real life, and finally found it under my pillow. Just in time, I punched the *talk* button.

"Hello. At least I could understand myself.

"Hello!" It was Tiffany.

"What's up?" I tried to put as much clarity into my voice as I could.

"You wouldn't believe who I went out with last night."

"Nick."

"How'd you guess?"

"He called and asked permission."

"Oh. Are you all right? You sound really–"

"I'm fine. My mouth is just dry." Which was true, but only a symptom, not the diagnosis.

"Well, you wouldn't believe how it went. Unless he told you that too."

"No, he just said he had an idea."

"Well he did. You *really* don't sound good. Are you sure you're–"

"I'm fine. Really. Tell me what happened."

"Well, let me tell you about his call first. At first, I didn't recognize who it was, and then, when he first told me who was calling, my first inclination was to say, 'What're you calling me for? I can't stand your place.' But I didn't say it. He told me you had said we were bro —we weren't engaged anymore, and that you had told him some of the things I'd said. He said after he heard that, he was interested in getting to know me a little better."

She giggled. "Of course, I remembered what he

looked like, and I was tempted to say that it would be kind of like Beauty and the Beast, but I didn't.

"And do you know what was neat? He didn't say a thing about my appearance. He told me to expect something unusual, and I said I was looking forward to it. I kind of was. I mean, you gotta admit, he's a different sort of character."

"Yep," I managed to answer.

"Then I got to thinking. What kind of "unusual" activity would a quirky guy who runs an offbeat sandwich shop come up with? I got to fretting, and I almost called him back and canceled. I'm really glad I didn't."

In spite of the headache, I was getting really interested. "What'd he do?" I blurted.

Tiffany ignored my outburst. "At 7:00 last night, I heard a knock at my door. With a sense of dread, I answered it, and saw not Nick, but a middle aged woman with no expression on her face."

"Bev," I murmured.

"I couldn't see anyone but her standing there. She told me she was Nick's mother, and she was to be our guide that night. I had no idea what she was talking about until she held up a strip of cloth she held in her hand. 'Turn around,' she said. Then she blindfolded me."

"What?"

"I know. That's what I thought. After making sure I couldn't see anything, she led me down my sidewalk to

the car, where she opened the door for me and helped
me in. As it turns out, it was in the back seat of her car.
'Nick's on the other side,' Bev said. 'He's blindfolded
too.'"

I was beginning to see Nick's genius. "Wow."

"Yes. He told me the blindfolds were to keep us
from gauging our feelings based on appearance, and to
keep us from letting the body language of the people
around us effect our opinions of what was going on.

"Michael, we spent the entire evening blindfolded,
and you know what? I didn't try once to see anything.
We talked and we talked. Bev drove us to a restaurant,
and she ordered something by pointing to it, so we had
no idea what we were going to get. You might have
thought we would have been embarrassed with all the
people that must have been staring at us, but I didn't
even think about it. I tried to imagine what every food
would look like, but I noticed, when my salad came,
that I couldn't tell which kind of dressing I had. All I
knew was, the lettuce was fresh, (but it might have been
baby spinach) the tomato, (I believe it was a tomato)
was juicy, the lime or lemon was sour and the
conversation was excellent. We had a better talk than
you and I have ever had. Even with his *mom* there."

A pang of jealousy stabbed me, but I pushed it back.
Nick was my friend, and—so was Tiffany, and if they
had that kind of a good time together, why should I feel
—cast off? Just because I had never thought of
something like that?

"Nick's voice is so *gentle*, Michael. At the end of the night, we held hands in the car while we were going home, and I felt a thrill of excitement. I wanted him to put his arm around me, I wanted to snuggle up to him, I even wanted him to kiss me. It was the best date I had ever had!"

"That sounds great, Tiffany. Why didn't I think of stuff like that?"

"Because you've never had to scratch for your own worms."

"What?"

"You've just let your prettiness wow the girls, and never had to depend on your wits. In a way, this was kind of like Cyrano de Bergerac."

"It really is," I said. "And that makes me Roxanne's handsome, witless boyfriend who can't tell the girl why he loves her."

Tiffany laughed nervously. "I'm not saying anything against you," she said.

"I know it. I'm implicating myself, and that hurts all the more."

"I'm sorry, Michael."

"Please, don't be. I've pretty much proved that stereotype true anyway."

"You have? How?"

"Let's just say I've learned from my stupidity."

"What've you learned?"

"That I'm not as great a guy as I was thinking I was."

"Like what?"

"Please, Tiffany. I'm not really ready to talk about it."

"I'm sure it can't be that bad."

"Well, it just depends on what your definition of 'bad' is."

"Michael! Tell me."

"I'm keeping it all to myself for now. If I get out of this with greater wisdom and growth, I might write out a confession."

"I'm dying of curiosity."

"All right. Let me put it this way. I indulged my vanity."

"Is that all? I do that all the–"

"Not like I did it. Believe me."

"Where are you now?"

"I'm in Kansas City, and I have a horrible headache."

"I've never know you to get a headache."

"I know. But this one is not unexpected and it is deserved."

"I'm going to burst if you don't tell me what's going on."

"Let me make a deal with you, Tiffany. When I get myself completely out of the mess I've made for myself, I'll tell you."

"When will that be?"

"Maybe never." Even as I spoke, I sat up in bed, and realized, to my horror, that I was naked. "Oh, no."

"What?"

"I'm in more trouble than I thought. I'll see you later.

And you won't get any more information out of me if you call right back."

*How did this happen? How did she get me in here, and where in the world are my clothes?*

*Could those be they?* I had looked at a closet that was only a few feet away. It's door was open.

Looking around to make sure nobody saw me, I scampered across the room, grabbed the clothes (they were mine, all right) and got back under the covers. Then as quickly as I could lying on my back, I donned my wardrobe, (it was the same set I had worn when I had left my home—how long ago? I didn't know)

Once I had my pants securely fastened around my waist, I checked my wallet, particularly the credit cards, and found everything there. I even called the 800 number of my bank. All was well.

*Then what did she want out of me? What could she have possibly thought I was going to do for her?*

A chill went through me. *All drunk and everything, I wasn't able to do* that, *was I. Oh I hope not, please, I hope not.*

But how was I to know what I had done? Unless Bella Cherie were to come back, and I were to ask her–

I didn't want to see her again. I had already seen her, in the short span where I had full command of my faculties, far too much. I had to get out of there.

While I was putting on my shirt, I heard a rattle, and found about a quarter page of torn off paper in my pocket. It was a note:

*Sorry to get you drunk. You seem like a nice guy, and you might have some good things to say to me, but I don't know how to treat good people. If you give me another chance, I'll do better. If you decide to meet me again, I'll be at the bar where you first saw me. If you don't come, I'll understand, but I'd like it if you came. Bella Cherie Shafer.*

Immediately, in spite of all my discomfort, my KISAS kicked in. Bella Cherie was a DID, and if she were to give me a chance, I could probably help her.

*Yeah, but do I want to help her? Does she deserve any help from me after what she did?*

*What did she do, or even try to do with me?*

I just didn't know, and I didn't dare to ask. What if I had, in my drunkenness, compromised myself more than I–?

When I went outside, there was a car waiting for me. It was a limo, and the driver was dressed in some kind of livery. I opened his door. "Do you work here?" I asked.

"Yes sir. The lady of the house has told me to take you wherever you want to go."

I climbed in the back seat. "Just start driving," I said. "I need to get back to my hotel room, and I don't remember the name."

As it turned out, Eddie, my driver, knew Kansas City inside and out, and by my description of the surrounding buildings, he dropped me off at the doorstep of the hotel. Before I got out, he cleared his throat. "Um, sir," he said. "I'd like to ask a favor of you."

"What's that?"

"I think Miss Bella Cherie likes you."

"Why do you think that?"

"Because she doesn't usually pay attention to men, especially like this."

"What do you mean?"

Well, usually, I drive important people back and forth, people like the mayor, the senators, the governor, but never someone like you. You're not anything are you?"

"That's a very good assessment of me, Eddie. I think you have it just about right."

"I beg your pardon, sir. I didn't mean to–"

"No offense taken. "It's just true, that's all. What's the favor?"

"Will you please go back to the Swimming Turtle, sir?"

"Why was I in that huge bed?" I said suddenly.

Eddie looked down. "I don't know, sir. I helped her take you to the manor house, but one of the inside people helped from there."

He was looking back at me from his driver's seat, and I saw the anguish in his face as well as the pleading. "She might have done something shameful, and she's probably not sorry, but you have a chance to help her be sorry."

I saw tears appear in Eddie's eyes. "She's *dying*, sir.

She drinks enough to kill an ordinary man, and she hates everyone."

He shut his eyes for a moment and shook his head back and forth. "She said she likes you. If you go back there and talk to her, I think she'll listen a little bit. Please sir, please, give her a chance."

It was a little bit hard to do, but I looked at Eddie steadily. "I'll think about it. I promise to think about it."

It was very little short of telling him I would not, and he knew it, and so did I. He dropped his eyes again. "Yes, sir," he said. The moment I shut the door, he hit the gas and shot away.

It was the most subtle way he had of expressing his anger and disappointment, and it took the strength out of my legs. *Does he think of her like his daughter? Even though she tells him what to do all the time, I'm getting the feeling he's been in the family for years, through all the—whatever she's been through and loves her like his own child.*

*Should I go back to the bar? I think she might feel guilty enough over getting me drunk that she might listen to what I have to say.*

*But I'm such a hypocrite! I've gone on this quest to upgrade my life, and I think I'm making all this progress, and then I do a bunch of stuff that shows I've not only not made progress, I've prabably fallen back a mile or so. Can I redeem myself now by letting my KISAS take over, and try to rescue a woman that is undoubtedly more than I can handle?*

*No. This is a job for better men than I am.*

*But she seemed so vulnerable in her note to me! What if what Eddie said about her is right, what if I'm her last chance for anything good? Do I want it on my conscience if she just dies, because I didn't do what I could for her?*

*I can't use that argument on myself. It applies to every DID in the whole world. Why am I not out on my white horse, going into everyone's lives like Santa Claus? Because I can't take care of everyone.*

*Yeah, but this one, for better or worse is now part of my life. Don't I have an obligation to help her, now that I've met her? Isn't that how the universe works? And don't I have an obligation to redeem myself somehow?*

*Redeem yourself with whom? The bartender and that woman that hates everyone. What're my chances?*

I went to my room and showered, considering the entire time. I didn't want to go back, I didn't want to have to face all the shame...

But I felt the shame anyway. Leaving now would increase the shame. I got dressed in different clothes, and, with a shuffling step, headed back to the Swimming Turtle.

*I'm hopeless in my KISAS. Absolutely hopeless.* Still between the embarrassment on the one hand and the shame on both hands, I felt better about going back than not going. *I can't stand to have her think all men are going to give up on her. Eddie and I won't. Tom won't either.*

*But she might have raped me! How can I talk to someone, how can I try to help someone who forced me, took advantage of me...*

Suddenly I was filled with a shame so great it smote me about the knees, rendered me helpless. I couldn't go back into that bar, look the woman, *the rapist* in the face and see there, and see–

For a moment, I slumped to my knees, bereft of feeling as well as strength, my energy, seemingly my very manhood, stripped from me, taken by a woman, a beautiful black widow, who had robbed me of my virtue. How could I look at any woman, any person, much less *her...*

I could feel the cold of the sidewalk in my knees, through my pants, and it was soothing to me, a strange comfort. *I can feel.*

For several moments, I let myself feel it, let it soak into my legs, doing my best to concentrate on it, letting it permeate through, capturing my full attention, pushing away the shame, the guilt. Slowly, slowly, I felt the paralysis and numbness leave me. Only the slightest bit shakily, I rose up to my knees.

*If I'm going to go in there, I can't think about what she did. I have to take my own responsibility, regardless of the guilt it brings up in me.*

I grasped the bumper of a car directly in front of me, and used it to help me stand up. After I was standing, I leaned on the same car, feeling my strength returning.

When I finally looked up, I realized I was leaning on the very same limo that had carried me away. Eddie was still sitting in the driver's seat.

*_____*

*Los Angeles, California*

Wilma actually let me guide her to a seat. Then she sat with her face in her hands and had a fresh episode of crying. I don't think she had any idea where she was.

My father let her cry for as long as she wanted. Only when she put her head up and looked at him did he say anything. "Thank you for coming in here, Wilma," he said.

"Who are you?"

"At the moment, that isn't important. Would you like to talk to me?"

Her eyes filled up again. "What good would it do?"

"Let me tell you what I know about you," my father said. His voice was very gentle and soft.

He paused, as if waiting for her to respond. "I've been a good worker!" Wilma said, screaming more than speaking. "I've been on time every day, and I've stayed late lots of times without getting paid. I treat the customers really well, and I–"

My father held up his hand. "I know all that. You've been an excellent employee."

Wilma started to cry again. "Hold on a minute, Wilma," my father said. "I can think of only two reasons why someone would do what you've done, and you probably did it for both of them."

"What's that?" There was a sudden sarcasm in her voice.

"First of all, you have an extraordinary need, and second of all, you're angry with someone who has authority over you. You justified yourself by saying they deserved it. Tell me about the extraordinary need first."

"Why would you care?"

"Good question. Why do you think I care?"

"You're a nosy friend of Henry's that wants to enforce your ego by doing a little counseling on the side?" Sarcasm, but probably some real belief too.

My father raised his eyebrows. "That could be part of it, I suppose. But let's just suppose you're mostly wrong, and I can help. What's the need?"

"Why should I tell you?"

"Because I really care about the answer, and at this point, I don't think there're very many others who do."

Tears came into her eyes again. "I don't know why I was even considering it!" she said, her voice rising in volume. "He's a worthless, ungrateful–"

"But he's your son," my father said.

"How did you know?"

"Women don't usually use the term 'ungrateful when talking about their husbands," my father answered. "Did he need bailing out?"

Wilma nodded, not speaking.

"What was he in the clink for?"

"He's still there," Wilma said, laughing even as she

cried again. "For DUI. His bail was set for twelve hundred and I was only able to *steal* nine hundred. I had two hundred on hand, and now I'm out of a job, and–"

My father held up his hand. "Where's the nine hundred?" he said.

Wilma laughed again. "Right here in my purse. I may as well give it back."

"Do that," my father said. Then he reached into the breast pocket of his coat and pulled out a checkbook. He wrote out one of them, tore it off and gave it to Wilma. She looked at it for a moment.

Her eyes opened wide. "Iago Salvadore? You can't do this sir."

"It's a note of appreciation," my father said. "For all the good work you've done."

"But I just stole–"

"Yes, but I have a very strong feeling you won't do it again. Who were you mad at?"

"You, sir."

"Me?"

"Yes, sir. We've been the top of the list in business over the past three months and you haven't given us any recognition."

"Who told you that?"

"Henry, sir." Pause. "I hope I'm not getting him in trouble."

"Not a bit. I need to recognize my people."

"Does this mean I'm not fired?"

"I'll talk to Henry.   But you will have to be on probation for six months."

"Yes, sir!"  She started crying again.

"Oh, and Wilma."

"Yes sir."

"I'd like to give you a little advice.   Are you up to hearing it?"

"Very much, sir."

"All right.  Take the twelve hundred and put it in the bank."

"But my son—"

"—is in jail because he ought to be there.   You have no obligation whatsoever to pull him out so he can get on the road and endanger all our lives again."

"Why give me the money then?"

"Because it's your choice.   I think you need to have the cash in the bank for emergencies.   If you bail him out, you will be back to being penniless, with nothing to do if a real emergency comes up."

Wilma bit her lip.  "He'll be awful mad—" she said.

"Yes, he will."

Wilma stared at my father for a moment, then leaned forward over the desk and kissed his cheek.   "Bless you," she said.

She left, a total contrast to what she had been in when she arrived.   Once more, *I* was crying.

"My father looked at me, his face serious, but a smile in his eyes.  "I'll be back in a moment," he said, and went out the door, closing it behind him, leaving me alone with my tears.

*What are you bawling for?   All you're seeing is your father trying to be a hero.   He's got extra money and he spends it on thieves.*

*I'm crying because I've seen a side to my daddy I've never seen before.   I could have known it if I'd thought about it, but I haven't bothered up to now.   Right now I'm finding I love him.   No, I adore him.   What's been the matter with me?*

*You know perfectly well what you're doing.   You're splitting.*

*Maybe I am, but since he's been on the other side of it all my life, that means I'll be cherishing him for at least twenty four years.*

*You've never held it for anyone that long.*

*Why is it so important for you to criticize everything good in my life?*

*We're not wor–*

*Yes, I know.   You've said it plenty.   Don't bother.*

*You're just arguing because you know I'm right.*

*In what way?   I still love my mother, even though she was never that nice to me.*

*You were both victims together.*

*Still.   And I'm going to love my father as long as I live.*

*We'll see.*

*We will see.   (Just wait)*

About five minutes later, my father came back into the room.   He was smiling.   "You know what's funny," he said. "Henry was so happy to have me tell him to keep Wilma. Now he can tell anyone who knows what she's done that it was because of my intervention that she's still here. Nobody will have to think he's been soft."

I went up to my father and took his hands. "Let's eat here," I said. "I want to know how well Wilma does her job."

# *Chapter XVII*

## Redemption

*Kansas City, Missouri*

I gave a small wave to Eddie, who sat in his limo, reading the comics. His expression showed a sudden surprised pleasure, and he jerked on his paper, ripping it half way down its middle. I walked on past him, into the bar. My heart was pounding as furiously as though I'd just finished wind sprints.

She was sitting there, staring at five empty glasses in front of her. A glum-looking Tom was carrying a tray to her. The same mud colored liquid he had given me the day before was in two tumblers. *Doubles.*

I cleared my throat. Tom looked up, a glint in his eye. "You know what?" he said as he put the tray down at Bella Cherie's table. His voice sounded conversational, matter of fact. "I hate this job."

Bella Cherie looked up, something like interest in her face. "Why?" she said.

` "Because of people like you," Tom said. "And because of what I did to Michael yesterday."

"You didn't do it," she said. I thought I could hear the slightest bit of slur in her speech. "I did."

I cleared my throat again. "No," I said, a little louder than I needed. "I did."

Still feeling a great nervousness, I stepped up to the table. "I am the one responsible for my own life," I said. "I could blame either one of you for my cowardice, but then I would be a liar *and* a coward."

Bella Cherie opened her mouth to reply, but I held up my hand. "Yes, I know you both played a part," I said. "But that's probably true of everything in life."

I closed my eyes for a moment. "And if I blame you, I'll take away my chance to grow."

Tom came up and sat down opposite Bella Cherie. "You're a good man, Michael."

"I'm about dying of embarrassment from what you've seen of me. I don't know why I woke up on that monster bed in your house stark naked, because I don't remember anything beyond getting out of the car."

I was going to ask her directly, but decided it might be better to leave it open ended.

"That's private," Bella Cherie, said, her face reddening slightly.

"It may be private, but since it's about me, don't I

have a right to know?"

Then, in spite of myself, I laughed.  Tom laughed
too.  Bella Cherie looked indignant for a moment, but
then she smiled.  In a moment, she laughed too.

The laugh cleared the air, established a small amount
of intimacy, allowing me to speak the shameful thought
that flitted like a pesky mosquito around the corners of
my mind.  "I feel like I've been violated."

Immediately, Tom and Bella Cherie's laughter
stopped.   Bella Cherie's eyes opened wide in
startlement.  "Men always want–" she began.

"How'd you know what I wanted?" I said.  "I was
drunk."

Bella Cherie's face fell.   There was about thirty
seconds of silence.  Then, "I thought you weren't going
to blame anyone," Tom said.

*He's got KISAS too.*  I opened my mouth to retort
that I wasn't blaming anyone for getting me drunk, but I
was pretty helpless after I got that way.  Instead, a
miracle happened.

So many times, to my great chagrin, I have betrayed
myself with my need to get in the final word.
Afterward, I kick myself and wish to have the moment
back again, so I can do better.  This time, I remembered
*before* I spoke.  Maybe it was my condition slowing my
reaction time.  If so, I suppose I have to be grateful to a
*hangover.*

"You're right," I said.  "Sorry."  They were some of
the hardest words I had ever spoken.

The stinging remark I had planned sat there a moment, angry it had been ignored, but then it shriveled away. I had just done something very well. By letting the ugly go before it escaped my lips, I had cemented a new friendship I would have lost if I had satisfied my ego.

All the aggression I had seen building in Tom's body vanished, Bella Cherie's misery dissipated, and all three of us were sitting at  a table, perhaps the strangest combination of new friends ever assembled.

Maybe it was a reward for holding my tongue, I don't know, but I had a sudden clear insight.  In the brief, almost random interactions between us, a subtle but fundamental change had taken place.  Bella Cherie had felt some small attraction to me perhaps, maybe because of the care I had shown her the day before when I had a silly wager going with Tom.  But now, because Tom had defended her, she felt a debt of gratitude toward him, a debt that had potential.  Infinite potential.

We were coming to a time of the day when business probably picked up, and Tom's services were required behind the bar, but it was like the moment of grace held. Nobody came in, and we had a two hour long discussion.

It was like we were the pilgrims on the road to Canterbury, each of us sharing our own tale. Starting with me, we each told our stories.  I told about my engagement to Tiffany, about my father's agreement with Iago Salvadore, about my quest to find a word of honor, about the unusual messengers I had received as I traversed the country, and about the message each had given me. I ended by telling my shame about exploiting the knowledge I had gained to manipulate the hearts of all the spectating women at the contest, and the resultant inability to tell anyone about it, leading to my decision to tell Tom, a stranger.

Tom went next, telling his own story, giving a lot more detail than he had the day before. His father was a physician, as was his father before him, going back generations to before the Revolutionary War. It had been expected, since before he was born, and his parents had discovered, through ultrasound, that he was a boy, that he would follow dutifully in the family tradition. He told us how his father, through all the years of his growing up, had pulled him aside, giving him "man to man talks," telling him how he had sacrificed his talent as a musician to honor the tradition, and how, just like he, Tom had to sacrifice his artistic talent to do the inevitable.

"You're an artist?" Bella Cherie said. In answer, Tom took out a receipt, and on the back of it sketched a picture of the three of us sitting at a table, discussing as we were. We all three looked like ourselves, and each of our expressions seemed to contain our souls. It took him less than five minutes.

Bella Cherie looked long at the picture. Finally, she said, "This is me. And you haven't even heard my story yet."

Her father was a gambler. A plumber by trade, he had been successful, eventually owning his own business, marrying a stunningly beautiful woman, an aspiring singer, whom he had financed long enough for her to discover her talent was sufficient to earn her the attention of a wealthy casino boat owner. She had left Bella Cherie's father, leaving him behind the one child of their union.

At that point, her father hadn't cared much. He bet on everything, but unlike the stereotype, he often won. It was part of his obsession to research the objects of his betting, finding wagers that seemed hopeless, and then betting against enormous odds.

Eventually his winnings were spectacular enough to attract attention, so that it became more and more difficult for him to find betters. So he gave up his business, bought an RV, and toured the country with his daughter. From city to city, they would travel, and her father would find possible items of betting, research them thoroughly, then find suckers to wager on the outcome.

It was in that very bar that the sentinel event occurred. Bella Cherie's father had told her sometimes he had "gut feelings" which he trusted more than anything else. When those came, he would make the most extravagant of bets possible, virtually certain of success. On this fateful evening, a mayoral election had been about to take place, and he had had a gut feeling about the candidate that was the underdog in the race, a man with a speech impediment. He had engaged a local group of small businessmen in an argument, wherein he had presented his opinion, leaving out the points that were the most telling. During the discussion, the brother of the favored mayoral candidate had come into the bar with a friend, had overheard the conversation, and gone to her father's table, and had argued with great scorn against him. Finally, her father had offered to wager the man, who had replied Bella Cherie's father couldn't possibly have anything he could possibly want.

It was then, Bella Cherie's father had made the fatal mistake. Rather than just back down, and fleece the local businessmen, who were plenty eager to engage, Bella Cherie's father had gone out to the RV, taken his beautiful twelve year old daughter by the hand, led her inside and offered her as stakes in the bet: against the man's palatial estate.

The man with the speech impediment had, in an unexpected series of events that shed unfavorable light on the favorite, won the contest for Bella Cherie's father. He had won an enormous mansion with twenty perfectly groomed acres on the outskirts of the town, and he had earned—the hatred of his daughter. From that moment onward until his death ten years later, she had not spoken a word to him. Even as he had died, begging her for a word of forgiveness, or even farewell, she had stubbornly refused.

The day after he died, guilt had come into her life. Every day since then, she had come to the same bar where her father had won his biggest bet, the bar where he had drunk himself to death, and she had begun the same pattern that had destroyed him. Because of her whole attitude about men, she had deflected any possible romances by putting them through "tests." Up until that day, no man had ever come back.

"You've given me a little hope, Michael Marson," she said. "If you can forgive me humiliating you, maybe my father can forgive me not forgiving him. Maybe the universe or God or whatever you call the supreme power can forgive me."

She smiled, and her smile was beautiful. "You stood up for me, Tom Fairbanks. I know I come across as hard-hearted, like I don't need anybody, but that meant something."

*_____*

*Los Angeles, California*

I realized if I were going to change myself, I needed to make some major lifestyle adjustments. So the next day, I went down to the gym and exercised for an hour. Then I came home, planning to work in the garden. Our gardener, Ray, had worked there for years, and I really believe he was almost ninety years old. Arthritis had slowed him down a great deal, but still he worked, weeded, planted flowers, cut grass and kept the place up. The edging wasn't done as perfectly as it had been in times past, but it was good enough, especially considering Ray's age.

Even as a little girl, I had enjoyed going out and

watching him. He was short and had been somewhat portly in times past, but he was thinner now, and as I went outside to speak to him, I thought he was almost gaunt.

"Hi Ray!" I said, expecting and getting a delighted smile from him. "How are you today?"

"Even if I'd been doing bad, I'm doing good now," he said, which was his standard reply, but I think it was totally serious. "What can I do for you, Garden Olive? (A nickname only he used)

"I want to grow a garden," I said.

His eyes lit up even more. "Ah, what kind? Flowers or vegetables or both?"

"Both. And I'd like to grow some strawberries and some raspberries.

"What brought this on?"

"Because it gives me joy to see what you do. I thought it might give me and Daddy joy to do it ourselves."

His smile grew absolutely huge. "How big a plot do you want?"

"I don't know. Big enough to grow all that, small enough that we don't get overwhelmed."

"Where do you want to start?"

"I want to do everything. Till the soil, fertilize, plant the seeds, weed, thin, harvest, and everything in between."

"You're ambitious."

"Yep. And I want to use the Mittleider method.

"What?"

"The Mittleider method. It was made up by a guy named Jacob Mittleider. He figured out the exact nutrition a plant needs. I'll print off a copy of it so you can pick up the materials, even the micro ingredients."

"Where'd you hear about it?"

"I ran across it when I was surfing the web one time. It sounds like the perfect thing to do."

Ray shrugged. "Whatever you say, Garden Olive."

"You'll be happy with it. I promise."

"Whatever you say," he repeated, sounding like he didn't like new information at this time in his life.

"Thanks a lot, Ray." I gave him my most brilliant smile. It's going to be really fun working with you."

He had the rototiller for me later on that day, along with a bag of fertilizer, (non-Mittleider) and he showed me how to use it. He had decided on a thirty by thirty foot plot, which necessitated us digging up a corner of the lawn. It was a corner that was behind the house and the garage, and could not even be seen from the street, but it was also shaded on all four sides. Nothing was going to grow very well.

The berries were to be on one side and the flowers on the other, with the vegetables in the middle. That seemed fine to me, except as the berries started vining outward, they could quickly choke out the garden. It needed to have more space, and it needed sun.

Any time I asked Ray about the garden's need for sunlight, he would divert my question, steering it back to the way he had decided to do it.  *He doesn't want to affect the visible yard.  Only if it's completely out of sight will it be acceptable.*

*One of the reasons I like him so well is because I haven't worked with him in his territory.  He has a definite way he likes to do things.*

*I don't want to have to push this issue.  This is going to be an enjoyable experience for my father and me.*

*One advantage I have.  He doesn't get here until nine o'clock.  Daddy's and my gardening hour will be from eight to nine.*

# Chapter XVII

## Loss

*Kansas City, Missouri*

At the end of three hours, one thing had become quite clear to me. I had become a third wheel in the relationship we were forming. Whatever my flawed reason for coming back to the Swimming Turtle, it had been sufficient to begin something Tom had desired a long time: a relationship with Bella Cherie. *I have a feeling it's going to end up being more than he wants, and certainly more than he's expecting, but it's giving her a chance for living, and I think it'll free Tom up too. I bet he finds a way of keeping in touch.*

Customers had started to filter in, but the magic had been accomplished. During the time of our three way tale relating, the bar had, miraculously Tom said, remained empty, and Bella Cherie's heart had been softened. She hadn't drunk another drop during our meeting. How much credit could I give myself?

I shrugged, then stood. "I need to get back to my quest," I said.

Both Tom and Bella Cherie nodded and looked up, bidding me farewell. Bella Cherie's smile would have earned me all the liquor in the bar if the bet had still been on. I walked out into the western Missouri twilight, feeling like a new man.

Eddie was asleep in his limo when I left, but I rapped on the window and said goodbye. His advice had made a difference to me, and now, as I walked out, the anger, shame and weakness I had felt when I walked in was gone. If I looked back at my circumstances two hours earlier, I was embarrassed, but if I thought about the situation I was leaving behind, I felt great, and the embarrassment was bearable.

"It's going to be fine, Eddie," I said. "Go have a look,"

My headache was gone. I went back to my hotel, worked out hard, showered, then slept again. My stomach was still queasy so I didn't eat. Nine o'clock in the evening, I was on I-70 again, heading westward.

Night driving had become quite enjoyable to me. The air was cooler, there was less traffic, and so far, there hadn't been any shortage of messengers for me to pick up, or any lack of adventures.

This time, however, I drove for half the night without

incident. An hour after midnight, it was actually hunger, rather than fatigue that impelled me to stop, somewhere in eastern Colorado, at an all night diner. Having eaten nothing the day before, I ordered two meals, but was able to eat only one, having found, as I almost always did, that my eyes were bigger than my stomach. As I was putting my second dinner into the Styrofoam container, I saw, across the aisle of the cafe, someone that looked familiar. He was eating his dinner, and his head was down, concentrating on the food in front of him.

*Where in the world do I know him from? Here in Nowheresville, thousands of miles from my home, what are the chances of me knowing somebody?*

But I couldn't help staring at him, because the more I looked, the more convinced I became that I knew him. It seemed I had seen him in profile sometime...

*Is it possible I have picked him up–?*

*Yes! It's my first hitchhiker!*

*What's his name? We introduced ourselves, I'm certain.*

*Clyde? No. Clint? No, but close.* "Cliff!"

He turned and looked up, not as startled as I thought he would be. *Maybe he recognized me, but didn't want to bother me, or was afraid I wouldn't remember.*

Oh, hi," he said, much less enthusiastically than I would have thought.

"Do you remember me? I'm the guy that picked you up in the '63 Corvette."

Oh yeah," he said.   Again, not nearly as much animation as I would have expected.  I thought we were kind of friends.

"How in the world did you happen to be out here?"

"I've been hitchhiking across the country."

"Well, you've done pretty well."

"Not bad, although I've had to wait a few times. How's the old car running?"

"Better than ever.  I picked up an old timer who worked on them when they were new.  He fixed it with more power and better mileage in less than a minute."

"Really?"    Now he was starting to sound enthusiastic.  "What kind of shape's the oil in?"

"Great.  I had it changed less than a thousand miles ago."  *He really cares about my car.*

"Wow, that's great.  You've been really kind to the old girl."

"Well she's worth it.  I had a policemen friend I've made take her up to the top."

"One eighty?"

I nodded.

"How'd she sound and feel up there?"

"Perfect.  The speedometer was pinned but there was still accelerator left."

"That old boy must have really done some good work."

"I think so.  Hey, do you want a ride again?"  It had been so pleasant before, and so much fun to talk about cars.

"Sure. You don't mind?"

"No, I'd be glad of the company. Talking about cars should keep me awake all night long."

"Cool. My favorite subject."

"All right. I'll meet you at the front door." I paid for my meal, went to the restroom, then went to the front of the cafe. He wasn't there, so I waited a minute until he showed up.

"I can't wait to get back inside that masterpiece of machinery," he said.

"Let's go enjoy it together."

So we went. I noticed this time, something I had not consciously noted, but when I saw it the second time, I recognized it as what he had done before. He opened the door slowly, like he was relishing the experience. It was with reverence that he sat down in the seat. With equally great care, he set his shoulder bag in his lap.

How could I not like this guy? He loved my car, and I had put so much into it, it felt like he had reverence for me.

Neither of us said anything as we drove to a gas station and I gassed up, then bought us both a bottle of exercise drink. He merely nodded his thanks, and did not open his. I thought it a little odd that he watched me drink mine so vigilantly.

Then we were off, cruising the eastern Colorado stretch of 70. Again, we spoke about cars, and I think he was at least as enthusiastic as before, once he got going. He told me all the different opportunities he had to ride in various exotic machines from across the world and across time.

*He must spend a lot of time at this,* I thought, and realized suddenly that I was not as interested as I had been before. My journey had awakened me to other things, things more important. A few times, during the first hour that we drove, I tried to bend the subject in a different direction, but Cliff took it right back to automobiles. *It isn't his favorite subject. It's his* only *subject.*

Finally, at the end of the first hour, during a brief lull in the conversation when Cliff finally opened his drink and carefully took a few swallows, I decided I had had enough.

"You know what I've found out on this journey?" I said, pouring as much sincerity as I could into my words, knowing that my audience was, at best, only mildly interested.

"What's that?" Cliff said. "You haven't found anything you like better than this sweet machine, have you?"

"Oh no, that'd be infidelity," I said, and we both laughed, but both sounded forced. "I've found out what I'm more afraid of than anything."

"Oh yeah?" His reply was more interested than I thought he would be.

It was easier to talk about intimate things to perfect strangers I'd never meet again, but it was harder than I thought it would be. Maybe it was because I'd thought him someone in that category when I first met him, and here I was, riding with him again. *How many times am I going to run into him?*

"I found I'm afraid if someone were to take away my appearance, my great job, my education and"—I decided I'd say something he'd identify with—"my car, I wouldn't know who I was. I'm afraid I'd be nothing."

To my great surprise, Cliff started laughing. "That is amazing," he said.

I was perplexed and a little annoyed. "I don't get what was funny about that."

"You'll get it in a minute," Cliff said. He reached into his shirt pocket and pulled out something that in the dark looked like a small piece of paper.

He held it out, as though he wanted me to read it. "I know you can't see this," he said. "But I'll tell you what it says in a minute."

"I don't know what–"

"Just be patient," Cliff said. "Let me start by telling you this: I've found a buyer for your car."

"My car's not for sa–"

"Oh, it will be. And that brings me to the subject of what's on this card I'm holding. It's my business card. It says, "Cliff McDonald, professional car thief."

"What!?"

"Well, in this case, it isn't really true. It ought to say 'professional car jacker.'" As he was speaking I saw, with terror, his hand move smoothly into his bag.

"Pull over now," he said. "I've got some good news

and some bad news."

All I could see of what was in his hand was that it was black and bulky.

"It's a 38," Cliff said. "Loaded lovingly with hollow tipped bullets."

I was signaling my pulling over, even though we hadn't seen another car in a long time.

"The good news is, you're going to be able to meet part of your fears. The bad news is good news for me. I'm going to be rich and you're going to have to buy a new car."

I braked to a stop. Cliff gestured with his gun. "Go ahead and get out," he said. "If you're good and do what I say, I'll be good too. And I want you to know something, Mike. Up to now, everyone's been good."

If I had been prepared, I might have got out quickly, and lost myself in the darkness, but I was nervous about the lovingly loaded gun and stray bullets. I turned off the car, opened the door and stood, wishing the night were not clear and the moon full. Cliff was right behind me, and now, in the light of the moon, I could see clearly the shape of the weapon in his hand. "Come over to this side," he said.

Without hesitation, I obeyed. *This is so surreal, I'm not sure I'm not dreaming.*

"Now, take your clothes off," Cliff said. There was no emotion in his voice, and I realized he was transacting his business as usual.

As I slowly unbuttoned my shirt, Cliff watched me.

He didn't seem to mind that I was taking my time. "You know, if ever I thought of feeling bad about what I do for a living, I would now," he said. "You know almost as much as I do, and you've cared for your car so well."

"But, I can't afford to feel bad," he said, matter of factly, like he was talking about his favorite seat cover. "And I better tell you to hurry so I can get good and gone before it gets light. This car is the kind people are going to remember seeing, so I like darkness until I get to Denver. My partner has a garage where we can hide it until we make the sale."

"How much?" I said.

"Two hundred grand," Cliff said. "And don't go offering me more to let you go. It doesn't work."

"Oh," I said. "I guess I can see that."

I was working on my pants now. "Get a move on," Cliff said. "I'm going to let you keep your shoes, so you don't hurt your feet. That's my gift to you for keeping this beautiful lady beautiful."

I took off my shoes so I could get my pants off. When I had them lying on the ground next to me, I started to put my shoes on, but Cliff waved his gun. "Sorry, Mike. Underwear and T-shirt too."

"But then I'd be–"

"You'll still have your shoes. And leave all your stuff in your pockets. I'll make a deal though. If this sale goes through like I think it will, I'll cut up your credit cards. If it doesn't, I'll use them only to make up the deficit."

*You're a generous one,* but I only thought it. I was too leery of the gun to say something smart.

"Can I keep my belt?"

"Why would you want that?"

"Well, I was thinking, it might be easier to arrange something to wear if I have it."

"Good point. No. I want you naked as long as possible. Where's your cell phone?"

"In my shirt pocket. I guess it would be silly of me to ask for that, wouldn't it?"

"Yep. Get your shoes on, then push everything over to me with your feet."

I complied. Keeping the pistol perfectly trained on me, Cliff opened the passenger door, then placed everything inside. I noticed, for the first time, that there was a breeze cooling my backside.

"I have to be honest," he said, then laughed. "That's gotta sound funny coming from a guy in a business like I'm in. I let everyone have their shoes."

For a moment then he stood, scanning the ground all around me, making sure nothing had dropped out. Then he nodded and, keeping the gun trained on my chest, moved around to the driver's side. "I want you to run up the road now, one hundred steps," he said. "I wanna be able to get in the car without having to worry about you doing something stupid."

Of all the things I had done, this was the hardest. I had never felt more vulnerable than at that moment as I turned my back. I don't think I've ever run faster than the hundred steps.

Well over a hundred yards behind me, I heard a car door shut, than an engine start. *Goodbye old girl,* I thought, as loud as I could. Then fearing he might decide it was more convenient if I weren't around, I got off the road and hid behind a large clump of sagebrush. A moment later, my car sped by, and I felt violated for the second time in two days.

"NO!!!" I stood up and sprinted to the road, following the rapidly disappearing lights. Even when they were gone, I ran, sobbing the whole time, until the tears blurred my eyes, and I got so winded I sprawled on the road. I lay there, sobbing, sobbing. *This isn't fair! What right does he have to take my car? It's mine! And how can he take my ID?*

It was like I didn't exist. No car, no ID, no *clothes. Nothing!*

And suddenly it came to me. I was facing my worst fears.

*_____*

*Los Angeles, California*

Daddy and I rototilled the plot, (plus a little more) that Ray had designated, in spite of my misgivings about lack of light. It was actually more difficult than it looked, but we were able to finish going through it twice in an hour and a half, long enough for Ray to come and approve of what we were doing.

"If you keep at it, you'll be good enough to take my job," Ray said, laughing loudly, as though he were really funny.

I managed to smile, even though I didn't feel it. "We'll work the preplant mix in tomorrow," I said.

The look on Ray's face was total puzzlement.

"The pre plant mix. You know the gypsum, Epsom salts and Borax." I said.

Again, his expression was completely blank.

"Never mind, I'll take care of it," I said, trying not to let my annoyance sound in my voice. I don't think I succeeded very well.

"Oh, that's good," Ray said. "You start using all this fancy stuff, I don't want any part of it."

That remark didn't help my mood any. "Yeah, I'll have Daddy pick it up in town. Is that okay?"

"I'd be delighted," my father said. "This is really fun. Thanks for all your advice, Ray."

The truth was, he hadn't said anything we both didn't know, but it was all right. My father was really good at finessing, and he was showing it at that moment.

"My pleasure," Ray said, but it sounded like he knew he hadn't done much.

This wasn't working out quite like I wanted. Ray had always been my casual friend, but I was feeling some definite icicles from both of us. So I drew a deep breath, and made a supreme effort.

"All my life, Ray, you've been outside keeping our place lovely and orderly. Now, all of a sudden, I'm coming out here and digging up some of the lawn you've nursed into something that belongs in the Garden of Eden.  This has got to be hard for you, and I'm really sorry."

Maybe I was laying it on too thick, but I was trying my best for sincerity.  Ray shook his head.  "It's all right," he said.  "I probably need to retire."

"No you don't!" I said, feeling a sudden great anxiety.  "This is your yard, and if you don't want us messing around in it, we won't.  Will we, Daddy?"

"No we will not," my father said.  I don't know why, but it seemed his eyes were shining.

"Naw, it's okay," Ray said.  "Change happens.  It's part of life."

He said it, but his heart wasn't in it.  Without saying a word, my father and I went inside, leaving an old man to grieve over the marring we had just done.  I cried, and I think my daddy did too.  Ray Corelli died that night.

*Eastern Colorado, Roadside*

It feels awkward, telling about myself, naked in the desert, in a position where I had to solicit a ride, but unable because of my nakedness. I'm not really keen on someone reading this, imagining me in—well, it's probably obvious.

Interestingly enough, I did not feel despair.  I had already considered the fear, during long hours of driving, and now that I was actually facing it, my desire and need to survive took precedence.

For several reasons, not least of which was the

September breeze that blew fitfully, reminding me winter wasn't too far away, my first priority was clothing. *How does a person with no knife, no tools of any kind, improvise clothing out of the stuff in a desert? How am I going to make a loincloth out of sagebrush?*

At that moment, I saw the headlights of an oncoming car. Quickly, before the driver, (it was most likely a semi truck) saw me, I ran out into the desert and hid behind sagebrush again. *Isn't it strange that right now I'm afraid of what I'll welcome if I can figure out how to cover myself?*

Once the truck was past, I came back to the road, stepping through some broken glass on the way. *Thank goodness for my shoes. It sure was nice of him–*

Those were, interestingly enough, genuine thoughts, without guile. I was feeling grateful to the man that robbed me.

*And what kind of creep would throw a bottle out their window? Don't they care that they're trashing up Amer–*

Trash. Something I had despised up to that time now would be my greatest friend.

A plastic grocery bag was the first treasure I found. It had something in it, which I emptied out on the ground. Then I took it and studied for a moment. I could tear it into three strips of more or less equal width, and tie them together to make the start of my belt.

I tried to do it with my hands, and found something

wet and sticky on the bag. I sniffed my hands and found out what had been inside. Dog poop.

*People are amazing. They don't want to have their pet's excrement lying bare on the ground where it will dissolve in a week or two, so they put it into a bag and throw it out their window.*

As best as I could, I scraped the residual doodoo on the road, then more or less successfully tore the grocery bag into strips. While I was tearing it, I was walking forward, my eyes scanning the roadside, grateful for the same moon I had resented only fifteen minutes earlier.

In less than half an hour (Cliff had forgotten to take my watch) I had found another plastic shopping bag with beer cans in it, several large fast food soda pop cups, a 'For Sale' sign made of thin cardboard, a cardboard drink holder, a dead crow and a black sock.

*Here I am, rejoicing over* garbage, *some of it stuff I would have thought gross less than an hour ago. Now it's like the greatest treasure in the world. Stuff I would have never even noticed before has become personal, my intimate belongings, each with a story behind it.*

*I walk in a world of wonder, and I never would have noticed if I hadn't been robbed.*

At that moment, I came upon the greatest treasure of all, and my task became easy. I found a plastic shopping bag full of plastic shopping bags.

And if Cliff had felt reverence when he sat down in my car, I felt it at that moment. *If you're up there God, and at this moment, it sure seems like you are, I'm grateful.  Really grateful.*

*Los Angeles, California*

The word came to us the next morning, at 7:30, from Ray's daughter.  I answered the phone, and she identified herself.  Immediately, I knew something was dreadfully wrong.  "What's the matter with Ray?" I blurted, but I knew her answer before she said it, and in my mind, I cursed her for calling and telling me.  *Why did I have to be the one to take this call?  Where's my father when I need him?*

Ray's daughter's voice was slightly emotional, but not overly so.  "My father had a stroke last night," she said. "He died sitting in his favorite chair."

"Why'd he have a stroke?" I demanded, unable to keep hysteria from my voice.

Of course, it was an unanswerable question, and Ray's daughter hesitated a long moment while she answered. "It was just his time," she said, slowly, with almost a question mark at the end of her statement.

"Did he say anything about me?" I asked, my voice shrill.

Another long pause.  "Yes, he did."

"What?"

"Well, are you sure you want to hear now?"

"Why wouldn't I want to hear it?"  I was frankly screaming.

She sounded even more uncomfortable.  "Well, I was thinking I would have it part of his funeral."

That set me back a little. *What could he have said that would be funeral material? It wouldn't be bad, surely.* Exerting all my effort, I brought my voice down a few notches. "As you can tell, this has me devastated. Please tell me what he said."

Instantly, she sounded mollified, and as she relaxed, so did I. "He said 'My Garden Olive has finally grown up. She's become a gracious woman.'"

"Oh." *She'll never believe it now.*

"He really loved you."

Tears are such treacherous things. I didn't want to start weeping now, on the phone with Ray's daughter, while Jean, the housekeeper was standing nearby. But I did, of course. Crying is just like laughing. When you want it the least it's the most threatening.

So, my voice full of emotion, I answered her. "I love him like a grandfather."

Then, too embarrassed to continue the conversation, I hung up. Putting my head down to hide my oh too obvious emotion, (whom did I think I was fooling?) I ran upstairs to my room, buried my head in my pillow and cried my grief out. Somehow though, by the time eight o'clock came, I was sitting at the table, my usual meeting place with my father, still in my pajamas.

He came in dressed in the same work clothes he had worn the day before. His eyes lifted in question when he saw my attire.

"I'm not sure I can," I said.

"Why not?" His voice, as usual, was mild, not

hysterical. I could learn a lot from him.

"Ray died last night," I said, trying to put as much neutrality in my voice as he had.

"He did?" My father was surprised and grief stricken.

"Yes. And you know how he felt about us doing what we're doing?"

"He was maybe a little reluctant, but I think he was happy you were out there working."

"I'm not sure, Daddy. We've been tearing up the lawn he worked so hard to keep perfect."

My father considered a moment. "What happens when we die? Does our consciousness continue?"

"Nobody knows. Why bother asking?"

"Let's just consider both scenarios. First of all, let's assume there's nothing there, that death is the end of existence."

"Okay." It really frightened me to hear my father say it, even if it was only hypothetical.

"What point is there in honoring a thought or custom that was unreasonable?"

"Aren't *we* the ones that are being unreasonable?"

"Not at all. This is our property, and he's our employee. Isn't it more important for him to keep *us* happy than to keep the yard looking like it always has?"

"I guess so."

"So I ask the question again. Are we honoring someone that no longer exists by doing their wishes, when their wishes are no longer there?"

I bit my lip. "Well, I guess not."

"All right, now let's take the opposite supposition, that there *is* a life beyond this one. What kind of a place would Ray be in now? A good place or a bad place?"

In spite of myself, I smiled. "Well, we found out he's a little stubborn, but most definitely a good place." My father had so much serenity, so much confidence, it was hard, now that I was paying attention to him, for me to be with him without feeling some of his exuberance for life.

"So if he's in a good place, he's undoubtedly seeing that his desire to keep our garden plot as a stretch of boring old grass is unreasonable, and the opportunity for a father and daughter to work together, creating beauty and delicious, nutritious foods is worth the sacrifice of a stretch of lawn nobody sees anyway."

This time, I laughed. "I'll be out there in five minutes," I said. "And we'll work in honor of Ray."

My father was like that.

*_____*

*Eastern Colorado, Roadside*

It wasn't difficult at all to find a stick, a broken stem of sagebrush as it turned out. I sharpened it on the road, until I had a point I could use as an awl. Because of the treasure trove of plastic bags, I had indulged in the luxury of tripling my strips, so my belt was very strong. Then I had tied the other bags together to form a rude loin cloth, which I ran between my legs and draped over the front and back of the belt, leaving essentially equal lengths to hang down on both sides. Finally, with the three remaining bags, I made another belt. This I threaded through holes I punched with my awl in all the other stuff I'd found, that would help to cover me a little more. When I was finished, I had a skirt, composed of all of sorts of objects.

I had to look really funny, but when I stood, now able to request a ride from a kind motorist, I also felt an indescribable sense of accomplishment. It was, in a sense, like I had conquered my fear and the wild, and I had won.

The next vehicle that came along was another semi truck. "Clothed," (in what had to be the most ridiculous outfit ever) I stood somewhat timidly, at the side of the road, my thumb out, at 2:45 in the morning.

Suddenly, I felt a chill of extreme embarrassment. *My attire, my first time hitchhiking. What am I going to say to someone that picks me up? Why did I have to use the sack with the dog crap on it?*

I was tempted to run off and hide in the bushes, but I was very cold, and I had no water or food, and a thief was about to sell my car and run up my credit cards.

I wasn't sure whether it was a good or a bad feeling when I noticed the truck slowing. It seemed like it slowed far longer than it needed, and stopped still out in the road. I stepped forward and pulled the door handle, but it was locked  Then I saw the driver inside, (he had turned the light on for a moment) motioning for me to step away from the truck. Really puzzled, I complied.

The passenger window rolled down, and a man's face appeared. By the light inside the cab, I could see he was holding a cell phone. He lifted it up and snapped a picture. The light flashed in my eyes, and I put my hands up to avoid it. Once more I took a step toward the vehicle but he motioned me away again.

"You might have a good reason to be dressed up like that," he said. His voice was nasal and obnoxious, enough that I noticed it in spite of my embarrassment. "But you're probably a weirdo, so I'm not going to let you in my truck. My wife'll get a kick outta this picture though."

He rolled up the window, and a moment later was gone. I will admit, I was tempted to express my feelings for him with sign language.

I was shivering now, and the meal I had eaten in the cafe a hundred miles away seemed an age ago. Interestingly, as I consider it now, it was kind of symbolic of my situation. I was further away from the world I had left behind than I had ever been in my life, with no car, no fiancee, no phone, no money, no clothes, no food in my stomach, and nowhere to go. I was so far from where I had started, it seemed foolishness to go back, and yet, the thought of going into a strange city garbed like I was–

I felt despair begin to well up inside of my throat, threatening to spill out into my eyes. I was so alone. Why didn't I–

No! This wouldn't do. I turned toward Denver and

started to run.

*_____*

*Los Angeles, California*

I had never been to a funeral before, not even my
mother's. Death was such a permanent thing, such a
slap in the face of routine, of control. And this death
was one for which I felt responsible. If I hadn't argued
with Ray, insisted that he do things my way...

*But here I am, on the front row, sitting with the
family of the man I had a hand in killing.* Thank
goodness my father was beside me, but still. *Is
everyone going to think I'm part of his family?*

The meeting was different than what I expected.
There was some kind of song, something about praising
the greatness of God, and celebrating the beauty of the
earth. It was vaguely familiar and strangely comforting.
Then some woman from the congregation, presumably a
family member, not the preacher, to my surprise, got up
and gave a prayer.

It was unlike any prayer I had ever heard before. I'd
made it a practice all my life to despise all religion,
viewing it mostly as Karl Marx called it—the opiate of
the people. But if I had ever received evidence that
there was a God, Someone that was caring for the
universe, I was persuaded by this woman's prayer. She
spoke to her "Heavenly Father" so simply, so directly, it
sounded like she was talking to a real person, someone
she knew and loved. I heard her say something like,
"Thanks so much for taking Grandad home. We know

he's happy with you.    Please put him to work right away. You know how much he likes to work hard..."

There was nothing affected in her words. She could have been talking to me. I actually looked up to see if she was speaking to someone I hadn't noticed. I didn't see anyone, but for a strange moment, I wondered if there was something the matter with my eyes. *Can she see someone I can't?*

# *Chapter XVIII*

## Found

*Between the Eastern Colorado border and Denver, Colorado*

In some respects, it was an ideal time for running. I had eaten waffles and strawberries for my meal, long enough earlier that it didn't sit like dead weight in my stomach, and I had drunk plenty of fluids. The air was cold on my bare skin at first, but as I ran, I didn't notice it anymore. My shoes were what I wore everywhere except formal situations, a pair of higher end running shoes, and though I had another pair I ordinarily worked out with, these were only a little older and still in great shape.

I ran for a long time, and only two cars passed me. Both times, I stuck out my thumb, but they seemed to even speed up rather than show any sign of stopping. After an hour, I quit, worried about dehydration, not sure how long I was going to have to hold on. Besides, my loincloth (more accurately my loin*plastic*) had really started to chafe. Only as it was starting to get light, (and also starting to get embarrassing dressed the way I was) did I see a car start to pull over.

I breathed out my relief, but only cautiously. It could be another jerk only wanting a picture.      This   time, however, the car pulled up right behind me, well onto the shoulder, and stopped completely.    With great gratitude, I went to open the door...

"Get in back!" the voice called through the window. Obediently, but a little concerned (the voice hadn't sounded very friendly) I complied. The inside of the car was warm. "Ahhh," I said as I sat down."

But only for a moment. There was a cage in between me and the uniformed man driving. I was in an unmarked police car.

"What's going on?" I said. I had a hard time keeping the hysteria out of my voice. As soon as I had sat down, the car had pulled out onto the freeway.

"You tell me," the officer said, his tones no friendlier than they had been when he told me to sit in back. "Is this some kind of fraternity initiation?"

I put my head down. Now that I was in a more stable environment, the sheer gravity of my situation began to settle on me. To my great chagrin, I started to cry.

"I've been carjacked," I said, my words barely

understandable.

"How much have you had to drink?" the officer said. There was no softening of his tone at all. In spite of my strange circumstances, I remember thinking that drunks cry all the time.

I shook my head. "I don't drink—usually." Just in time I remembered the debacle of a couple of days earlier.

The officer's tone was sarcastic. "How much did you drink in this *unusual* situation."

"Nothing sir." I didn't like his tone or his assumptions, but he was holding all the cards. All of them.

"All right then, what is it?" he said, an impatient note entering into his voice. "Weed? Meth? Coke?"

"Nothing sir. I don't do that kind of stuff."

"That's what they all say," he said, but his tone softened a little. "Okay, tell me what you're doing."

"I was carjacked," I said again. "He had me take off all my clothes but my shoes."

"A real gentleman, eh?" He still sounded like he didn't believe me. "Where'd your getup come from?"

"Roadside trash," I said. "Mostly grocery bags."

"Hmph," he said.

We drove in silence for a moment. "All right, then. What's your name, what's the make and model of your car, and do you happen to know your license number?"

"Yes sir," I said. "But he told me he had a partner in Denver that would hide it for him until he sold it."

"Just give me your information."

"About five minutes later, he had radioed everything in, and verified that Michael Marson, indeed owned the car I was reporting as stolen. His manner had softened some, but not much. "Look man, I don't have anywhere to take you," he said. "Except to the station. And I have to get a positive ID on you, I have to verify your story somehow, and meanwhile, there's a complaint out on you."

"What?"

"One of the people you tried to get a ride with called in and said there was a naked man hitchhiking on the freeway, which is illegal in Colorado."

He hesitated a moment, then chuckled. "Hitchhiking at all. But doing it naked doesn't help."

We were about two hours out of Denver, so eventually, unable to sleep, I started talking to the officer, whose name was Coleman. At first, he wasn't terribly talkative, but he didn't have anything else to do, and he could tell I wasn't intoxicated, so he told me a story or two about some of the experiences he and his colleagues had had. I could tell he was exaggerating a bit, but it was still interesting.

One case in particular was particularly intriguing. It had happened to one of his colleagues, so he didn't feel any need to aggrandize himself in the story. It kind of reminded me of my own experience.

Coleman said his friend, Curt, was out on patrol one night, when a hot, red sports car passed him, going about ninety.  He said he could see the woman (by the light of her phone) inside was paying very little attention to the road, and appeared to either be dialing or texting.

He turned on his lights, and got up right behind her, but she didn't pull over for about five miles or so, even after he turned on his siren.  During that time, he clocked her with speeds up to 101 mph, but never under 85.  When she finally did stop, she was still talking on the phone, and just as he came up to the car and she had rolled down her window, he heard her say, "I've got to get off because some *expletive* cop just pulled me over."  Then she turned to look at him, flashing him this smile that would have melted butter.  It was a smile completely incongruous with what she had just called him.

"What can I do for you, *officer,?*" she said.

This was a hardened patrolman, and he said she was so incredible appearing he was speechless for a few moments.  "Um, ma'am, you've been going over one hundred miles an hour in a 65, and you were not paying attention to the road."

"How about you just give me a *verbal warning*, and I promise to be good?" she said, smiling again, wriggling her body as if making sure it got some attention also.

"Um, ma'am, I need to see your license," he said. "And your registration and proof of insurance."

"I left all that at home," she said.  "Why don't you just let it go for now, and I promise, I'll make it up to you later?"

"Um," he said, and that's all he got out. Her smile got even broader, and she was staring at him like he was the most manly, desirable man that's ever lived. He said he just nodded his head, and the woman took off, laying scratch as she did. Curt gazed after her, as befuddled as if she had injected him with some kind of hallucinogen or something. He got back in his car, with fantasies of the woman calling him back and repaying his generosity to her. With a woman like that...

According to Officer Coleman, Curt was a happily married man. In about five minutes, he was back to himself, shaking his head, wondering what in the world he was thinking. He had just compromised his own integrity, but also the safety of everyone that was driving at the same time as the woman. *Am I willing to sell my soul for the smile of a seductress?* he wondered. Fortunately, according to Coleman, he never saw the woman again.

I was very uncomfortable listening to this story. Essentially the same thing had happened to me with Bella Cherie. How much power did an attractive woman have, if she turned on her flirtation and seduction to full power? Would I compromise myself–?

How could I possibly look down on Curt when I was so nearly guilty of the same thing he had done? Again, thank goodness for his sake that the woman didn't try to make it up to him. In essence, she "made it up to him" by never acting on her promise to do it.

Officer Coleman told the story as if his associate were some kind of a dupe or something, but I found myself really liking Curt and identifying with him, especially since I knew in my heart that I probably would have done no better.

The implications of the story, and the opportunity for thinking it gave me were actually quite welcome under the circumstances. It distracted me away from my very vulnerable and actually terrifying situation. After my first emotional reaction, the rest of the time, I was able to talk without embarrassment.

As we drew near to the city of Aurora, however, I started getting nervous. From the way Officer Coleman was talking, I was going to jail. What had I done to deserve jail? Picked up hitchhikers.

*Everyone advised against it. Maybe I had it coming.*

But the irony of the situation was galling. Here I was, trying to help someone out, giving them a ride in the middle of nowhere to somewhere, and they betray me and steal my car, my money, my clothes and my ID, and here I was, on my way to jail.

"Am I going to be treated like an ordinary criminal?" I said.

Coleman hesitated a little before answering. "I don't know that we have any other options until we get you ID'd and cleared," he said. "But I don't think it'll be too long."

Even after our conversation, and him finding that the information I gave matched me, his voice still had the trace of a growl in it. *Even though there's good evidence of me being innocent, he doesn't like to give up on his first impression.*

When we got to the police station, it was still early morning, about 6:45. Officer Coleman took me in to the desk sergeant, who was about ready to go off shift. That was not good for me, because he refused to hear anything about my extenuating circumstances. "You'll get your chance to say what you want to say," he said, without even looking up. Do you want to make your phone call now?"

I thought for a moment. "Not yet," I said. I was going to call my father, of course, and it was early out in California. He was going to chew me out for continuing to pick up hitchhikers after he had advised me not to, and I thought I'd rather not wake him to tell him my situation.

But then, as they led me to the cell, another thought occurred to me. *Am I going to just call Dad over all my troubles? At some point, don't I have to strike out on my own?*

*And what better time than now? I'm in a situation where I'm just about starting out fresh. I'm about as broke as I can get–*

No wait. I had a fat check in the back pocket of my lost pants. If I could get that canceled, and have it placed in my account–

"Excuse me, sir," I said to the middle-aged uniformed man escorting me to my cell. "I decided I would like to make my call now."

My jailer mumbled something about inconvenience, but he turned us around immediately and led me back to the sergeant. "Change of heart Sarge," he said. "He wants to make his call now."

The sergeant gave as sour look. "One of those, eh?" he said. "There's the phone. We're going to be standing right here listening,"

I nodded. "I need to call Information first."

He waved his hand. "I'm glad you don't have his number memorized."

"Whose number?"

"Your lawyer."

"I'm not calling a lawyer."

It was kind of fun to see the curiosity that suddenly appeared on his face. "You only get one call, you know."

"I know."

Somewhat to my surprise, I didn't have any trouble getting the number of the Mr Stud USA contest. A minute later, (someone was there because they were in an earlier time zone) I was talking to the woman who had checked us all in. The gamble I was taking was that Janice was still employed at the place. Of all the people I'd seen, she was the only one I was certain would be able to identify my voice.

"Is Janice–" I suddenly remembered I didn't remember her last name– there?"

"Which Janice? Weiss or Zubresky?"

Uh oh. "The one I interviewed with in the contest. This is Michael Marson."

"Michael Marson!" I was aware that her voice was loud enough for the two men that were flagrantly eavesdropping to hear. "You talked with Janice Weiss. This is going to make her day!"

Out of the corner of my eye, I saw the two men exchange puzzled yet knowing glances.

I waited less than fifteen seconds. Then, "Hello!" sounded on the other end.

"Hi, Janice," I said. Suddenly, the sound of a familiar voice, even one I knew only a little, was a very welcome sound.

"What's the matter, Michael?" she said. "You sound–"

"Yeah, well, I've run into a bit of trouble. Can you do me a huge favor?"

"Of course."

"You know the check?"

"The check you won day before yesterday?"

"Is there a way to find out if it's been cashed or not?"

"Wouldn't you know?" she said, her curiosity evident in her voice.

"No. It was stolen. Along with everything else I was carrying, including my car."

"Michael!"

"Yeah, well the hitchhiker I picked up happened to be a car jacker."

"Let me find out." Even though I knew she liked

me, it was gratifying how quickly she was taking care of my needs.

It took long enough that the two waiting men started getting fidgety. "It hasn't been cashed," she said.

A warm relief passed over me. "Good. Can I get you to cancel that check and deposit the money directly in my bank account?"

"Of course. Do you know your number?"

"Yes. My father insisted I memorize it."

"You're just a Boy Scout, aren't you?"

"Well, someday I'll tell you the whole story. Then you decide." I gave her my number. I was trusting her, and it was obvious to both of us. I knew she wouldn't dip into my money, but that kind of trust was almost implying more to our relationship than I wanted. Still–

"Do you need me to wire you some money?"

"No, I'll be okay. Look Janice, thanks a lot."

"Are you just going to leave me in the air, not knowing–?"

"I've gotta go. The desk sergeant is going off duty." That kind of gave her a hint. "But I promise I'll give you the whole story someday."

She hesitated a moment. "All right. I know you keep your promises. Stay in touch, please."

"All right. I'll talk to you later."

"Good-bye Michael."

"Good-bye Janice."

And that was it.

"That was your one call?" the sergeant said. "How's

that going to help you now?"

"I am being punished for doing something right," I said. "I'm no criminal, and by the time you finish my I.D., you'll know it."

"Who was that chick?" the jailer said. "Your girlfriend?"

I shook my head. "She interviewed me two days ago in the contest I was in."

"The Mr. Stud USA?" the sergeant said.

I nodded. "I wanted to at least secure that much of my money," I said.

"How much?"

"One hundred grand."

"You won the contest? What're you doing out *here*, dressed in–" he looked closely at my outfit– *grocery bags*?

"I was carjacked, and the only clothes I could find was the trash on the side of the road," I said.

"So this isn't some drunken prank or something?"

"Do I act that way? Do you smell any alcohol on me?"

They both sniffed. "I think I smell dog poop," the jailer said.

I grinned ruefully. "That's what one of the bags had in it."

"That really stinks!" the desk sergeant said. There was a pause, and then we all realized he had made an inadvertent joke. They laughed, but I didn't feel like it much.

"Look at the bright side," the jailer said. "No matter what, you're not going to get more than eight days, and a little probation for this."

"For what?"

"For hitchhiking on a Colorado freeway. "You're not naked, even if your outfit's a little crappy."

They both laughed again.

"What was I supposed to do?" I said. "I'm stranded out in the middle of nowhere, with no food, no water and no clothes."

"You don't hitchhike," the sergeant said. "It's breaking the law."

"Is that a law in every state?"

"I don't know," the sergeant said. His eyes shifted back and forth as he said it.

*He does know.* But he couldn't do anything about my situation, and wouldn't right now, even if he could. So I shrugged. "Oh." I said.

The jailer gave me a little shove in the direction of my cell. "Come to my place," he said.

I nodded without speaking, and he took me through a set of doors that opened only when he pushed a button and told someone he was there with a prisoner. I didn't like the sound of that. We went through the doors, and the loud click they made when they shut felt like a permanent closing.

There were three cells, and one man in each. One great big fellow was standing at the doorway to his, gripping the bars. "What are you bringing in, Larry?"

he said. "Is this guy wearing a diaper?"

Larry, the jailer, just grinned, but didn't say anything. The big guy kept his eyes on me.

"His diaper stinks, Larry. Don't put him in here with me!"

The warmer air inside was carrying the odor of the dog donation into every corner of the place.

The man in the second cell came and stood at his bars. "Don't put him in here either, Larry."

"Hey, can I get some different clothes?   I don't exactly like parading around in this."

"This is your unlucky day," Larry said. "I broke my closet key just yesterday, and the only other guy with a key doesn't come in until noon."

"Great. I can't get the smell out until I get this thing off."

Larry shrugged, and led me to the third cell, where the prisoner was lying on one of the two cots. Whistling tunelessly, Larry opened the door and let me in, but immediately, the recumbent man became unrecumbent, and said. "I don't want to be in here with *him!*"

"It don't make me no difference," Larry said, even though there was a hint of irritation in his voice. He took the prisoner by the elbow, (the guy was tall and lanky) and led him to the first cell. "Is this okay?" he said. I didn't hear an answer, but the door opened and closed, and I had a private room. In jail.

*_____*

*Los Angeles, California*

Surprisingly, the rest of the funeral was good. Four of Ray's five children gave speeches, and Debbie, the one I talked to on the phone, read some of her father's words that she'd recorded. I found myself weeping as she repeated what she had told me a few days earlier. To my great surprise, the speeches were not lamentations and sobbing, they were more of a celebration of his life, with a strong hope of an eternity of bliss. They acknowledged the stubbornness I had just seen and told stories about it that made everyone laugh.

"Are all funerals like this?" I whispered to my father. He shook his head. I didn't think so either.

When it was over, everyone stayed around, talking in small groups. Many people came up to me and embraced me, telling me how Ray loved me. A few told stories they remembered him telling.

I was astonished. *Was I really that important to him? Did I do anything to merit all the love he claimed he had for me?*

To my great shame, the memories that came in answer to my silent question made his supposed feelings for me seem impossible. I had been rude, thoughtless, bratty and disrespectful so many times that the fact he was even pretending was miraculous. *Is it possible to love another when that other does nothing to merit that love?* I hadn't thought so beforehand, but now....

The graveside service sounded unpleasant, and I did my best to duck out of it, but all three of his daughters came up to me and insisted that I was part of family, and Dad would have wanted me to, like it was a great privilege or something. I started feeling panic...

But again, perhaps more than at the funeral, I was pleasantly surprised. It was very sweet and dignified. One of the husbands of one of the daughters stood at the edge of the grave and said a simple, humble, quiet prayer. I remember his using a phrase like "the morning of the first resurrection," but that's all I remember. This time, I could feel the sorrow of the people, but it seemed like the sorrow of separation not annihilation. I found myself weeping again, but it was not unpleasant, and to my delight, I found my father's arm around me.

As we drove away, I felt quiet inside. "I just thought of something, Daddy."

"What's that, Sweetheart?"

"Those people seemed to know God pretty well." God."

He nodded. "It seems like it, doesn't it?"

"Is that possible if He's not even there?"

He thought for a minute. "It's not possible to be intimate with nothing."

"That's what I think. And yet that daughter that prayed talked to God like He was right there."

"Right. I thought so too."

"Since she couldn't be intimate with nothing, she had to be knowing God. That proves He exists."

"Interesting," Daddy said. "But true only if your assumption about her expressing intimacy is correct."

He was right, of course. Still, my thought hung about me for a long time. *Could the lives of the worshipers of God show Him to others?*

# Chapter XIX

## Resolution

*Denver, Colorado*

I discovered several things in the next few hours. First of all, prison food isn't bad. I was quite hungry, but the bacon and eggs they gave me tasted real, and the orange juice was cold and refreshing. Performing the ritual of eating was also very good for me, I thought. It relaxed me, and it tied this unreal experience to real life.

I had not slept the night before, and I found when I lay down on the cot in my cell, just to try it out, that it was comfortable enough to sleep on. In spite of my inadequate clothing, the blanket kept me warm enough, and in less time than it took to realize I was fairly comfortable, I was out. A few hours later, when I awoke, I was refreshed, like I had slept on the most comfortable bed in the world.

Lunch came, tuna sandwiches with tomato soup, and again, it was good. Still not enough but far better than the alternative. I ate slowly, trying my best to relish each bite, knowing that when I finished, I would have to face my situation. So, with careful chewing, I was able to postpone the inevitable an additional half hour. Just as I finished my lunch, the guy with the costume closet key arrived, (he was forty-five minutes late) and I was able to get showered and changed into attire matching my fellow inmates. It felt strange, being dressed like a criminal, no different than any other crook in any other jail, but it was better than having a stinky diaper as my sole clothing.

The trouble was, with all my creature comforts (or necessities, whatever they were) seen to, refreshed, full, clothed, I was brought face to face with my reality. I stared upward at the rough ceiling of my *jail* cell, and realized I had brought to pass my greatest fear—here I was, dressed like a jail bird in the government's clothes, penniless, despised, rejected, robbed.

In front of my eyes, the bars in my peripheral vision seemed to grow thicker until they were solid, encasing me in a cocoon that was shrinking around me, even as I watched. In a moment, it was going to engulf me, to squeeze my chest and my throat, to take away my ability to breathe, to live...

I put my hand over my mouth to block the scream that threatened to erupt forth from the bottom of my soul.  I found myself breathless, like I had just sprinted a 440.

*Who am I now?  I am nobody.  Oh, wait a moment. I'm Mr. Stud U.S.A.   All I have to do to restore myself to all the worldly acclaim I could ever want is to call the Hollywood agent and let him place me in a movie. Then the whole world will know that I'm a phony for a living.*  My breathlessness threatened to choke me.

*I could be a sex icon, a toy or at least a toy of fantasy for thousands of women across the country. Just the kind of thing to make my father proud of me, to make Iago and Olivia Salvadore admire me, and to make me respect myself.*  I spat.

"Hey none of that!" Larry's voice said.  There was a bit of an edge to it.

*I've lost my dignity, I've lost my incredible car, I've lost my beautiful, desirable fiancée, I've lost all the outside respect and envy I've enjoyed all my life.  I have no idea how I'm going to get out of here, much less how I'm going to get to either coast.  Who am I?*  "Who am I!" I repeated, but this time aloud.

"You're a prisoner in my jail!" the voice called out again, more cheerfully this time.

It was like the voice was a catalyst, because tears started to flow from my eyes.  I was totally alone.  I was nobody. *Nobody.*

*\*_____\**

*Los Angeles, California*

Daddy and I worked in the garden later on that day.

I had drawn out a revised map of where I wanted everything to go, and now we planted, corn on the west, then beans, then peas, then squash, then cucumbers, then tomatoes and peppers. We used nursery grown starts for the latter two. The theory was that the tomatoes and peppers would take advantage of the morning sun, while the corn would get the evening. It would have been a good idea, except for two factors: the lateness of the year and the wall.

In my reading, I had heard that I could prolong the remaining heat in the air using a series of plastic tubes attached together and filled with water. I spent the afternoon filling them and placing them around the plants, hoping that somehow, magically perhaps, they would be able to bring enough sunlight and warmth to my plants for them to survive.

I had a strange feeling that Ray was out there with me. He had been part of our family for so long, he had overseen the grounds of our place for so long, he had been such a part of every outside activity, it seemed he could not allow me free access to his domain without close scrutiny.

The feeling did not go away, and became stronger after my father went inside for a conference call. And it was strange. Rather than a haunting by a ghost or something, it felt like a visit from an old friend, one who was very interested in all I was doing.

It's a little embarrassing to relate, but I started talking to him. I had been talking to unseen entities all my life, so it was not terribly strange, but this was different than usual. For one thing, I had so little experience in conversation. Most of my life, I had either made impervious demands or listened to plaintive requests for good behavior. With my classmates at school, I had stayed aloof from any real friendships, limiting my relationships to people who would basically do as I told them without questions, or to girls with basically my disposition. With the latter group, we understood and despised each other.

So it was awkward. *Um, Ray, I enjoyed your funeral.*

*I did too.* Was it his answer, or just what I fancied to be his answer?

*Did your kids do a pretty good job talking about you?*

*Sure. They're good kids. They kind of knew me better than I thought they did.*

*Um, Ray, I'm sorry I've been such an unpleasant person around you.*

*Thank you for that, my Garden Olive.*

*It sounds really good to hear you call me that, even if you are only in my imagination.*

*It's as close as I'm allowed to get.*

*I'm trying to be better. I think your daughter's prayer helped me a little.*

*She knows how to talk to God, doesn't she?*

*Does he love me?*

*I can't tell you how much he loves you, because it is*

*beyond my comprehension.*

*I want that to be true now.*

*Now? Is that a change for you?*

*I've hated Him most of my life—if He were real. Is He real then?*

*God? Yes, as real as either of us. But you can't take my word for it.*

*Why not?*

*Because you're doubting my reality. And even if I'm not real, He still is.*

*That's very interesting.*

*What?*

*If you're my imagination, and telling me God is real, that means I want Him to be real.*

*I believe you're right.. It's a good thing to believe in Him.*

*Why?*

*Because He is the source of all happiness.*

*For my imagination, you very lively and opinionated.*

*You'll be more obnoxious than I someday. It's my legacy to you.*

*Great.* But I smiled when I said it.

*_____*

*Denver, Colorado*

*How hard is it to define a man without the definitions of others? Who am I without my trappings?*

"Stop bawling in there? You're giving my hotel a bad reputation!" It was good natured enough, but still, it stung.

"He stinks and then he whines. What kind of a wimp did we get?" It was the voice of the big guy in the first cell.

*(Now, you must indulge me, but I am not going to move the following thought train to the fourth book. It is so much a part of the changes you will see in the next two books that I feel I have to leave it here)

*I'll cry if I want to,* I thought defiantly. *No matter where I go, I'm free to do that.*

Like cold water to a parched throat, the import of my thoughts flowed into my mind. *I was free to cry or not cry, to laugh or not laugh anywhere in the world. Even if I have to cry or laugh inside, I'm free to do it.*

*Take everything else away, I'm still free. My thoughts, no matter what my outward circumstances, are mine and only mine. Nobody can take them away from me. They are subject to my will. Only my will.*

*Then my will is more basic than my thoughts. Yes. I always have my will. It's there even before the thoughts are formed. No matter my appearance, my wealth, my companion, I have it. It is the only thing I always have. Someone outside me can try to make me think I have none, but that's all they can do. And they're wrong. I have will. I can't be erased as long as I have will.*

*I will never cease to be will. My will has always been.*

The feeling of panic that had come with the tears began to subside. Suddenly, knowing I was something outside the perceptions of others, somehow, knowing I was something solid at the very foundation of my being gave me a strange confidence. I drew a deep breath, feeling like I was drawing in a strength I had never known.

I would build on this core that none could take away. *It gives a feeling of invulnerability, a place inside me where I am unassailable.*

*I like this feeling. I am my will. No matter what else happens.*

*What other qualities do I desire to place upon my foundation, qualities that strengthen this being of will?*

*I wish all that comes in to me, and all that goes out to be known to me. I wish to know every aspect of me. I wish for personal transparency, for self-intimacy.*

*Very well. What next? What else can I lay upon my foundation, that will add to my strength, that cannot be taken away?*

*I cannot remain transparent with myself if I let deceit pass out of me. Self intimacy therefore is contingent on intimacy with others. All others.*

*If deceit does not pass from me, I will also have truth built on my foundation of will, self-intimacy and intimacy with others. And if I live strictly on those principles, I will always have joy.*

*Exercise of will, self intimacy, and intimacy with others and obedience to the principles of truth are requisite for joy.*

*I cannot feel joy without the intimacy I have sought*

*and found. Good. Very good.*

I stroked my chin. *But I also could feel no sorrow without it. Is it worth–?*

*Yes. It is most definitely worth it. Intimacy is requisite for depth.*

*Why do I desire depth?*

*Because I must find meaning in my life. I must know that my life makes a difference to the universe. Without personal depth, which comes with intimacy, I could not have such a knowledge.*

*If I have intimacy in my life, what would be the natural consequence?*

*Love. Love? Why?*

*Because if I allow only truth to leave me, I allow only truth to come in to me. And if I see the truth in others, I will know them. And if I truly know them, I cannot help but love them.*

I thought about my interview with Janice, and I realized that I needed that interaction as part of my quest. My motives had not been pure—my motives had started out vain and selfish, but I had discovered something vital, something I could not have learned without the experience.

*Love means oneness. It means I am able to adopt the needs, the quest for meaning of another and make it my own. It means I know that other or those others so well I feel as they feel, I see as they see.*

*No, more than that. It means I have put in the effort to see them clearly, without the bias they might have developed. It means I will seek for their meaning in ways that will aggrandize them, not myself, even when they might not perceive my doings as beneficial. It means I am able to persist in my efforts with my mind single to their ultimate joy, their ultimate benefit, even knowing they might be initially angry with me.*

*Love means oneness.* I repeated the thought in my mind. *I cannot find oneness unless I find intimacy, unless I let myself be known, even as the people with whom I'm intimate allow themselves to be known. The more perfectly I allow myself to be known, the greater I am able to love. The more I am able to love, the more lovable I become.*

*Whom do I love?* It was appropriate to ask it now.

*For whom would I be willing to bare my soul, every last vestige of it?*

*My father. I have perfect trust in my intimacy with him. He would not use what I gave him for anything but my good. I have perfect conviction of that.*

*And I have known it all along. It was because of that conviction that I began this quest. I knew he wouldn't give me something not for my benefit. Therefore, even though I do not know Olivia Salvadore, I know and trust my father. He trusts his friend, with whom I have spoken only once, but since he trusts him, I trust him. Since Iago Salvadore, whom my father loves and trusts, loves his daughter, though I have never met Olivia Salvadore, I am ready to love her.*

There. It was out now. I had known it all along, but

it had taken—all that had happened for me to recognize it. In the process, I had become a man.

I stood up and stretched, and suddenly I laughed. I was in the best shape of my *life.*

"Hey, none of that either. We don't want people *signing up* to come to my hotel. But I'd rather that than the boobin.'"

The walls of my cell no longer threatened me. In fact —placing my toes on my cot, I grasped my bars and began climbing upward. It would make an excellent upper body workout...

*_____*

*Los Angeles, California*

I noticed two things, as I gazed at myself in the mirror. I was able to see and judge my appearance without having to slip into an alter ego. And I was more beautiful. Still too thin, but not as much. Ten to twelve more pounds would be perfect.

It was astonishing to me. "I am beautiful." It seemed like a miracle coming out of my mouth. *Yes, my nose is prominent, but it's not offensive. But that is not the source of my beauty. There is a light in my eyes, a hope I have never seen, a hope that shines like the glory of heaven.* And suddenly, I could see it no longer because of the tears that obscured it.

A knock sounded at my door. "Yes?" I tried my best to hide the weeping in my voice.

"There's a beautiful sunset out there, Sweetheart. I didn't think you'd want to miss it."

*I don't care if he sees my tears.    They're shed because he's loved me enough to give me opportunity for happiness.  To him, they're precious, even sacred.*

"Come in, Daddy," I said, standing and pushing my hand through my hair.  It would have to do for this unplanned outing, but it was good enough.  The light of day may have been disappearing from the sky, but before it had left, it had kindled its flame in me.

# ABOUT THE AUTHOR

In the process of deciding what to do with his life, Mark E. Mitchell has tried a variety of positions, including rock mason, carpenter, janitor, maintenance worker, home health care aide, designer of sporting goods and soldier. For the past twenty years or so, he has tried being a medical doctor, and he says that's okay, but it's only his day job. He has been writing all his life, but his early attempts have all wound up in the bottoms of some old cardboard boxes of memorabilia he might never look at again. Altogether, he has written 21 novels.

The most important thing in Mark's life is the Lord and his family. The Former has blessed him immensely in giving him the latter, and the latter has given him many occasions to talk to the Former. It is his hope that his writing will give you a taste of some of the joy and exuberance both the Former and the latter have brought to his life, and will perhaps give you greater ability to find the same in yours.

Other Books by Mark E. Mitchell: